'I don't need anyone,'

Dev said defiantly.

Anger surged through Kulani. 'You are as stubborn as a mule, Dev! Morgan said you are not to go on that mission alone. Are you in the habit of disobeying your boss's orders?'

Kulani stood there breathing hard. Fear warred with hurt inside her. 'I'm going down there with or without you. You can't stop me from coming, but it would be better if you just agreed to let me come along. That way, if I needed you, you'd be nearby, Dev.' Her throat closed off with tears as she watched his eyes soften with her admission. 'Please…I *need* you on this mission, Dev. Will you be there for me?'

His conscience railed at him. Kulani needed him. How long had it been since someone needed him? Swallowing hard, he grappled with her request.

Because it was tearing his heavily guarded heart wide open…

Dear Reader,

Welcome to the spot where you get a brief glimpse at the titles now available in Silhouette Special Edition®.

Our **That's My Baby!** book this month comes from the talented pen of veteran author Sherryl Woods and is an absolute delight; it features an older child and a father who isn't ready to be a father, yet! It's another in the author's novels about the Adams family, where **And Baby Makes Three**.

We also have a new novel from the small town in **Montana** full of big secrets—*Cinderella's Big Sky Groom* by Christine Rimmer. There are, of course, more of these to come at Christmas and in January's books.

Lindsay McKenna has the third of her Hunter family stories *Hunter's Pride*, part of her **Morgan's Mercenaries** mini-series, the next one of which is coming next month in Desire™.

There are also terrific books from *New York Times* best-selling author Patricia Hagan, Penny Richards and Jodi O'Donnell.

Happy reading!

The Editors

Hunter's Pride
LINDSAY McKENNA

™ SILHOUETTE
SPECIAL EDITION®

*First published in Great Britain 2000
Silhouette Books, Eton House, 18-24 Paradise Road,
Richmond, Surrey TW9 1SR*

© Lindsay McKenna 1999

ISBN 0 373 24274 3

23-1000

*Printed and bound in Spain
by Litografia Rosés S.A., Barcelona*

To all my readers.
Thank you.

LINDSAY McKENNA

is a practising homeopath and emergency medical technician on the Navajo Reservation in Arizona. She comes from an Eastern Cherokee medicine family and is a member of the Wolf Clan. Dividing her energies between alternative medicine and writing, she feels books on and about love are the greatest positive healing force in the world. She lives with her husband, David, at La Casa de Madre Tierra, near Sedona.

Lindsay McKenna

brings you four exciting, adventure-filled missions
for the rugged men of the Hunter family!

MORGAN'S MERCENARIES:
THE HUNTERS

HEART OF THE HUNTER
June 1999
A wounded, brooding marine finds his heart while
guarding a vulnerable beauty.

HUNTER'S WOMAN
September 2000
A determined military man wants his woman back—
and she's carrying his child!

HUNTER'S PRIDE
October 2000
A sexy mercenary takes on a lovely partner whose
passion rivals his own.

Look for the fourth book in the series,
THE UNTAMED HUNTER
in Silhouette Desire® in November 2000

Chapter One

Would Kulani Dawson say yes? Morgan Trayhern's hand hovered over the phone as he hesitated, his mouth pulled in a slash, his brows drawn. A month ago, he'd asked her to do some low-key detective work for him on the island of Kauai, where she lived, and she'd come through with valuable information for Perseus. Morgan knew that Kulani had done it because of their friendship, even though she no longer worked for him.

How could he make this next request of her? She would think him heartless. But Kulani had been a high-powered, ambitious woman at one time. Before the accident she'd been a highflier, and now she was living what he considered a desultory life flying tourists around her island. That was a helluva comedown from what she had been. In his gut, Morgan felt she needed the mission he was about to offer her. She needed *something* to bring her life, and herself, back into sharp, pas-

sionate focus once again. Besides, he had no choice.
Not one damn alternative. Kulani was the best merc for
this job.

With his heart wrenching, Morgan withdrew his hand
from the phone and wiped his damp palm against his
dark, pinstripe slacks. He didn't try and minimize how
Kulani would react to his request.

She was like a daughter to him. He hoped his own
daughters would someday grow up and be a lot like her.
She was a woman of incredible courage, having taken
part in the Gulf War, where after being shot down, she
still managed to bring her helicopter crew back to
safety. And she was just a kid back then. Hadn't even
seen thirty yet. Her career in the navy had been mete-
oric. How lucky Morgan had counted himself in wooing
her over to Perseus, afterward.

Sitting down at his desk, he felt his gut tightening.
He had to make the call. Thousands, maybe hundreds
of thousands of lives rested on it. Still, how could he
do this to her? He knew the awful tragedy of Kulani's
past. After the accident, she had quit Perseus abruptly.
Now she was trying to rebuild her life, and Morgan had
done what he could to help her do that. She had gone
home, where her heart was, to the place she had been
born—Kauai, Hawaii. Morgan knew she was trying to
pick up the pieces of her shattered life and he was about
to blow it all to hell.

"Damn," he muttered. His low, growling voice echoed around the large, walnut-paneled office. Raking his
fingers through dark hair touched with silver at the temples, he fixed his gaze on the photo of Laura, his wife.
Her blond hair mussed by a playful breeze, she sat on
the steps of their cedar home, high in the Rocky Mountains. Their son Jason sat to her left, and their second

born, Katherine Alyssa, or Katy, at her right. In Laura's arms were their youngest children, a set of fraternal twins, Peter and Kelly. Laura had always wanted a large family, and they were certainly on their way to having just that. The twins, at eighteen months, looked like healthy little pink butterballs in Laura's loving arms. The light shining in his wife's eyes told him just how proud she was of them. Of him. Together, out of their love, they were creating more love in the image of their children.

Smiling a little, Morgan sighed heavily as he picked up the photo. Without his family, he wouldn't want to live. How destitute Kulani must have felt when she lost the man she loved to such a horrifying accident. Worst of all, she had watched him die. Fingers tightening momentarily around the oak frame of the photo, Morgan could imagine all too well the trauma of losing Laura or his children. Actually, he'd nearly lost them once to vicious drug lords when he and his family had been kidnapped years ago. And how would he feel if someone called him less than a year and half after such a tragedy and asked him to go back to the very scene of the accident? To the place where his life had been ripped irrevocably apart?

He had to be some kind of unfeeling bastard to call Kulani and do just that. Would she understand? Would she be able to get past her grief in order to understand the dangerous nature of the mission he was going to speak to her about? Would she be able to see how necessary it was for him to ask her to take on such danger? How would he react to such a call? He'd tell the caller to go to hell.

Making a grab for the phone, Morgan cursed himself. Cursed his job. He was asking the impossible of Kulani.

And she had every right to hate him for what he was going to ask of her.

"Hello?"

Morgan's fingers tightened around the phone. "Kulani? This is Morgan. How are you?"

He heard the gasp of surprise and then the pleasure in her low, soft voice. "Morgan! It's so nice to hear from you. I'm fine."

"Am I catching you at a bad time?" He wiped the sweat off his upper lip.

With a slight chuckle, Kulani said, "I'm having my morning Kauai coffee. I've got to leave for the airport in about ten minutes. To what do I owe the pleasure of hearing from you? Are the twins okay?"

How like Kulani to inquire about his children. She loved all children, which made her loss even more devastating. With the man she'd hoped to marry gone, Morgan didn't know if she'd ever have children of her own. His heart pounding, he continued, "The twins are fine. And so are Laura, Jason and Katy. My call is business, Kulani."

"Oh." Her voice fell flat. "I got you the information you asked for on that professor."

"Yes, the information you got us was vital. And I'm grateful." He hesitated, thought to hell with it and dove in. "I need your help again, Kulani."

"Morgan..." she pleaded softly, "I don't want—"

"Please, Kulani, hear me out. You're the only one who can help us. And if there was anyone else I could ask to take this mission, believe me, I would."

"A mission? I don't work for Perseus anymore, Morgan. I'm done with that part of my life."

The raw desperation in her voice gutted him. "Just

hear me out, Kulani. That's all I ask," he pleaded, clenching the phone.

The silence was serrating. Finally, Kulani whispered, "I'll listen, Morgan, but I won't change my mind. I can't...."

Heartened, Morgan began what he hoped was a story that would make her change her mind. Sweat beaded on his wrinkled brow. He didn't have much time, so he made his description of the planned mission succinct. When he was finished, he halted abruptly. Wiping his upper lip again with the back of his hand, he said in a rasping voice, "Now you see why I need you, Kulani. You've done the preliminary work on the professor, anyway. You're familiar with the territory. Only you can do this." He held his breath.

Over the phone line he heard Kulani sob once. "Damn you, Morgan! I can't. How could you even think of asking me? It's just too much." Her voice cracked. "Too much!"

The phone line went dead. Morgan hissed a curse and gently placed the receiver back in the cradle. Kulani's cry squeezed his heart. Only the sound of Laura's tears could make him feel worse. And now he'd wounded Kulani—again. On purpose, though his motives had been pure. Patriotic. So many lives were at stake. And he needed her. So why did he feel like the worst kind of turncoat son of a bitch?

Looking angrily around the office, Morgan picked up the phone. "Get me Dev Hunter," he ordered his assistant heavily. "Now, please."

"Morgan, I hope you've called me in for an assignment. I'm bored as hell." Devlin Hunter stretched his hand toward the big man who sat behind the wooden desk in the secluded office. Perseus, the covert branch of the CIA that Dev worked for and Morgan headed, had gone underground since Morgan, his wife and son had been kidnapped years ago. Instead of being in Washington, D.C., its original 'home,' Perseus was now located in a tiny, sleepy community of Philipsburg, Montana.

Morgan grinned sourly and gripped the younger man's hand. "Oh, I think I have something that will unglue you from your boredom, Dev." He pointed to a large leather wing chair to the left. "Have a seat." Morgan noticed that Dev, although casually dressed, still wore designer clothing, as was his penchant. Of the four Hunter brothers, all of whom worked for Perseus, Dev was the clotheshorse among them. Plus, in Morgan's opinion, Dev was the only one of them with the kind of model-handsome looks that seemed to attract women like bees to honey.

Dev sat down on the edge of the chair, relaxed but alert. Folding his large square hands between his opened thighs, he waited expectantly as Morgan took his seat and opened the file that sat in front of him. Maybe it was Dev's imagination, but Morgan looked more tired than usual. His black hair, cropped short and always military neat, had more silver at the temples. Despite that, however, Morgan looked just as fit as ever. Dev knew his boss worked out at the gym daily as if he were still in the Marine Corps, which he'd left a long time ago. When Dev was between assignments, he ran five miles with Morgan most mornings along dirt roads in the area, among huge, fragrant Douglas fir.

"I hope it's a good assignment," Dev said. "To tell you the truth, I'm getting flabby." He patted his hard gut with a grin. Dev, too, worked out conscientiously at the underground gym that was available for Perseus employees. Morgan had had a condominium built in Philipsburg to house incoming and outgoing Perseus employees. To the outsider, it looked like a time-share facility for vacationers coming to the magnificent Rocky Mountain area of Montana. Morgan was very good at camouflaging things to protect his people and to protect his own family from global enemies who wanted to see Perseus and everyone associated with it destroyed.

He thumbed through a number of e-mail messages lying near the file, his thick, black-and-silver brows dipped in concentration. His mouth tightened momentarily and then he raised his craggy head and met Dev's intelligent gaze. On the surface, Dev Hunter looked less the mercenary and more like a Wall Street broker. And he always wore a lopsided grin, the left corner of his mouth slightly hitched upward, as if he knew a joke that no one else did. It wasn't a sarcastic smile, more one of a playful imp from Ireland. Dev Hunter's easygoing nature was one of the things Morgan liked about him. And in this forthcoming assignment, Dev's charm and laid-back personality were going to be tested to the limits—and then some. Morgan wasn't even sure Hunter would take the assignment, but he was prepared to apply a lot of pressure on him to do so. Inhaling deeply, Morgan considered his words carefully. He knew that, in order to get Hunter lured into the assignment, presentation was everything. Morgan prided himself on knowing his people—what snagged their attention, what connected with their passion in life, what made them *want* to undertake a mission.

"Take a look at this," he told Dev in a casual tone as he picked up a color photograph and handed to him.

Frowning, Dev took the large photo. "Hey, this is

some looker,'' he rasped as he sat back, his gaze riveted on the picture. It showed a woman in a Hawaiian grass skirt and a bright red halter top, her wrists and ankles surrounded by garlands of pale pink plumeria, her arms raised skyward as she swayed gracefully on a golden beach, the deep blue of the Pacific Ocean behind her. Her black hair, shining with blue highlights, was encircled with a wreath of white plumeria and greenery, which set off her dusky gold complexion and warm black eyes. Her gaze, too, was turned heavenward, her full lips, a ripe pink color, parted, as if she were caught up in some sacred dance with the spirits of nature and the mighty, placid blue ocean that lovingly framed her.

Dev's gaze moved in appreciation over her tall, lithe body. One of her knees peeked out from the grass skirt, parting the yellowish strands and displaying her long calf and delicate bare foot. Her exquisitely long fingers curved upward in honor of the sky she danced beneath. Her arms, firm and slender, arced gracefully above her head, as if in tribute to the golden sun that embraced her. She was small breasted, her torso long and her hips slender beneath the flowing grass skirt.

As his gaze moved to her face, he felt a wrenching in his chest. That caught him off guard. Hunter was used to being around attractive women. He drew them like sunlight opened flowers. It was his gift, he supposed. Certainly, his other brothers did not possess the charisma he had with women. But something about this woman moved him as no one had before. He studied her features—the square face with high cheekbones, the dark black brows arching above her wide, shining eyes. Everything about her shouted of aristocracy, from the fine thin nose to the confident way she held herself as she danced the hula. Dev had been to Hawaii a number of times, and because of his curiosity about other cultures, he'd learned quite a bit about the traditional dance. It was a sacred custom among the Hawaiian people, not the touristy thing that visitors thought it was. And there was no doubt the woman dancing in this photo was moving in a deeply sacred communion with the unseen.

Releasing a low whistle, he raised his chin and pinned Morgan with his gaze. "Tell me she's my mission."

Smiling a little, Morgan said, "She's half of it."

Dev sat up expectantly. His hands tingled as he held the photo, and he was amazed once again at his reaction to the woman pictured there. She looked like an ancient Hawaiian princess—or maybe the daughter of the fire goddess, Pele. "Okay...you got my attention. Is she my tango?"

Morgan smiled to himself. *Tango,* a military term that meant target, was used to identify the person a mercenary would be protecting. "No," he said slowly, "she's your partner." Steeling himself, he saw Dev's expression go first, to surprise and then to mild shock before he set his jaw firmly. Hunter was a loner among the elite personnel of Perseus; he didn't work with a partner. He never had—until now.

Glancing briefly down at the photo, Dev bit back an automatic "No." He knew Morgan too well, and he sensed his boss was trying to trap him into taking the mission by showing him an incredibly beautiful woman. Morgan knew a pretty face was Dev's Achille's heel. Anger sparked within Dev and tension ran through him momentarily. Yet, as he looked at the photo, those shining eyes filled with such life and awe, he found his anger dissolving. That shook him. No woman had ever had that kind of hold on him. He took that back—one had, but not to this powerful degree at first glance—and that relationship had ended up in a disaster of untold proportions that haunted him to this moment.

"What's her name?" he demanded gruffly.

Morgan was surprised. He'd expected Hunter to instantly put up a fight and flatly turn down the assignment. Something must have captured his attention. Smiling to himself, Morgan answered, "Kulani Dawson."

"Kulani..." Dev muttered, more to himself than to Morgan. He repeated the name over and over in his mind. The funny thing was, his heart pounded a little bit every time the word spun through the halls of his mind. Was he just having a purely male response to this photo of her? She *was* stunning looking. More ethereal than real to Dev. He wanted her. For him it was that primal, that straightforward. Yes, it had to be his desire for her that had caught him off guard. That was all.

"Kulani used to work for us. She's a helicopter pilot," Morgan continued. "She was one of the first women to fly helos in the U.S. Navy. I found out about her, managed to convince her to leave her military career behind and work for us." His voice grew sad. "A little over a year and a half ago, she quit. She runs her own tourist helicopter service over on Kauai now."

Dev grinned cockily. "This is one helluva dessert to be putting on my plate." He placed the photo back on Morgan's desk. "You know I don't do partners. And even though I'm intrigued, I'm not changing my mind about how I operate."

Holding up his scarred hand, Morgan said, "Hear me out first, Dev, before you make a final decision."

Shrugging his broad shoulders, Dev replied, "You're the boss. What's up?"

Becoming grim, Morgan said, "Your brother Ty and the team from the Organization of Infectious Diseases—OID—confirmed that a genetically altered form of anthrax was sprayed upon an unsuspecting Juma Indian village south of Manaus as a 'test' case for Black Dawn, the international terrorist group."

"Damn," Dev whispered painfully. "I didn't know the details. I suspected what was going on, but Ty didn't say for sure."

"He couldn't. This is top secret information. But it's been confirmed through five different governmental agencies, including our own. It's only a matter of time until Black Dawn picks a top event target."

"Like delivering anthrax by air over a major city?"

"Yes, and probably a U.S. city—that's our best, educated guess." Morgan tapped the pile of e-mail messages on his desk. "But we've got a lead. A strong one. And I hope this isn't a wild-goose chase this time. The light plane used to deliver the aerosol spray over the Juma village in the Brazilian jungle had numbers on the side of the fuselage. We were able to trace those numbers."

Dev's brows shot up. "That was a pretty basic mistake on Black Dawn's part not to disguise or change the lettering on the plane."

Morgan agreed. "No plan, no matter how carefully thought up, is without mistakes and screwups. And this is theirs."

"Who does the plane trace to?" Dev asked, unable to keep his gaze from wandering to the photo of Kulani Dawson. There was such incredible life in her. There was a radiance about her face, as if she were caught in the throes of something so sacred that Dev could not even begin to connect with it. That didn't matter. He knew with sudden insight that just by being next to her, hearing her voice, and looking into her eyes, he could somehow possess it. Possess her. Shaken, he forced himself to pay attention to Morgan.

Pulling a paper from the file, Morgan rumbled, "A Professor Jevon Valdemar. A refugee from the Balkans granted asylum by our government to continue his work in biochemistry." The derision in his voice was heavy. Tossing the paper toward Dev, he added, "The turncoat son of a bitch has sold us out. We gave him asylum, grant money in the millions and what did he do? He joined Black Dawn, perfected the genetic anthrax to kill millions around the world." Morgan's nostrils quivered as he glared across the desk at Dev, who picked up the paper and looked at the photo of the professor on it.

Eyes narrowing, Dev studied the thin-faced man with round, gold, wire-rimmed glasses. The professor appeared to be in his late fifties, his hair gray and helter-skelter across his broad forehead. "Funny how faces never tell the whole story," Dev murmured philosophically. "You'd think a killer would look like a killer. You'd think they'd have pig eyes, hard faces, their features broadcasting just what kind of people they were."

Morgan's eyes were icy. "Valdemar looks like a radical in my opinion."

"How does this top event tie in with her?" Dev asked as he slid the paper back to Morgan. Again, his gaze drifted to the beautiful Kulani Dawson. He'd been over on Hawaii, the Big Island, and Oahu, but never on Kauai. He'd seen his share of hula dancers, but no one like Kulani. *Was* she the daughter of Pele, the fire goddess? She looked it, with the fire in her heart, her passion, written across her lovely face, in her shining eyes.

"She did a little of the legwork for us already, because after we traced the plane back to the professor, we discovered it was originally bought in Kauai. Since then we've found out Valdemar was paying rental at Lihue Airport for his plane. *How* it got from there to Brazil, we don't know. It could have been transported in the belly of a large cargo plane. In any case, Professor Valdemar disappeared a year ago from Kauai, where he was doing his work at a local lab that was part of the CIA efforts. His plane disappeared from Lihue Airport about the same time he did. Rafe, our contact in Brazil, found the plane after a search of the Manaus airport with that city's police detectives. Rafe, who is one of our deep mole Perseus operatives, showed a photo of the professor to Manaus airport employees and Valdemar was positively identified. And now we have another lead. Kulani saw Professor Valdemar back at Lihue Airport three weeks ago. Further, she's reported an unmarked black helicopter coming and going just at dusk or dawn around the Na Pali Coast area, on the north side of the island."

"Even though she doesn't work for you anymore, it sounds like she keeps pretty good tabs on the island for you," Dev said with a slight smile.

"Well," Morgan hedged, "let's put it this way. I was the one who contacted her. I sent the professor's photo over the Internet to her. I asked if she'd seen him around the airport she flies out of, and she said she had. When I asked if she'd seen anything unusual by way of flights or airplanes, she mentioned the black helo."

Intrigued, Dev asked, "So you think the professor is on Kauai right now and you want me to verify that?"

"Yes, and I want you to persuade Kulani to join you." Morgan held up his hand in warning. "And before you say no, hear me out," he growled. "This mission is going to absolutely take both of you. I'm choosing you because of your mountain climbing skills. I need her to help you because she has equal skills in climbing. Plus she knows those damned dangerous valleys where the professor's lab is located and the sheer lava cliffs you're going to have to climb down to get there, better than anyone."

Morgan slowly stood up and turned around. Pulling down a screen, he pointed to the detailed map of Kauai pictured there. "These lava cliffs on the Na Pali Coast are twenty-two hundred feet high. They're sheer, vertical faces with nothing but lichen, grass, moss, ferns and brush clinging to their surface. Kulani grew up climbing these cliffs. She knows them like the back of her hand. And she knows the Kalalau Valley, where we believe the professor has his lab hidden. We can't go busting in there with a military force. If the professor is there, and he hears us coming, he's liable to let loose some of that anthrax and put the entire island's population at risk. I'm working with FBI headquarters, as well as with their field office located on the Big Island. We've got the green light to try and get in there and insert a team to verify the professor and his lab are there. If you can take 'em out, you'll do it. Quickly, quietly and cleanly. I want Valdemar alive, if possible. We know he's making enough anthrax for a top event. You and Kulani will stop him."

Dev shook his head. "Morgan, I've climbed every mountain in North America. Climbing is a single sport."

"No, it's not. It's teamwork between you and the

others you're roped with, and you know that." He scowled. "Besides, I've got other problems. This mission is far from stable at the moment."

"Oh?" Dev gazed down at Kulani's photo. Damn, but she was a delicious-looking woman. And what a dichotomy she was—part goddess of the old Hawaiian culture, part modern-day woman and helicopter pilot. Hell, it would be worth taking the mission just to meet her, he thought, grinning to himself. Outwardly, he kept his expression carefully neutral and monitored because he knew Morgan could read a person like a book, quite literally sometimes.

Grumpily, Morgan said, "Kulani doesn't want to take this mission."

Dev couldn't help himself; one corner of his mouth lifted—just a tad. That wouldn't stop him from meeting her, however. She was too much of a looker not to check her out. Dev liked women. All kinds of women. But while he enjoyed them, he refused to get entangled—ever. After a good time, maybe some good, mutual loving, it was time to part company.

"That's okay by me. I can handle a little rappelling down a cliff to get what you want."

Morgan sighed. "It's not that easy, Dev. Don't you think, if it was, I'd tell you to undertake this mission alone? The sheer walls of lava that embrace these deep valleys on Kauai are unlike any other mountaineering challenge. That's why you need Kulani." Running his fingers through his hair, Morgan muttered, "And she refuses to help us. To help you."

"It wouldn't hurt for me to go and meet her. Maybe I can change her mind." But Dev had other things in mind he'd rather persuade her to do, like have dinner with him. Hell, if he was going to undertake this mission in Kauai, he might as well go down and meet her.

"I hope," Morgan said, leaning back in his chair and intently studying Dev, "that you can talk her into working with you. Use that considerable charm you've got to persuade her."

"Morgan, I can't promise you anything." Dev wasn't about to twist Kulani's arm to work with him. He wouldn't promise Morgan that. Dev Hunter worked alone and that was that. But there wouldn't be any harm in meeting her.

Eyes narrowing, Morgan growled, "You will *not* go on this mission alone. If you can't get Kulani to agree to it, you call it off and we'll turn the problem over to the FBI." Morgan held up his index finger. "We have *one* chance. And it involves *two* people or it's a no-go. Do you understand?"

The heavy warning in Morgan's voice put Dev on alert. He wondered if his boss was reading his mind. No, that was impossible. Closing his fists, he said, "I'll do my best. That's all I can tell you."

Nodding, Morgan relaxed slightly. "Okay, you fly to Kauai, get in touch with Kulani and then let me know what goes down. If she's not on board for this mission, then we're out of it in a heartbeat."

Rising, Dev smiled slightly. "I'll do my best to charm her. Usually, women can't resist me."

"Kulani isn't like most women you know," Morgan warned. "She's like a daughter to me. I admire her. I respect the hell out of her. Lately, life has dealt her a pretty rotten hand. You're going to have your hands full, Hunter, and not like you think."

Dev's grin widened boyishly. "I just can't imagine

any woman turning me down. That hasn't happened in so long I can't remember the last time.''

Morgan chuckled. ''I'll give you an A for confidence, Hunter. There's more info in the file you need to read up on. But do that on the flight to the islands. Be in touch.''

Dev nodded. He picked up the folder and placed the color photo of Kulani inside. ''This assignment definitely has perks. I'm looking forward to persuading Ms. Dawson to work with us.''

Well, maybe that wasn't exactly the truth, Dev admitted as he left the office. Kulani Dawson would make his life interesting, but he didn't need her help going into that dinky little valley and finding the turncoat professor. He'd get as much information about the climb from Kulani as he could, without having to partner up with her. So, he'd mix wooing a pretty lady with a little business, and then head out on the mission alone. No woman was capable of the sustained and dangerous demands this mission would make on her. Anyway Morgan was just being overcautious, as usual.

Nope, dinner, definitely. But as to making Kulani his partner, that would never happen. Not *ever.*

Chapter Two

Kulani Dawson greeted the morning with dread. The phone call from Morgan Trayhern the night before had left her raw and hurting. As she moved around her bungalow, the bright orange-and-purple bird-of-paradise blooming outside the kitchen nook looked strong and resilient compared to how she felt as she prepared her coffee.

Normally, Kulani eagerly looked forward to the delicious quiet of this time of day. The bungalow lay at the end of a dirt road, a mile from the main highway that encircled most of the garden isle of Kauai. From the kitchen window of her home, which sat high atop a hill surrounded by pink and red begonia bushes nearly three feet tall and slender palms silhouetted against the sky, she could see the hint of an apricot dawn lovingly lavishing the Pacific Ocean.

Dressed in a pair of comfortable khaki slacks and a

peach-colored, short-sleeved blouse, she swept strands of her thick, black hair, still loose and falling almost to the middle of her back, away from her face as she sat down and sipped the fragrant coffee. The glass slats of the window were open to allow the cool morning air into the bungalow. Because Kauai lay in the middle of the ocean, there was always a breeze. Kulani leaned back in the well-worn, white wicker chair, resting the colorful cup decorated with red hibiscus between her long fingers and watching the breeze move the mighty fronds of the palm trees that surrounded the property.

This place was her haven. Her healing. Her mother, one of the most beloved kahunas in the islands, had birthed her here thirty years ago with the help of several of her sister kahunas. Kulani had been brought into the world with welcoming love, in beautiful, natural surroundings. As she thought of her mother now, her gaze moved to the black-and-white photo on the wall near the window—a picture of her parents with their arms around one another, smiling. She'd purposely placed the bamboo-framed photo of them there where she could see it each morning, and it always made her smile. It also brought sadness over the memory of their early demise in a car accident five years ago.

Sipping the coffee, Kulani's midnight eyes darkened with pain. She'd lost her parents. And then... Quickly, she swerved away from the emotional powerhouse of thoughts and feelings surrounding the loss of her fiancé a year and a half ago. Struggling, she forced the memories deep down inside her. Morgan's unexpected call had torn loose the heavy steel door she'd placed against that terrible day when she'd lost the rest of her world. Lost her will to live her life with the passion she had before.

Normally, she savored the sweet, nutlike taste of the Kauai plantation coffee she drank each morning, but her peace had been shattered. Why had Morgan asked the impossible of her? Kulani had come to think of Morgan as an adopted father. He'd certainly treated her like a daughter. If not for him, for his flight to Kauai after the unthinkable accident, Kulani would have been alone in the aftermath.

Morgan's presence had been a balm to her during the ordeal. He'd organized the funeral, taken care of the paperwork, the police and the insurance people when she could do little else but sit in shocked, almost catatonic silence or suffer incredible storms of weeping, anger and guilt. Morgan had been there for her through it all. Oh, she'd heard of his famous care when mercenaries who worked for him at Perseus got into trouble. And Kulani had talked to more than one merc who had been blessed with Morgan's presence during some traumatic event. But she had never expected Morgan to be there for her as he had.

Closing her eyes momentarily, Kulani took in a deep, shaky breath of air. Morgan had helped her piece her life back together after that tragic day. He'd put her on leave with full pay. He got Dr. Ann Parsons, a flight surgeon and psychiatrist, to fly over to Kauai and help Kulani through the worst of her grief. When all was said and done, Kulani could not force herself to go back to work—at least, not the type of work she'd done before.

She'd flown to Montana, to that little mining town nestled deep in the Rocky Mountains where Morgan made a life for himself and his growing family. Save for her father, she'd rarely seen such family devotion in a man, as she saw in Morgan. And it was then that she began to realize she was like family to Morgan and not just an employee, another cog in the wheel of Perseus. She and Morgan had sat deep underground, in the war room of his facility, and talked. She knew he was a terribly busy man, yet on that afternoon he acted as if she were the only focus he had in his complex and pressing world. Laura, his wife, was pregnant with the twins back then and she had gone into labor the day Kulani was there. The call from the midwife came in just as she and Morgan were finishing their meeting.

Opening her eyes now, Kulani let her gaze drift to another photo below that of her parents. It was of Laura, looking very tired but happy, with her twins, Peter and Kelly, in her arms. Morgan sat behind her, his massive arms around her and the newborns, making the babies look tiny in comparison. His eyes shone with pride and happiness. Kulani had been privileged to be at their home while the midwife, along with Morgan, had helped Laura welcome their newest children into the world. The photo was one of the many she'd snapped that day with her camera. And she'd rolled up her sleeves and helped out around the house. Not that Morgan and Laura didn't have nearby friends who also came to help. But Morgan had made Kulani feel part of his family and she'd wanted to be there for him and Laura.

Swallowing hard, Kulani avoided Morgan's smiling countenance. The next day, when she was preparing to leave her motel and fly home after telling Morgan she was quitting Perseus, she'd gotten a phone call from him. He'd invited her over to the house for lunch. She'd gone over and watched him bungle through making soup and crackers. Morgan wasn't exactly a hausfrau, but in her eyes and heart, his awkward attempts made him even more lovable. He'd proudly made Laura, who was spending the first day after the births in bed, the same fare. Kulani was sure it was welcomed, despite its simplicity. The heart behind the offering was what counted.

When Morgan had sat down to eat with her at the kitchen table, he'd asked her what she wanted to do as a "civilian." Trying to smile, she'd told him of her dream to buy her own helicopter and start a touring business on Kauai. She wanted to share the incredible beauty, the sacredness of her island, with those who were drawn to the place she called home.

It was Morgan who suggested that he float a loan for the 1.3 million dollar Aerostar helicopter for Kulani to start her business. She'd sat there, mouth agape, stunned at his offer. There was no way she could afford to swing such a loan herself. Who had a million dollars to throw around?

Perseus did. Morgan told her to fly home, contact the aircraft manufacturer, put in her order for the Aerostar, and he'd handle the rest of the paperwork. It was a loan in his name, and she could send him monthly payments at a very low rate of interest, to pay him back. She'd accepted his incredible generosity.

That was a year and a half ago. Kulani had come home, accepted the Aerostar at the Lihue Airport and built a lasting name on the island for her touring services, Rainbow Air. All thanks to Morgan, who had picked up the pieces of her life and given them back to her. But there was still a huge, gaping wound in Kulani. She could feel the emptiness sometimes when she waxed philosophical. Every time she had to fly past the Na Pali Coast, the most beautiful and dangerous part of her island home, her gut would clench. Over time, the clenching stopped, and so had a lot of the emotional turmoil that flying near the scene of the tragedy caused. Maybe the fact that her tour route took her past the coast every day, five days a week, had helped some of her initial emotional reactions toward it to fade. Her flight service was so popular that she had a third of the loan to Morgan already paid off. Just the day before Morgan's recent phone call, Kulani had been thinking that for once her life was steady and predictable. No more chaos. Just doing what she loved most: flying. Yesterday she would have sat here and said she had nearly everything she could ever want in life. Almost.

Today, the taste of ashes filled her mouth. Her heart felt bruised when she thought of the wrenching phone call, like someone had placed a belt around her chest and was tightening it. Torn between her loyalty for Morgan, and her own still unhealed grief, Kulani felt shaken to the core. She knew Morgan needed her help—desperately. He wouldn't have asked her otherwise. And yet she'd hung up on him like an immature teenager who hadn't yet mastered her emotions. She needed to call him back. But something whispered to her not to try it today. Still feeling too raw, Kulani honored her own need to take time to get down off the roller coaster of emotions Morgan had torn loose in her once again. She couldn't take the mission, but she could at least apologize for her behavior and let him know that she just didn't have what it would take to help him. Kulani knew Morgan would understand. He was one of the most insightful human beings she'd ever had the privilege of knowing.

Looking at the simple gold watch with the dark brown leather band on her wrist, Kulani realized it was time to go. Usually she looked forward to her work—

taking six people five times a day on one-hour flights around her beautiful island. Today her heart wasn't in it. She wanted to stay home. Maybe do some cooking, which she loved but rarely had time for anymore. Or to putter in her mother's herb garden, which she had replanted after she'd come home to stay. There was something soothing and nurturing about sliding her fingers into the rich, warm volcanic soil of the island. It was healing. And right now, she needed a little time out to do just that. But a million-dollar helicopter did not get paid off by her sitting around and feeling sorry for herself.

What would today bring? What kind of people? Any quirky characters? Today it would take everything for her to remain pleasant, to pretend she was enjoying their company as much as they were falling in love with her beautiful isle.

Dev hoped he didn't look too conspicuous in his bright red, short-sleeved shirt liberally splashed with white hibiscus. Donning a pair of aviator-style sunglasses, he hoped that he looked like a tourist—more aptly, a fish out of water. He stood at the back of the small group of people, all thrilled and excited about their upcoming flight around the gorgeous, green-mantled island of Kauai. Dev's gaze was riveted on the Rainbow Air Aerostar, a white helicopter with a brilliant rainbow painted across the fuselage. Inside it, he could see the pilot, Kulani Dawson, with a clipboard in hand, apparently finishing up some last-minute paperwork. He couldn't see her well from this distance, but his heart hammered a little every time he remembered that luscious photo of her dancing the hula. In fact, she had haunted him during the six-hour flight across the deep blue Pacific to this little island hideaway.

Dev told himself that his reaction to her was so strong simply because he was between relationships. He truly enjoyed women—the way they thought, the way they reacted—and he liked trying to adjust his world to fit theirs. There were definitely differences between men and women he acknowledged. And maybe those differences were the reason his first marriage had been destroyed. Or maybe it was…other things. Frowning, he adjusted his sunglasses. The bright sun was angling toward the west. It was 3:00 p.m. and he knew this was Kulani's last flight of the day. After rearranging the camera he'd slung across his shoulders, he pulled the bill of his baseball cap low over his eyes, shading them. The hat, an old, beat-up Orioles' baseball cap that he wore religiously, probably didn't look exactly tourist-like. But he'd been a fan since a little kid and now that he was a big kid, he enjoyed the sport just as much. He certainly wasn't going to give up his favorite hat for the sake of his ruse.

As he stood waiting and wishing Kulani would emerge from her Aerostar, he noticed the trade winds were deliciously warm at this time of day. He looked up to see the central volcano, Mount Waialeale, long extinct, and clothed in the green of jungle trees and brush, rising from the center of the large island. At the top of the volcano were the perennial white clouds that formed because of icy temperatures at that altitude. Around him, the airport throbbed with the coming and going of other helicopter services, which operated like ceaseless, busy bees, onloading and offloading six passengers at a time. Though all the helicopters were on the same tarmac, Rainbow Air had the first landing apron and seemed to stand apart from the hustle and bustle.

Indeed, Dev had been impressed with the calm, the quietness of Kulani's employees at her office, situated across the street. The mobile structure had beds of colorful flowers around the entrance—definitely a woman's touch, setting it off from the concrete buildings, steel fences and angular aluminum structures that comprised the rest of the airport. Inside, a beautiful young woman, crisp and efficient, had smilingly welcomed the clients. It was obvious to Dev she enjoyed people and her job. There had been comfortable rainbow-colored seats to wait in, and another young employee had prepped them for the coming tour. There was real Kauai coffee and papaya-laced iced tea for those who desired it. Every detail and amenity for the paying passengers had been lovingly attended to.

His curiosity about Kulani had only grown while he'd waited for the flight to return and disgorge its passengers. Dev had thumbed through a huge photo album of people—all smiling as they stood beside the Rainbow Air helo—who had flown with Kulani and written glowing letters of thanks to her. So, was she really an old Hawaiian goddess in the guise of a human being? Her touch, a rainbow touch, was everywhere.

He snapped out of his reverie as he saw her open the door and emerge from the pilot's seat. Finally he was going to get to meet her in person. His heart thumped once, underscoring his reaction to her as she rounded the nose of her aircraft and walked briskly toward them, the clipboard pressed to her breast. She was tall. Much taller than he'd realized—possibly close to six feet. And slender, like the palms growing all over Kauai. Yes, she was as graceful as a palm, he thought, but it was more than that. She was comfortable with her body, with the fact she was a woman. The slight sway of her hips, the flowing walk as she approached them, made his heart trip unexpectedly. As his gaze moved upward, Dev felt smothered by an unfamiliar feeling. His chest expanded with a wild euphoria that took him completely by surprise. It was as if a shock were being jolted through him as he absorbed her features. Her hair, black with bluish highlights in the strong sunlight, was twisted up and neatly pinned in a French roll behind her head. Tendrils touched her temples and high cheekbones, and soft strands brushed her broad forehead, nearly touching her arched eyebrows. She wore aviator sunglasses, so he couldn't make out her eyes, but there was plenty more about her to occupy his piqued interest.

Her face was square, her chin stubborn looking and her lips, breathlessly parted, were full, reminding him of a lush orchid just opening for the first time. Her nose was fine and straight in the midst of her beautifully symmetrical features. Everything about Kulani suggested grace and overall harmony. As she came closer, she gave everyone a slight, welcoming smile, but somehow he sensed her heart wasn't in it. Why? Was she tired? Burned out on tourists? He knew he could never do what she was doing. Working with the public wasn't his idea of a great job. People were always so picky and demanding. However, as Kulani slowly approached, he sensed she truly enjoyed people. Just like that employee she'd hired to manage her office.

Kulani reached up in one graceful motion, her long fingers curling gently against the sunglasses as she removed them from her face. Dev felt as if he was being struck in the chest. He sucked in a deep, shaking breath. Kulani's eyes were huge, as black as the heated tropical nights and shining with life. Her thick black lashes framed them beautifully. When her lips curved upward, Dev was very glad he'd taken this assignment. She was dessert. The best kind. The obvious intelligence in her eyes marked her as someone who knew about life, and the light in them showed that she was no stranger to laughter. Dev knew she had a sense of humor. Maybe he could coax it out of her?

Suddenly, his trip to Kauai wasn't looking so bad, after all. Kulani Dawson was worth the flight and then some, in his opinion. His own mouth curved recklessly. From a purely male standpoint, she was worth chasing, capturing and hotly loving. As she came to a halt before the group, her smile warm and engaging, Dev automatically stepped forward to be in the sunlight of her presence, as did the rest of the eager passengers, who crowded into a tight semicircle around her.

"Good afternoon, everyone. I'm Kulani Dawson, your pilot." She turned and gestured gracefully toward the helicopter. "I hope to give you a magical tour around the island I was born on. This is our 'steed' for today's ride. Let me check the manifest here and get to know you a little before we are whisked away on our rainbow journey."

His skin prickled pleasantly. Kulani had a low alto voice that reminded him of honey—honey trickling moltenly across his flesh, making him want to reach out and slide his fingers along the slope of her cheekbone. She wore absolutely no makeup, but with her natural beauty, Dev felt it suited her not to. Her movements were unhurried and always graceful, her eyes engaging with whomever she spoke as she went through the names on the roster she held. His heart began picking up in beat as she reached his name, the last on the list.

"Mr. Jack Carson?"

"Roger that," he said with a grin. Unaccountably, he felt like an awkward teenage boy. His palms grew sweaty in anticipation. Because Kulani had worked for Perseus at one time, he didn't dare use his real name. If she got wind that he was a Perseus merc, she might balk at giving him any background information. Morgan had warned that she had cut herself off from her former life. And because of that, using an alias was Dev's only option. He didn't like doing it, but he had no other choice at this point.

Kulani felt her heart gallop unexpectedly at the reckless, little-boy smile the tall man at the back gave her. Her intuition niggled at her. He was out of place here. He looked like a tourist, but the way he stood, tall and erect, his knees slightly flexed beneath the navy blue Dockers he wore, said differently. Assessing him keenly, Kulani moved past his warm, devastating smile. His hair was cut military short and he stood like a boxer ready to make a lightning-quick move. Her senses had rarely been wrong. Even though he wore the loud red Hawaiian tourist shirt, he was no vacationer to her island, a voice told her.

Looking down at the manifest, she asked, "How much do you weigh, Mr. Carson?"

He chuckled and placed his hands on his hips. "How much do I have to weigh in order to sit next to you?" Dev knew that the people who weighed the least sat up in the two front seats with the pilot. He knew he'd never get such an opportunity, but wanted to let her know he liked her. But though he'd thought she'd find his reply funny, because the rest of the group chortled over it, he saw her brows dip.

"You could be the weight of a sparrow and you still

wouldn't get a front seat, Mr. Carson.'' Kulani's heart
was beating a little harder now. Damn, she couldn't see
his eyes behind those very dark sunglasses. That bothered her. Already the day had been long and harrowing.
Emotionally, she was raw and simply wanted to go
home, take a hot bath and be alone. This man, whoever
he was, unsettled her for no discernible reason. Kulani
admitted he was drop-dead handsome. Not in a pretty-
boy way, though—not with his darkly tanned face
weathered by life, and the crow's feet at the corners of
his eyes. Deep dimples flashed whenever he gave her
that heated, teasing smile. Really, there was nothing to
dislike about him. She could see a lot of scars and nicks
on his large hands, the muscles of his arms confirmed
his terrific athletic condition. There was no fat on this
man—at all.

''How about a canary?'' he replied with a grin.

Again the group laughed heartily, glancing back and
forth between the pilot and Dev.

''How about no?'' Kulani said sweetly. She smiled
despite how she was feeling. Who could resist this man?
Her heart certainly couldn't.

''I'm crushed, Ms. Dawson. Here I was told you were
the closest thing on the islands to Amelia Earhart.'' He
held up his camera in jest. ''I was hoping for a photo
of you standing next to your bird.''

She regarded him seriously. ''Bird'' was a military
term. Was this guy in the military? A spook? CIA? He
was something, that was for sure. So why did she feel
bothered by it? She had nothing to hide. And then she
recalled Morgan's mission and stiffened internally.
Maybe the other intelligence agencies knew about the
mission, too. But why would someone like him be here?

She'd told Morgan no. She shook her head. None of it made sense.

"Sorry, Mr. Carson. I'll be happy to take a photo of *you* and my bird after the flight, but that's it."

Dev felt a little guilty as he saw her eyes darken with censure over his pushiness. Looking more closely at her, he saw the beginning of shadows beneath her eyes. And there was strain around her tender, soft-looking mouth. The urge to reach forward, slide his hand across her slumping shoulders, almost undid him. Normally he wasn't that eager to run to the aid of a woman he didn't really know. Maybe it was that photo of her dancing that made him bolder than usual.

He nodded deferentially to her. "I'm in your capable hands, Ms. Dawson. You are more than worth the price of admission."

Kulani tried to ignore the handsome stranger's teasing. He certainly thought a lot of himself. Still, that engaging smile of his touched her deeply and she couldn't shake the warmth in his voice as it blanketed her, making her feel just a tad better than before. "You will be the last to get in, Mr. Carson. I'm giving you the rear right window seat."

Dev realized that was the most prized position in the rear of the aircraft. The flight over the island would entail all right turns, and the window was large enough so that a passenger with a camera could take some breathtaking photographs. Dev waited patiently as she stood at the door and ushered each passenger inside. When his turn came, he gave her another glorious smile.

"I think I'm in heaven. No, I take that back. Heaven is standing right in front of me."

Kulani felt his larger-than-life presence as he brushed past her and climbed into the aircraft. "Heaven begins when we lift off, Mr. Carson.'' She smiled a little. What a ham he was. He was playful without being derogatory, and she really had no need to feel uncomfortable. Yet something about him unnerved her.

"Tell me," he said with his most charming smile, "what does your first name, Kulani, mean in Hawaiian?"

Kulani felt red-hot heat strike her cheeks as she stood anchored to the spot, unable to move. The man was positively glowing with a "gotcha" expression on his face. She laughed self-consciously. "It means 'heavenly,' Mr. Carson."

With a gloating grin at all the other passengers, Dev said, "See? I was right—heaven is here with us, right now."

"You're incorrigible, Mr. Carson."

With a slight bow of his head, he murmured, "Why, thank you, Ms. Dawson."

After she got all the passengers in, Kulani circled her aircraft, looking for any telltale leaks or anything else out of place. Satisfied the helicopter was air worthy, she climbed into the left-hand seat. More than a little aware of Jack Carson staring at her from behind his sunglasses, she felt the side of her neck prickling pleasantly. All the rest of the passengers were smiling and chatting excitedly as they put on their protective earphones, hardly able to contain their anticipation over the forthcoming adventure.

Dev watched as Kulani's hands flew with knowing ease across the instrument panel, switching on this or that toggle. He put his earphones on his head and heard soft classical music in the background. No detail was too small for her, he realized. As the rotors on the aircraft began to turn faster and faster, the vibrations went through him. He was enjoying watching her—maybe a little too much. Kulani Dawson was more than a looker; she was enigmatic, he decided. And he had seen her assessing him, too. Being able to coax one tiny smile out of her made him feel like Mark McGwire when he'd hit his seventieth home run.

Suddenly, Dev felt happier than he could ever recall. Since his devastating divorce years ago, a pall had hung over him. But simply by being in the general vicinity of Kulani Dawson, he felt his life take on a new, keen joy. It was something Dev had never experienced before. As the aircraft lifted off the tarmac and headed upward into the deep blue sky, he laughed softly and sat back. Morgan Trayhern sure as hell knew how to pair him up with the right woman. But Dev would never have her as a merc team member. Now, as far as a relationship was concerned, that was another matter—a honeyed one oozing with promise.

Chapter Three

Kulani began her formal introduction to her eager passengers as she gently lifted the helicopter off the asphalt tarmac of Lihue Airport. Ascending quickly to one thousand feet, the prescribed altitude for her aircraft, she started off on her usual route. Kulani wasn't surprised to hear gasps of pleasure from the women passengers as the immense size and grandeur of Kauai came into view. They always appreciated Kauai's incredible green beauty.

"Kauai is called the Garden Island for good reason," she said as she moved her aircraft toward the western, drier side of the island. "You can see the magnificent dormant volcano—Mount Waialeale which we'll visit later—in the middle of the island. As we fly around it, south to west, you'll find a lot of sugar cane being grown below."

"Not pineapple?"

Kulani's neck prickled pleasantly. Jack Carson's deep voice was like the rough lick of a cat's tongue on her flesh. It wasn't unusual for passengers to ask questions, but she'd never had such a response to a question before. "Not pineapple, Mr. Carson. Just a lotta sweet sugar cane on this island."

She continued her talk. Kauai Community College sped by beneath them and they crossed the major road that encircled two-thirds of the island, the Kaumualii Highway. "As we go south, it gets a lot drier. There's not as much rainfall down here as up on the north coast of Kauai. The main tourist hotels down in this part are located around Poipu. You can see the clear turquoise and emerald colors of a healthy ocean below us."

"How about whales?"

It was Carson—again. He was leaning forward in his seat, his camera balanced between his very large hands.

"They come in from about November through May every year to calve their babies here. The north shore, the Na Pali Coast area, is where most of the sightings take place." She licked her lips. Carson was so close. She felt vulnerable to his warm, vibrant presence. As if sensing her unease, he sat back in his seat. Internally, Kulani breathed a sigh of relief. Trying to concentrate on the changes of terrain taking place beneath her, she urged her helicopter toward the western side of the island.

The land below turned from green to the many different colors of dried earth. "What you see coming up beneath us is Waimea Canyon. When Mark Twain was here, he called it the Grand Canyon of the Pacific. The layers of earth represent different eruptions and lava flows. The canyon is ten miles long and one mile deep.

For those who are hikers, you can actually walk thirty-six hundred feet down into the bottom of it.''

"I'd like to take that hike with you. You look like you could handle it.''

Carson—again. Kulani found his intrusions unsettling. Not in a bad way; rather, a good way. She absorbed his low, vibrating voice into her body and, surprisingly, into her heart. Maybe it was just because she was feeling vulnerable. After all, they were getting close to the Na Pali Coast, and Kulani dreaded this part of the trip. Already, her chest was beginning to feel as if a band were around it. And Carson's voice somehow, almost miraculously, had dissolved her fears—if only momentarily.

"I don't do hiking, Mr. Carson. I like to fly,'' she teased back, her voice a bit off-key.

He chuckled deeply and took a few snapshots out the window. "If I pack the sandwiches, the bottle of wine and bring along some great desserts, will you go with me?''

The other passengers all chuckled at his joking. Kulani felt heat crawling up her neck and flooding her face. Blushing! Of all things. It didn't look very professional, she was sure. Keeping her focus on the instruments before her, she laughed a little. "I know a whole lotta ants that would love to take you up on your offer, Mr. Carson.''

"Shucks, shot down again.'' Dev grinned at his audience, who were all smiling and laughing with him. He saw the redness creep into Kulani's soft, golden skin and he saw one corner of that incredibly luscious mouth pull slightly upward. Sensing that he had his foot in the door, he decided to work on getting her to go out to dinner with him tonight. One way or another. Right now, he felt like a hunter on the track of an animal he wanted to bring down. There was always the thrill of the chase for him where women were concerned, but Kulani wasn't just any woman. She was unique. Sultry. Enigmatic. He didn't quite know what was going on in that head of hers. He wished he could look her in the eye, but from this angle, all he could see was her clean, aristocratic profile.

They flew over the canyon, then on toward the northern part of the island. Clouds that were forming like white cotton candy along the green-clad slopes mesmerized Dev. The whole scene was beautiful.

"What you're seeing right now," Kulani said, "are the misty forests of Koke State Park, woodlands that surround this incredible canyon. We're going to rise and follow the brush-and-tree-clad slopes to the top, on the other side of which is the Na Pali Coast." Her throat closed. She felt grief surge through her. Automatically, her hands tightened around the collective and cyclic. Her heart began to beat a little harder as the helicopter began to climb the verdant slope toward the top of the ridge that separated the canyon from the coast.

"Hey," Dev said, pointing his finger between Kulani and the passenger seated beside her, "isn't that a hiking trail right on top of this ridge?"

Shaken by his sudden closeness and his intensity, Kulani said, "Why, yes, it is…thousands of tourists hike that trail every year. It's a slippery track made of clay, and it's always misting rain up there. A lot of people get hurt because they don't wear proper foot gear or they're not prepared for the changes in temperature and weather, which happen almost hourly at that elevation."

Dev was less than twelve inches away from Kulani. He heard the breathlessness in her voice. He saw the corner of her mouth dig inward, as if she were hurting. And as he perused her more closely, he saw tiny dots of perspiration standing out on her brow. She was having a reaction to something. Him? He hoped not. His ego wouldn't be able to handle the possibility that he bothered her. The feeling around her was one of tightness. Even her lips were compressed, no longer soft and accessible as before.

"Is it possible," he asked, "to climb from that path down into the Kalalau Valley? It looks like the trail stops at the top of the ridge."

Stunned by Carson's question, Kulani felt an incredible surge of pain in her heart. She brought the helicopter to a hover well above the trail so that her passengers could get their first look at the Na Pali coastline. "Uh, yes...yes, I guess you could." Swallowing hard, she rasped, "The trail is a point where a climber could choose to scale that wall and descend into the valley below. It's a highly dangerous climb. The valley is twenty-two hundred feet deep, with steep, vertical, black lava walls on three sides. Your handholds are minuscule—little holes and cracks here and there. As the lava cooled, the rock became bumpy and concave, and you might get a handhold if you're lucky. You must rely on lines and pitons to scale it. It's *very* risky. People have died trying to descend from that trail into the canyon."

Dev heard the rattling in her low voice and saw her face go ashen. He frowned as he glanced out at the red clay trail that zigged and zagged along the top of the ridge forming the northern lip of Waimea Canyon. On the other side of the ridge was one of the most photographed spectacles in the world.

The Na Pali Coast looked as if, millions of years ago,

a giant had dug his sharp fingernails into the lava cliffs, leaving five gouged-out valleys in their wake. All were clothed in an incredible verdant splendor, with stubborn brush, grasses and orchids clinging to the sheer walls. Down below, he noted, was the Kalalau Valley—his target. His heart beat a little harder in anticipation as he perused the area with the eye of a mountain climber. Kulani was right: the vertical walls were covered in greenery—mostly ferns from what he could make out at this altitude. Gazing out the window toward the cobalt-blue Pacific, he saw a small trail winding across the landscape.

"What's that other trail to the right?" he asked, pointing toward it.

Kulani gulped and tried to get a handle on her galloping pulse, her grief. She wanted to get away from the coast as soon as she could. She used Carson's question to do just that. The deep, wide valley of Kalalau opened up beneath them in gaping splendor. On the valley floor was a river that splashed over smooth gray and black boulders, tumbling toward the ocean. "That's known as the Kalalau Trail."

"How do you get to it?"

"You can drive to it by going around the east end of the island. It's a two-mile hike into Kalalau Beach— one of the toughest trails anyone will ever try. I advise good hiking boots, rain gear, a hat, water and food."

"Not to mention a first aid kit?" Dev joked as they drew closer. They swept out over the blue-green ocean, which looked both emerald and aquamarine, depending upon the depth. White, foamy waves crashed against newly minted gold beaches uninhabited by human beings. The Na Pali Coast was forbidding from a mountain climbing perspective. But negotiable. Dev hadn't climbed El Capitan in Yosemite for nothing. The walls of lava were just different, that was all. He felt confident he could climb down into the box canyon where the anthrax lab was reputed to be.

Kulani tried to smile, but didn't succeed. "Yes, a first aid kit is very advisable. We get hikers all the time who trip over exposed tree roots or fall on the rocks and break an ankle." She wanted to cry every time she saw the Kalalau Valley. It held too many bad memories and she was still tied to it emotionally, whether she wanted to be or not. Aiming her aircraft in a southeasterly direction, she brought it inland and headed toward the center of the island.

"Next, we're going to fly very close to Manawaio-puna Falls. For those who saw the movie *Jurassic Park,* you'll remember the opening sequence. This is the waterfall they shot for the picture." Kulani concentrated on doing her job. She banked the aircraft. Below them and to her right was the spectacular waterfall.

Normally, the waterfall, which fell a thousand feet, thundering over gray and brown lava, always lifted her heart. Today, for some reason, it did not. And then she felt the gentle touch of a man's hand on her right arm. It wasn't a hard squeeze, but one that instantly soothed her grief.

"Ms. Dawson, any chance of hovering for a sec while I get a photo of this beauty?"

Jack Carson—again—only this time, she craved his touch. For as big a man as he was, with obvious strength and power exuding from him like a ten-million-watt sun, his touch was surprisingly gentle. *He* was a surprise, Kulani realized. As his fingertips left her arm, she stammered, "Well, s-sure..." and she halted the helicopter and turned it so that he could get a full view of the waterfall. There was a rainbow down below, in the mist near the oval pool at the waterfall's base, and she knew the shot would be breathtaking.

"Thank you, Ms. Dawson." Dev grinned broadly. He saw her nod, although her eyes never left the control panel in front of her. He felt the aircraft move gently to the left. What had possessed him to touch her? And he had *liked* doing it. In fact, his hand had been itching like fire itself to reach out and touch her. He was surprised at the firmness and muscle beneath that silky blouse she wore. The moment he'd touched her, she'd responded, and he had felt her strength, realizing there was nothing weak about this woman.

"I want to take you to the heart of my island," Kulani said in a softened, husky tone. "The heart of the Hawaiian people is bound by everything around them—the air, the birds that fly in it, the life-giving ocean, the fish and the land creatures." She banked the helicopter toward a large crater clothed in olive, avocado and emerald colors. "I'm going to take you inside the middle of Mount Waialeale, our largest dormant volcano. Only this isn't just any volcano. This is the soul of Kauai, and of our people," she continued in a hushed tone.

Dev was instantly snared by her low, honeyed voice as she told the story of her people, at the same time taking the helicopter downward. He saw a circular shaped, cavernous hole coming up. It looked like a dark, gaping wound in the landscape.

"Waialeale is the heart of our island, of our spiritual link with nature. Just enjoy as I slowly move the aircraft down into the central cone, where once, millions of tons of red-hot lava spewed out...."

Dev tensed. That crater was a good thousand feet deep. The walls were slick, gleaming with moisture provided by the clouds that hung above the volcano. The lava inside the walls was either black or a reddish, rusty color.

Kulani's control of the aircraft was impeccable, for they moved smoothly over the lip and then sank down, down, downward. The shadows deepened, and as he looked up, he saw bright blue sky and sunlight far above him, but now they were in the embrace of the volcano. The shadow swallowed them up. The sky began to recede more and more as they descended deeply into the sacred crater.

"I'm sure all of you can feel it," Kulani said with reverence. "We call this *manna*. It is the energy of spirit—of this volcano, of the old gods and goddesses of Hawaii, who still live here. We are privileged to experience it, to feel it...." She watched her instrument panel closely. The volcano crater was wide, but she only had about a fifty foot clearance on any side, so any abrupt move on her part would send them crashing into the mighty lava walls and tumbling to their deaths.

"In the olden times, when a king died, his body was dropped into this volcano. It was a sign of his greatness, and the living on of his mighty spirit." Kulani gently touched the controls, turning the helicopter in a complete circle. She heard the gasps of pleasure, the cries of "Look!" and she smiled. Some of the pain she'd felt earlier was loosening its grip on her. Just being able to descend into this volcano was a healing for Kulani. And she found herself thinking that Jack Carson was healing, too. His touch had had a profound effect on her, whether she wanted to admit it or not.

Then, just as slowly, Kulani urged her aircraft up and out of the crater. Moving the cyclic and collective gently, she flew up and out of the cone to hover above it, so that the people on board could take pictures of a view they'd never forget.

As she rotated the helicopter in a semicircle, three different waterfalls could be seen, each falling three thousand feet, from the volcano's massive shoulders to dark blue pools below. The crater was, indeed, a mystical place where dream met reality. Kulani loved this part of the tour. She could hear the soft sighs, the thrill in their voices, and she knew all of them had felt the *manna,* the power of the gods and goddesses. No one was left untouched by the ancient Hawaiian spirits in this experience—not even her.

Dev tried to quell his disappointment. All too soon, they were flying back to Lihue Airport. He checked his watch as they landed and saw that it was 5:00 p.m. Just in time for dinner. He smiled a little as Kulani shut down the engine after they'd returned to the tarmac of the busy little airport. Kulani was his—she just didn't know it yet, that was all. So he waited like a patient wolf who had his quarry in sight. He saw her open the door and give the okay to disembark once the rotor blades had stopped turning.

Everyone climbed out, breathless and excited. Dev stood over by the fence and watched as Kulani snapped shot after shot of guests standing beside her colorful aircraft. It was a nice touch, a great way to advertise. The trade winds were soft and warm, moving through her ebony hair and catching the blue highlights now and again. Dev feasted his gaze upon her. Her every move was so graceful, and again that photo of Kulani dancing the hula came back to him as he waited for the last patron to leave the tarmac and head across the street, the adventure at an end.

Kulani's back prickled. There was one customer left.

Jack Carson. Slowly turning, she saw him leaning languidly against the cyclone fence, one foot lifted against it, his massive and muscular arms crossed in front of his barrel chest. There was so much power and masculinity in this man. Yet Kulani had felt his touch, and it was anything but that. He knew how to be tender. Few men did, and that was a travesty. That was why she was drawn to him—that incredible sense of care and tenderness radiating like a beacon from him.

Kulani literally felt as if she were blanketed by his watchful gaze. Tilting her head to one side, she looked at him.

"Do you want your photo taken with my bird, Mr. Carson?" She saw a slow smile ease across his lips. He had a nicely shaped mouth and that careless little-boy hitch on the left side endeared him to her. Wishing once again that he'd take off his sunglasses so she could see his eyes, Kulani laughed at herself. It had been a long time since she'd been genuinely interested in a man. *Any* man, as a matter of fact.

"Well," he drawled, dropping his foot to the tarmac and unwinding slowly, "you could do me a favor, Ms. Dawson." He stood up and met her halfway. "I really would like a photo of *you* standing next to your bird here. How about it?"

Kulani smiled a little and gazed up at him. This man was so confident it sizzled out of every pore. "I don't normally pose for customers, Mr. Carson."

He saw her frown a little at his request and intuitively realized that his sunglasses might be offputting, so he removed them and looked deeply into her eyes. Instantly, he saw them widen with what he thought was surprise, and then...pleasure? Was that what he was reading in them? Dev was unsure. However, he was sure that he wanted Kulani.

Kulani choked back a little gasp of pleasure when Jack Carson spontaneously took off his dark sunglasses. His eyes, large, hard and intelligent looking, were the deep green of the jungle floor of her beloved Kauai, the pupils large and black, with a thin rim of forest green surrounding them. There were gold highlights sparkling deep within his gaze, and she could feel his playfulness, his warmth toward her. And she wanted more, but suddenly felt awkward about it. She hadn't felt like this since— She quickly squashed the errant thought.

"I'll make you a deal," Dev said in a husky voice tinged with humor. "If you'll let me take a photo of you with your bird, I'll spring for dinner tonight at the Kilohana Plantation. I've heard Gaylord's Restaurant has excellent food. How about it?" Never had Dev wanted a woman to say yes more than in this instant. He saw Kulani's beautiful ebony eyes widen.

"I don't normally go out with customers, Mr. Carson."

"Call me Jack," he said, and cringed. Dev wanted to tell her the truth, but he didn't dare. At least, not yet. He knew he could climb down into the Kalalau Valley by himself now that he'd viewed it from the air. He didn't need Kulani. At least—not in *that* way. He saw her in his arms, in his bed, her lips against his mouth. No, she definitely had a place in his life—but not at his side as a mountain climbing guide on a merc mission.

When he saw her lips part, sensed the protest coming, he held up his hand and said, "Okay, okay...no problem. No photo of you and your bird, but you *have* to agree to have dinner with me tonight. I understand Gaylord's is the place to take a beautiful woman. You can't say no, Ms. Dawson. I'll keep you well entertained and we'll have a lot of laughs.'' He held up his hands. "No monkey business. That's a promise."

She met and held his verdant gaze, which was shining with confidence. "I can handle monkey business, Mr. Carson. And no, I don't want to go out...." She was lying and she knew it. She hoped Carson didn't see that she was. Why on earth was she even considering his invitation? She'd had plenty of other male passengers make offers for dinner before, and it had been easy to turn them down. But not this time. Not with this stalwart, egotistical guy dressed in a bright red-and-white Hawaiian shirt, and wearing a crooked grin on his mouth.

"Now, I can't see you running home to just sit all night, read the newspaper and watch television."

She laughed a little and then shook her head. "You're something else, Mr. Carson."

"Call me Jack," he said again. "Am I right? You're not the homebody type?" He motioned to her arm. "You got a set of muscles under that beautiful veneer of yours. My hunch is you do something pretty physical and strenuous to stay in shape. Am I right?"

Her heart twinged. "I mountain climb. I—I mean," she stammered, "I did. I don't anymore." And she began to pray that the past would finally ease up and leave her alone. She saw his eyes glitter with interest. Almost like a wolf who considered her prey. Inwardly, Kulani trembled with anticipation.

"Ah, we have something in common. I'm a mountain climber, too." He gestured toward the dormant volcano. "I climbed Mount McKinley in Alaska just the other year. You ever climb El Capitan in Yosemite?"

All the talk of mountain climbing scared her. Kulani

felt her stomach twist into a knot. "Please—" she held up her hand "—I don't want to talk about the subject, Mr., er, Jack." Any topic other than that one. Kulani moved away from him. It was as if the past were haunting her. She liked Carson. She even entertained the thought of having dinner with him. But she couldn't talk about mountain climbing. The fact that he was a climber scared her the most. Hurriedly, she walked back toward her aircraft.

Dev was right on her heels. "Hey, slow down...." He reached out and gently snagged her arm. "I'm sorry if I stepped on some painful stuff."

Surprised, Kulani pulled free of his gentle grip. His eyes were narrowed and assessing, and she knew that he was genuinely sorry, although she saw a lot of questions in his gaze. If he was smart, he wouldn't ask. Holding up her hands, she whispered, "Look, you're a very nice guy, but I can't handle conversations about mountain climbing anytime soon, so let's just—"

"No problem." He grinned boyishly, hope gleaming in his eyes. "What would you like to talk about at dinner? I'm open. I'm a global traveler, so I'm sure I can handle a conversation about anything you'd like to chat about." He saw the wind ruffle her hair playfully and he had a maddening urge to tame the dark strands back into place, but he didn't dare. Kulani was holding herself stiffly, her arms crossed against her chest.

"I just got back from Hong Kong. Now, there's a place to go. Ever been there?"

Kulani frowned and allowed her arms to drop to her sides. "No...but I've wanted to go." She turned, opened the door to the cockpit and retrieved her manifest.

"How about if I give you a guided tour of Hong

Kong, then? We'll get a little dinner, enjoy the stars above us as we dine, have a nice bottle of wine to celebrate the sky, and maybe have a few laughs.''

Walking slowly, Kulani moved around the nose of the helicopter. The sun was setting in the west and the shadows were growing dark and long. Jack Carson shortened his stride to match hers, moving easily at her side. He had his hands thrust deep into the pockets of his cotton pants, his head turned toward her, his eyes— those large, intelligent eyes, so assessing, as if he could read what was in her soul—touching her vulnerable, hard-beating heart.

"I can promise you a night of damn fine food and even more excellent company.''

Kulani was scared and she admitted it. Oddly, she felt he was telling her the truth. And for whatever reason, she capitulated. She didn't look too closely at why. Her heart had been heavy with grief and depression minutes ago, but being around this man was making her feel buoyant once again. For the first time in a long time she wanted to live as she once had, to be out in a social environment, to participate in a world she'd closed herself off from so long ago.

"Well…''

"Listen," Dev whispered roughly as he slid his hand around her upper arm and opened the gate leading off the tarmac, "you do what you gotta do to tie up loose ends around here. I can wait in the car, the white Mercedes over there, until you're done. I'm new to the island, but I do know where Gaylord's is. I'll get you an early dinner and make sure you're home in time for a good night's sleep so you can fly tomorrow. Fair enough?''

He saw her face turn pink momentarily as he touched

her. Dev *wanted* to touch her. He liked the firmness of her body. Grace with incredible feminine strength. Maybe the quiet, deep strength he sensed in Kulani was because of the Hawaiian blood that ran in her veins. Maybe…well, he was looking forward to finding out a whole lot more about her over a nice starlit dinner, that was for sure.

Her mouth twisted a little. "This is rare. You're going to be *my* tour guide."

Chortling, Dev walked Kulani across the highway toward her office. He forced himself to release her arm. Touching Kulani was habit forming. In fact, downright addictive. "I'm pretty colorful once I get started."

Kulani's heart lifted a little more. She definitely felt lighter. In fact, she felt hope—something that had died almost two years ago. "What is it about you, Jack?"

Dev winced at her use of his alias. He felt bad for maintaining his cover, but he had to. "Oh, I don't know," he crowed confidently, giving her a wink. "I'm single, young and eligible. I make a decent living and I enjoy life. How about you?"

Wrinkling her nose, Kulani halted at the steps to her office. Holding the clipboard against her chest, she gazed up at him. Right now, Jack Carson looked more like a little boy who had just stolen a frog from the pond and was going to show it off to all his buddies. Only she was the frog. Would he be as good as his word? Would he be *just* a dinner companion and not try any moves on her? Kulani wasn't ready for that. She doubted she ever would be. But Jack Carson was an interesting man. Quickly closing the door on the fact that he was a mountain climber, she decided she could have an enjoyable night out with him.

"I live to fly," she told him simply.

Dev smiled down at her. "My instincts tell me you like to do a lot of things, but let's save dinner tonight for exploration, shall we?" He lifted his hand and moved toward his Mercedes, which was parked in the gravel lot.

Just the way he walked, his shoulders thrown back so proudly, the way he arrogantly lifted his head with that graceful, taut movement only an athlete had, made him very alluring to Kulani. With a shake of her head, she reminded herself that she had about thirty minutes of wrapping up details with her office manager before she could leave. As she climbed the wooden steps to her office, she smiled softly. She was looking forward to finding out more about the enigmatic Jack Carson....

Chapter Four

Dev was pleased with his surroundings. Gaylord's Restaurant was the perfect place to take the woman who'd been on his mind from the moment he'd first laid eyes on her. He felt guilty about continuing his ruse as Jack Carson, but it couldn't be helped, he thought, as he and Kulani walked toward the plantation headquarters, built in the 1930s during the golden days of the sugar cane era, to the restaurant. The lawns and shrubbery about the sprawling building were carefully manicured. Now the plantation had been turned into a number of boutiques, plus the famous restaurant. The two-story structure loomed above them as they walked up the marble steps and into the dimly lit foyer.

Without thinking, Dev placed his hand across the small of Kulani's back as the maître d' came to escort them to their table. Though Dev's fingers barely brushed the material, he felt the strength and firmness of her body beneath her silk blouse. She looked up at him, an expression of surprise on her face at his touch. Quickly, he removed his hand.

"Sorry, it's an old habit of mine," he said with a wry smile. "Take a lovely woman who looks like a goddess from old Hawaii to dinner, and I just sort of lose my perspective." When he smiled down at her, he saw her lips part. Groaning internally, he wondered if Kulani knew how damned provocative she appeared. Her hair, which had been pinned up earlier, now flowed like molten lava across her shoulders and upper back. The low lighting made it look like gleaming sapphires had been braided through the strands.

"Kauai inspires creative thinking," Kulani agreed. Her flesh tingled wildly where his strong, guiding fingers had brushed her blouse ever so briefly. She knew that Jack wasn't trying to grope her. He was a gentleman, a throwback to the men of the past who escorted a woman with a gallant flair. "And your gesture was a nice one. Thank you."

Relieved, he smiled again. Glancing around at the hundred or so laughing, chatting patrons, Dev realized they were enjoying their meals without the knowledge that a mad professor with a worldwide terrorist organization might be making deadly anthrax in one of the beautiful, pristine valleys along the coast. The reality intruded harshly for a moment as he followed the maître d' to the table. All these people could die, too, which was what made this evening with Kulani so important to him. Just for one night he was going to enjoy this woman completely, and then, tomorrow, he would face the raw reality of life in its worst moment.

Again he placed his hand in the small of her back as they were escorted out the French doors of the restaurant to a U-shaped terrace. Twilight was falling and he was delighted to see old-fashioned, turn-of-the-century lampposts spreading a casual, unobtrusive light. The dining area was filled with white-linen-covered tables and bamboo chairs with thick, cream-colored cushions. In the center of the patio was a cascade of flowers, ranging from yellow and red ginger, proud looking bird-of-paradise, spectacular red torch ginger thinly outlined in white, to delicate shell pink ginger. Plants that were easily ten to twelve feet high created a natural barrier from prying eyes around the outdoor restaurant. As Dev inhaled the delicate, sweet fragrance of ginger in bloom, he saw directly ahead of them the silhouetted mountains topped with a small dormant volcano called Kilohana Crater. Everything was clothed in purple and blue shadows in anticipation of the coming night.

Kulani saw the awe written in Jack's expression as he seated her at the table. She smiled a little at how easily she could read what he was feeling; not many men allowed that kind of access to themselves. But then, she told herself humorously as she picked up the pale pink linen napkin and placed it across her lap, Jack Carson was so full of himself that he shouldn't have any trouble at all showing how he felt at any time to anyone. The man's confidence radiated from him like the sun at high noon. Kulani had noticed how many patrons had looked up as he'd entered the patio.

After the waiter took their drink order of iced guava juice, Dev folded his hands on the table and smiled at Kulani. "You know, with the backdrop of that shadowed volcano behind you, you look more and more like a daughter of Pele."

She felt heat prickle her cheeks. Avoiding his gleaming, forest-green gaze, she picked nervously at the linen

napkin in her lap and rearranged it—even though it
didn't need rearranging. "Oh…thanks…yes, sunset and
sunrise are very dramatic on Kauai. Actually…" She
lifted her head and finally met his gaze. There was such
tenderness in his expression that she found her heart
fluttering in response. Carson was a visual feast for her
eyes. And Kulani was more than a little aware of other
women looking appreciatively in his direction. "Actually," she said again, clasping her hands in front of her,
"Kauai is really an artist's and photographer's paradise.
The light here is fantastic. I see changes in the landscape every time I fly over the island."

"Don't you get tired of flying the same route and
saying the same things?" Dev inquired. He saw her lips
draw into a slight smile.

"No, not at all. Every hour, the light shifts." She
waved her hand gracefully toward the spectacular
flower-filled garden near where they sat. "Look at that
incredible white-and-pink shell ginger."

Dev looked at the long spike of cuplike white blossoms tinged with dark pink inside. "Yes?"

"Watch how the light shifts and changes on them.
Every minute they're a little different." Inhaling, Kulani whispered, "I just love the fragrance of ginger. It's
wonderful."

"I think that's the perfume you were wearing today?"

She held his gaze. "Why, yes…I do wear ginger perfume." Because some of her passengers had perfume
allergies, Kulani was very careful to wear just a tiny
dab behind each of her ears. No one had ever com-
plained to her of it, so she figured no one could smell
it except her. "You've got a nose like a wolf," she said,
laughing a little and taking a sip of her iced drink.

Cocking his head, Dev watched the twilight bathe Kulani like an old-master's painting. The lamplight cast a golden color across part of her face while the twilight caressed her with darkness, accentuating the raw beauty of her full mouth and her straight, aristocratic nose and high cheekbones. "In my business, all my senses count." He groaned internally at his words. Somehow, he'd dropped his guard. *Damn!* He instantly saw Kulani's dark, thoughtful-looking eyes narrow a little speculatively. He didn't want to continue to lie to her. Yet if he told her who he was, she'd more than likely get up and leave. The last thing he wanted was an aborted dinner engagement with her. Later, he'd come clean. Now, as he saw the question forming in her eyes, he quickly distracted her.

"So, excellent tour guide from Kauai, tell me about this wonderful old plantation we're in. I like antiques, and judging from what little I saw as we walked in, this place was very expensive to build. Looks like the owners spared no expense. Teakwood floors aren't exactly cheap."

Perking up, Kulani gazed around the busy, bustling establishment. Around the ginger plants in the center of the garden grew bougainvillea of hot pink, bright orange and yellow. The thorny, climbing bushes had been tamed and pruned so that they looked like small, square splashes in a vibrant palette of colors. "You don't miss much, Jack. Kilohana was the inspiration of its owner, Gordon Parke Wilcox. A British architect by the name of Mark Potter designed this wonderful, sprawling estate." With a flourish of her hand, she said, "Kilohana was built in 1935 and was the most expensive and lovely home ever build on our island. The owner had furniture sent by ship from Gump's of San Francisco, which was *the* place to buy furniture in that day. We didn't get to walk around much, but there are many beautifully landscaped gardens as well.''

''The owners don't live here anymore?''

Kulani shook her head. She liked the way light carved half his face from the darkness. He had a strong, stubborn jaw, his eyes deep set and gleaming, his nose shaped more like a hawk's beak. There was nothing weak looking about Jack Carson, and she found herself relaxing within his aura, which was considerable. Somehow, Kulani knew that he would take care of her if she was in trouble of any kind. Her skin still prickled pleasantly at the memory of his healing touch.

''No, Kilohana rose and declined with the sugar trade. An enterprising entrepreneur restored the place to its original splendor, which you see now. There are many galleries here instead, and much of the Wilcox art is still in the plantation. It's a joy just to walk through this place if you have time. It's quite a celebration of art. There are other shops, as well, and this is where I usually come if I need a birthday gift for a friend.''

When the black-and-white-clad waiter came over, Dev looked at Kulani and pointed to the menus, which still lay unopened between them. ''Why don't you order for us? I trust your sense of things.''

Smiling a little brazenly, Kulani placed her hands over the large menus. ''My, do we lead a risky life?''

Her teasing made him feel hot and hungry for her. Would she smile at him that way when he slid his fingers along the dusky slope of her cheek? Enjoying her teasing, Dev grinned back. ''Risk is my middle name. Go ahead, order what you think I'd like.''

Opening the menu, Kulani devoted her attention to

the list of specialties printed there. "Humph. You look like a Midwest meat-and-potatoes man to me."

Chuckling, Dev said, "Not far from right. I was born in Colorado, and yes, I like beef."

Hence, his love of mountain climbing, a voice whispered to Kulani. Her smile slipped just a little, but she pasted it back on. "Okay, meat it is. I'm going to order you a filet mignon with papaya and brandy sauce drizzled over it, yam mashed potatoes, and a fresh romaine salad mixed with a mouthwatering papaya-and-poppy-seed dressing." She tilted her head. "How do you like your steak cooked?"

"Medium well, thank you." He was enjoying her taking over. She was a highly confident woman and he absorbed her presence hungrily. "What will you have?"

"Me? Oh, they have a wonderful tuna salad here that I'm mad about." She quickly gave the rest of her order, and the waiter left with the menus.

Clasping her hands together, she said, "Now, tell me a little bit about yourself, Jack. Why are you here on the island? Business or pleasure?"

Dev frowned inwardly. Damn, he didn't want to continue this charade, nor did he want to lie to Kulani. She was so sharp that eventually she'd catch him in his lies if he wasn't careful. Opening his hands, he said, "Oh, I'm a tumbleweed, you know? I promised to talk to you about Hong Kong. I just got back from there."

"Doing what?" Kulani asked. She saw the uncomfortable look in his eyes for a brief moment. He shifted in his chair as if to hide his nervous impulse.

"A little of this, a little of that. I do a lot of scouting for my company. It's a touring and travel business. I get sent all over the world." At least that wasn't a lie. "And I'm here to photograph certain places, take tabs on who's around, and stuff like that.'' That wasn't a lie, either.

"So, this is a business trip?''

"Sitting with you here tonight certainly isn't business. It's all pleasure.'' That wasn't a lie, either. Dev saw her blush beautifully. Kulani ran her long fingers through her hair, nestling the dark strands behind her delicate ear. She wore small pearl earrings, in keeping with her Hawaiian goddess image, he decided. Natural objects on a completely natural woman.

"Flattery comes easily to you, doesn't it?''

"That's not a sin, is it?''

Kulani studied him. "I feel you're uncomfortable, Jack.''

"Women's intuition at work?''

"Maybe…'' Kulani paused. She ran her finger in a circular motion on the linen tablecloth. "It's just that you seem out of place as a tourist here.''

Sighing, Dev was happy to see their salads brought by the waiter, creating a diversion. Eating always slowed down conversation. "What? You don't like my big red Hawaiian shirt with the white hibiscus on it?'' Pointing to it, he gave her a wide, boyish smile. "Well, you're right as rain about it. I'm usually in polo shirts and jeans and a good set of hiking boots. Coming from Colorado, where I either had my leg thrown across a good quarter horse or was up in the mountains climbing anything I could get to, I guess I do look out of place.'' Digging into the salad, he could see her expression ease a bit.

Kulani smiled a little and daintily ate her salad. Looking around, she saw that most of the tables were filled. Gaylord's, one of the most popular eateries on the island, was always busy. As she watched Jack eat, she felt her heart twinge. This was the first man since…the accident…that she felt actual interest in.

Shortly afterward, their main courses were served. Kulani's "salad" was actually a tuna steak laid out on dark green spinach leaves. The way the meal was presented reminded her of a rainbow. Red peppers arced like crescent moons on one side of the plate. On the other were delicious mashed yams with sweet honey mixed into them. She saw her pleasure mirrored in Jack's face as his steak was set before him.

"Look good?" Kulani teased.

"Brother, does it," Dev said with passion as he picked up his fork and knife. "I'm starving."

"A big man like you," she said, cutting into her tuna steak, "needs a big meal." Kulani looked at his left hand then. There was no ring on it.

"You strike me as the homey type, Jack. Are you married?"

Dev snapped his head up, the first bite of steak halfway to his mouth. "What? Me? No. Why? Do I *look* married?"

"Ouch." Kulani laughed, spearing the flaky tuna. "Looks like I pushed a hot button. You must be divorced?" She saw a number of fleeting expressions move across his broad, square face—naked grief at first, then heartrending sadness, and then confusion. Clearly he didn't want to discuss this aspect of his life, either.

Dev wanted to steer away from any conversation about himself. He was familiar with a woman's penchant for deep, personal exploration. Men never did that. They would never ask the kind of questions Kulani was asking him—but she was a woman, and women always communicated about highly personal topics.

"Mmm, this steak is delicious. Good choice," he told

her, his voice vibrating with satisfaction. He saw that she continued to wait for an answer to her previous question. After a few more bites and a forkful of the mashed yams, which were surprisingly sweet, he said, "Okay, I'm divorced."

"Any children?"

His heart clenched and Dev felt real pain across his chest. "Let's just say that yes, I was married. Actually," he joked, "I married not only her, but her family of seven brothers and sisters. Sometimes I felt like I was living in a commune and not with just my wife."

"So she came from a large family?"

He scowled a little and cut off another portion of the steak. "Yeah. I did, too. I've got three brothers, but this was…" he searched for the right word "…different."

"Oh? In what way?"

Dev would rather tell her the truth, even if it was painful for him, than to start down a trail of more lies. "Susan Gallardia was an incredibly beautiful woman and I fell in love with her many years ago. I got married shortly after coming out of the U.S. Naval Academy. I then joined the SEALs for the duration of my enlistment."

"The academy?" Kulani smiled. "And a SEAL. That's a very elite team. I'm impressed. That's why I'm picking up on a military background, then. When I first saw you today, and you used the word *bird,* I figured you might be ex-military. Or are you still in the service?"

"Uh, no, I got out after the mandatory six-year stint we promise the government." Feeling uncomfortable, Dev hesitantly returned to the subject of marriage. "I got orders for Imperial Beach, California, a real peach of a duty station. I met Susan at a party. She worked at a child care center in I.B.''

"Oh, so she really loved children."

Smarting, Dev nodded. "Yeah, she was a mother just waiting to happen."

Kulani felt his pain. She saw it as his eyes darkened and he refused to hold her gaze. Instead, he looked morosely down at his plate, pushing the last of his steak around on it.

"You...didn't want children?"

He shrugged. "Me? No. I love the little rug rats." He looked up and tried to smile, but his grin was lopsided and filled with old pain and memories. "Susan got pregnant a year after we married. Her whole family, who also lived in Imperial Beach, were pretty happy about it. She just kind of got absorbed by them during the pregnancy. I had to work weeks of nonstop duties training recruits, so it was a good thing she had them as support and company. Otherwise, she'd have been pretty lonely most of the time."

"Marrying someone in the military is always a hardship," Kulani acknowledged seriously. "I was in the navy myself for a while. So you and I share a common base of operation. How about that?"

Dev feigned surprise. "Really? We share something in common, after all."

Kulani watched him struggle with his past. She sensed something terrible had happened. "Look, if this is too painful for you to talk about, we can go to something else," she suggested softly. Without thinking, she reached out and laid her fingers across his darkly haired lower arm.

Her touch was galvanizing. Dev drew in a deep, shaking breath as her warm fingers touched his arm. He saw the tenderness burning like a dark fire deep in her eyes. She had such incredible eyes; they were fathomless and he yearned to lose himself in them. The fact that she'd reached out to the no-good likes of him touched him as little else could. Kulani was spontaneous. He was jaded and careful. Guilt ate at him more deeply.

"No, you deserve the truth," Dev said. When she removed her fingers, he continued, "Susan was nine months pregnant. I got sent on a mission, and hours after that, she went into labor. She was a worrier, you know? From the time I married her, she worried about me dying, because SEALs have a very short life span, usually."

"A lot of women have to wrestle with those fears," Kulani agreed quietly. "And it's not that their worries don't hold some truth, either."

"I agree," Dev said. He put the plate aside and wiped his mouth with the pink linen napkin. "In Susan's defense, I have to admit her worry wasn't blown out of proportion. I had a dangerous job. Granted, I was stationed stateside and I was training recruits, but sometimes I'd get called for duty overseas, too. I had to go and she knew it. I didn't feel good leaving her alone like that. What bothered me the most was her crying. That and her family making me feel like I was being cruel to her by leaving." Shrugging, he muttered, "I had no choice. I had to obey orders. Her family thought I was an unfeeling monster...."

"But she had a lot of family support in order to help allay her fears?"

Dev was amazed at Kulani's insight. "Well...yes, she did. Matter of fact, I felt like an outsider most of the time. She had this huge, protective guard-dog family that was always over there at our apartment when I had to be gone. She was never left alone. This is going to sound bad, but I felt like I was never needed by her, and that feeling was one of the reasons why the marriage fell apart—after..." He hesitated. Just one look into Kulani's dark, understanding eyes and he was able to go on. "I was on an assignment. I couldn't tell her where I was going, what it was about or what I was being ordered to do. She knew everything I did was top secret and I couldn't discuss it with her."

Kulani saw his face tighten, his mouth compress and the corners draw in. "You didn't make it home for her delivery?"

Looking up at the night sky, now quilted with huge, twinkling white stars, Dev released a pain-filled sigh. He glanced over at Kulani. In the soft golden lamplight, she really did look like an ancient Hawaiian goddess come to life. There was such energy and passion about life that seemed to radiate from her. Yet her voice was low and soft with compassion and he found himself, for the first time since the tragedy had occurred, spilling out the sordid truth.

"I made it home...pulled a lot of strings to make it happen. She was in labor for thirty-six hours. Things went from bad to worse," he muttered defensively. "Our baby daughter, Jessica, died four hours after she was born. By the time I got to the hospital, Susan was in hysterics. Her whole family was there. I walked in not knowing our baby had died.... Her family rallied around her. They told me that it was my fault our daughter died. If I'd only been there—" he waved his hand weakly "—then Susan wouldn't have worried like she did about me during the labor. The physicians had induced labor because they detected fetal distress. Susan was afraid I was going to die out there and leave her

and the baby alone. It was stupid…human, though…
and I felt so damned helpless. The whole family turned
against me.'' His voice grew sad and deep. ''I didn't
even get to see my baby girl…and I had to fight in a
court of law to get some photos of Jessica, taken shortly
after she was born. Thank God I have them, or I don't
think I'd have made it through that time in my life.''

Kulani's heart squeezed with pain. His pain. ''How
awful,'' she whispered.

He shrugged. ''When Susan was ready to leave the
hospital, she didn't want me to take her home. She
asked her family to do so. She didn't trust me any
longer, I guess.''

Sliding her fingers into his hand as it lay on the table,
Kulani saw Jack lift his head. Tears swam in his eyes
and she saw him visibly force them back deep inside
himself. ''It's one thing to lose a child, but to have your
wife's family shut you out like that and accuse you of
such a thing is ridiculous,'' she murmured.

''That's how tight they were. I told you, I felt like
an outsider,'' Dev said. He liked Kulani's easy way of
touching him, of assuaging some of his grief. Her ease
with him, her gentle comfort, made her just much more
special to him. Squeezing her fingers gently, Dev whispered apologetically, ''Talking to you about it, I guess
the bottom line I never realized until just now was that
I wanted to feel needed by Susan. But I never was.…
She had her family, who doted on her, took care of her,
and in the end, she really didn't need me.'' He hesitated.
''I didn't mean to make this night a downer. To wrap
up this conversation, Susan divorced me six months
later. She went back to her family and I went on my
way without her—or my baby. I carried a lot of pain

around with me for a lot of years after that. In a way, I still grieve over my baby daughter. Sometimes I wonder what she would look like now, what she would be doing, what kind of personality she would have developed—stuff like that...."

Studying him in the darkness, the lamplight carving out his strained features like the rugged, unforgiving Na Pali coastline, Kulani whispered, "It was a situation that was out of your control. You couldn't make Susan stop worrying. She knew what your work was like before she married you."

Dev wanted to keep holding Kulani's hand, but if he did, he was going to drag her out of that chair and kiss her breathless. He knew he'd find solace, even healing, with her lips molding hotly against his. "My head realizes that, but my heart still doesn't. Old wounds take a long time to heal. But you..." he smiled a little "...you are something else, Kulani Dawson. Every time you touch me, I feel happier. I feel better. Are you sure you aren't a healer instead of a helo pilot?"

She smiled and gently disengaged her hand. Kulani didn't want to, but she felt the charisma of his smile go straight through her—to her heart—and no man had ever touched her like that. "My mother was a kahuna, a healer, here on Kauai, until she and my father died in a car accident five years ago. She was beloved by everyone on the island. Maybe I have a little of her touch?"

Dev nodded. "I think a lot. I'm sorry you lost your parents like that. It had to be pretty damned devastating to you."

"Thank you. It was. I wasn't here when it happened. I was on a military mission when I got the call." She grimaced. "It changed my life."

"Yeah," Dev whispered as he moved his chair away

from the table, ''life has a way of doing that for us, doesn't it?'' He gazed deeply into her eyes for a moment. Then, with a glance at his watch, he realized he had to call this wonderful evening to an end. ''Listen, I've got to get going. I don't want to, but I have to. Let me drive you back to the airport to pick up your car, and then I've got to get some shut-eye.''

Kulani rose and placed the linen napkin on the table. ''Jet lag getting to you?''

''No.'' Dev escorted her to the front, where he paid the bill. Without thinking, he placed his hand in the center of her back as they left the premises and headed for the parking lot.

Kulani slowed her step as they strolled across the black asphalt. His white Mercedes was nearby and she watched as he fished the key out of his pocket. ''So, why do you need a good night's sleep?'' she teased.

Dev's mouth crooked a little as he opened the door for her. ''Because I'm going rock climbing tomorrow.''

Kulani said nothing as they got into the car. Her heart pounded with dread. Her mind shrieked at her that it wasn't any of her business what this man did. Yet, within heartbeats, Jack had become more than just a face in the crowd to her. She overcame her initial fear and asked quietly, ''What kind of climbing? And where?''

Dev saw the strain on her features. The Mercedes roared to life and then began to purr as he backed out of the parking lot. ''Tomorrow bright and early, I'm going to explore ways to get into the Kalalau Valley. I have it on good authority that it's wise to hike in early to miss the rain showers and higher humidity that develop in the afternoon.''

Terror struck Kulani's heart. "Kalalau?" The word tore in an agonizing breath from her lips.

Dev guided the Mercedes back onto Highway 50 and headed back toward Lihue Airport. "Yeah, why?" He saw her shadowed features turn ashen. "Kulani? What's wrong?"

"Why do you need to go into *any* of those valleys? Climbing there is dangerous. It can kill you. I've seen people die on those lava walls."

Her words came out in clipped undertones. He saw her breasts rising and falling rapidly beneath her blouse. Her hands were clenched into fists on her thighs, the knuckles whitening.

"Well, I'm here to scout out a situation," he told her slowly. "And I've got to look at ways to get into that valley. I really need to get into the box canyon area, the place where the valley ends and backs up against that ridge you took us over. That's why I was so interested when you flew over that real estate today. And that's why I was bugging you for answers to my questions during the flight." Dev smiled a little. Without thinking, he reached over and settled his hand over her smaller, clenched one. "Kulani? What's wrong? You look pretty upset. Is it something I said?"

Chapter Five

Kulani's expression was one of fear as she sat with her hands pressed into her lap while Dev drove back to the airport. Even in the shadows, he could see her face was tense and her eyes narrowed in some kind of pain known only to herself. After pulling into the parking lot next to her office at the airport, right beside her little red Mazda Miata sports car, he turned off the lights and shut off the engine. Being around Kulani meant having to deal with feelings—with his and hers—Dev was discovering.

He angled toward her and slid his arm across the back of the seat. As he cupped her drawn up shoulders in solace he could feel the tension she was holding in them. He could see strain in the planes of her face. As she lifted her chin, the anguish in her eyes turned visceral. It made Dev's stomach knot.

"Please...don't go exploring on the Na Pali Coast."

Kulani forced out the words from between thinned lips. "It's a deadly place...." She gulped against the avalanche of emotion threatening to overwhelm her. Kulani told herself she barely knew this man; yet Jack had opened her heart effortlessly and now she was afraid for him, fearful of the danger he was placing himself in. "There're so many other safer places to hike." She waved her hand nervously toward the dark silhouette of the volcano in the distance.

Moving his fingers gently across her tight shoulder, causing the fabric to slide across her warm flesh, Dev whispered, "Look, I didn't mean to upset you, Kulani. Hell of a thing." One corner of his mouth lifted. "Here I wanted to take a beautiful lady to dinner, to thank her for an incredible flight over her island, and then I go and say the wrong damn thing and ruin the whole night."

Holding on to her shredding composure, she honed in on his touch. Kulani felt his strength. Indeed, she welcomed it. She felt greedy, very greedy. How long had it been since she'd been touched in such a way that made her feel better? *Too long.* The past seemed to be trampling upon her present. Why couldn't Jack be anything but a mountain climber? Her heart was pounding as she lifted her lashes and met and held the gleaming, good-humored look that danced in those fathomless green eyes. She saw his concern; it was very real. Why did she feel like she'd known this man all her life? She shouldn't; he was a stranger who had walked into her life just this afternoon. Yet spending that special time with him at the restaurant, sharing his pain over the loss of the baby daughter he'd never been able to hold or say goodbye to, had created a different picture of him in her heart. He was a good man, and in many respects like— Kulani shut the door on the rest of that thought.

"Listen," Dev teased softly, "how about a good luck kiss?" He moved his hand more surely around her shoulder and drew her closer to him. "I could use the luck of an old Hawaiian goddess on this exploration. I know it's a tough valley to climb into. I'll be careful, I promise." To his surprise, he felt Kulani acquiesce as he nudged her gently closer.

Nothing had ever felt more right than this moment for Dev. The danger of his mission, the possibility of locating an anthrax lab on the island, the anticipation of climbing down the sheer lava wall into the valley, all exploded within him as he leaned down, down, down, to capture Kulani's parting lips. He had expected her to pull away, not ease forward. When he felt her hand come to rest on his left shoulder, her long, graceful fingers curving to follow the line of his tightening muscles, a shudder of need roared through him. Closing his eyes, he opened his mouth and drew in a deep, pleasurable breath because she was going to allow him the treasured privilege of kissing her.

Unprepared for the softness of her lips, Dev brushed them tentatively. He heard a soft gasp escape her. He felt the curve of Kulani's fingers tighten firmly against his shoulder as he slid his other hand along the clean line of her jaw and angled her head just enough so that his mouth could fit fully—and perfectly—along the contour of her lips. She was so soft and velvety! And he tasted the sweet remnants of the ginger sauce combined with the rich taste of coffee upon her eager mouth. Strands of her hair tangled against his cheek as he pressed his mouth more fully against hers. Her lips eased open like a shy orchid bloom, allowing him deeper entrance, and he groaned, the sensation rolling through every muscle in his body.

Dev had kissed a lot of women in his life, but this kiss was different. Provocative. Questing. He found himself boiling in a hot cauldron of violent need, his lower body tightening suddenly and painfully. Her lips were slick and parted, her breath coming in small, chaotic gasps—as was his. Those facts, and the hesitant, shy touch of her hand on his shoulder, served to warn Dev that she was new to this. Or, that she hadn't been kissed in a very long time. All those things registered within his barely functioning mind. He knew so little of Kulani. And he wanted to know more. Much more.

But now was not the time. This was a stolen kiss. He'd been thinking about ravishing the lips he held captive beneath his mouth right now all night long. Since he'd first seen Kulani's photograph, he'd wanted to kiss her. Now he felt like a penniless beggar who had struck gold. Her mouth was soft and flexible, giving as well as taking. Kulani was warm and alive and responsive. Something told him not to carry the first kiss too far. Usually, Dev overrode such a niggling thought. But tonight he didn't. He paid close attention to his intuition regarding this beautiful, ancient goddess, the royal Hawaiian princess. She struck him as being from another time and place, and in some wild, unexplainable way, he felt blessed to have met her.

"Sweet…" he rasped as he reluctantly broke contact with her searching mouth. He barely opened his eyes, lost in the pleasurable flow of heat pooling in his lower, hardening body. Her lashes fluttered and then opened. Looking deeply into her moonlit eyes, he saw stars shining within them. Caressing her cheek with his roughened fingertips, he heard her sigh. It was a sigh of pleasure, and that made him feel damn good about himself. He *wanted* to make Kulani happy, perhaps in trade for the healing she was giving to him. Lifting his hand from her cheek, he brushed several ebony strands of hair away from her face. In the moonlight she looked ethereal, from another realm and not really human. Yet the strong, sleek strands of hair that ran through his fingers were real. And so was the desire burning like molten lava in her eyes.

Kulani tried to get ahold of herself. She trembled violently as he ran his hand lightly across the crown of her head. There was such tenderness to this man! It shook her to her wounded soul. Fear merged with soaring and unexpected joy. Her lips tingled maddeningly from his strong mouth and she ached to reach out, slide her fingers around his thickly corded neck and draw him back within her reach. The wounding she'd experienced in the past warred with the tantalizing present.

"This was the best dessert I've ever had," Dev told her in a low voice as he held her sultry gaze. "And I hope you think so, too." Reluctantly, he glanced down at his watch. "I have to get going. Even though I don't want to.... But I have to get a good night's sleep, because I'm going to be on that trail at first light tomorrow morning."

He saw instantaneous fear leap to her eyes. "Kulani, do me a favor?" he said softly. Dev enjoyed speaking her name. It rolled off his tongue like sweet, hot honey.

"What?" She sat up, struggling with the collage of emotions that his heated, exploratory kiss had torn loose within her. His shadowed face was thoughtful, serious. He was no longer teasing her.

"Have dinner with me tomorrow night? How about if I pick you up here, after work? I'm staying at the

Princeton Hotel up on the north shore of Kauai, off Hanalei Bay.'' Once again, Dev had to touch her. Threading his fingers through her hair, he moved the thick, glinting strands across her shoulders. Kulani was incredibly alluring, more goddess than woman to him. ''Just say yes,'' he said in a rasping tone.

What was she stepping into? This man was a mountain climber, just like Stephen had been. Her heart couldn't take the loss of another man like that. ''Well…I—''

''Good, then it's settled,'' he said, a devastating smile of triumph pulling at his mouth, as he eased himself out of the car.

Shaken, Kulani emerged from the Mercedes after he opened the door for her. He looked so sure of himself as he walked her over to her car. ''Jack—I really don't think—''

''Shh,'' Dev whispered as he leaned over and placed his fingers against her lips. ''I see the fear in you, Kulani. What we have is good. You can't deny that. Can we take what we've discovered one day at a time?'' He saw the agony mirrored in her eyes. He also saw longing—for him. That made him feel good and strong. It also made him feel very protective of Kulani. She was holding a secret. A very ugly one, from the looks of it.

Gripping the car keys in her hand, Kulani moved away from Jack's persuasive and magical touch. Did he know how much he held sway over her vulnerable emotions? Kulani wasn't sure. Making her voice as firm as she could, she whispered, ''No, Jack. I'm not going out with you again. I can't.'' Looking up into his darkened, scowling face, she went on in an aching tone. ''It's impossible. I mean, *I* am. No…I can't do this again. I'm sorry. Please try and understand.…'' And she quickly climbed into her car, started it and backed out of the gravel driveway.

"I'll be damned," Dev muttered. He watched Kulani speed off down the road. Glaring around the parking lot, he wondered what the hell he'd done or said. What did she mean, she couldn't do "this" again? What was she talking about? Maybe she had a fear of heights, and mountain climbing scared the hell out of her? Maybe there was something in her personnel file that he'd missed? Dev had slept during most of the flight, and hadn't had a chance to read the file on her Morgan had given him. He'd go back to the hotel and check it out more thoroughly. Her reaction was too strong and he didn't understand it at all. One thing Dev did know was that he had a mission to fulfill. Kulani, as beautiful and competent as she seemed to be, wasn't cut out for this job, just as he'd originally thought. Mention mountain climbing and she went pale, like cold marble. No, he'd been right. He'd call Morgan tonight and tell him of his decision to perform this mission solo.

Kulani thought taking a hot bath would assuage the pain and the sense of loss she'd felt in her heart all day. Last night, after Jack's hot, wonderful kiss, she had barely slept. This morning she had been groggy. The flights today had gone well enough, but her heart hadn't been in them. Instead, she'd replayed her conversations with Jack, remembering his unexpected tenderness toward her and that world-altering kiss he'd shared with her. All day she'd yearned for his voice, his company. She still did. Not even her bath had helped soothe her, she realized now as she dried off and put on a rayon sarong with bright orange-and-purple bird-of-paradise splashed across the clinging material. Tying the cloth behind her neck, she padded barefoot from her bathroom to the living room. The place was small and filled with antique bamboo furniture with jade-colored cushions. The coffee table, also constructed of bamboo, held a little rock-and-fern waterfall that sang brightly through the room and reminded Kulani of her beloved ocean.

Moving a comb through her thick, damp tresses, Kulani wandered into the kitchen, where the windows looked out toward the distant Pacific Ocean. She could see the cobalt water, the evening grayish-white clouds, like plumped-up cotton balls, scudding in from the sea as the sun began to set.

She'd been home an hour, and her mind had never left Jack—or his mountain climbing expedition. Had he fallen? Was he dead? Shivering, Kulani put the comb in her pocket and placed her hands flat on the cool pink tiles of the counter. Hourly, she'd berated herself for turning down Jack's invitation to dinner. She was so scared. He at least deserved to know the truth, and she hadn't been honest with him at all. Her brows dipped. That wasn't like her; she based her entire life on honesty. Rubbing her arms absently as she watched the soft clouds race in off the ocean, Kulani decided she didn't like herself very much at the moment.

The doorbell rang. Kulani straightened and turned. Who could it be? She wasn't expecting anyone. Maybe it was Cappy, her climbing mentor, who lived a mile away. Usually, he came during the day to take care of her garden. Barefoot, she moved across the polished teak floor. Opening the door, she gasped. It was Jack Carson!

Dev stood there, grinning bashfully. In his arms, he had the largest bouquet of bird-of-paradise, red and yellow ginger, and purple and pink proteas that he'd been able to find. The fragrance washed between them, light and warming. He saw surprise—and joy—appear in Kulani's widening eyes.

"Well, I survived my little hike and I'm here to take you to dinner." He thrust the bouquet forward. She opened her arms and gently nestled it against her breast. How beautiful she looked! Her hair was damp and hung around her shoulders. The sarong she wore was colorful and revealing, the cloth falling to just above her knees. Right now, she looked like an island girl, a wahine, not a helicopter pilot from his world of concrete, steel and glass. Dev watched with pleasure as she leaned over and inhaled the fragrance of the colorful ginger.

"They're beautiful," Kulani whispered, a catch in her voice. "Thank you." Looking up, she met his warm green eyes, which danced with impishness. Today Jack wore hiking boots that were mud splattered with the red clay of Kauai. His jeans were dirty, too, and she saw a couple of tears in the material along one of his powerful thighs. The dark green, long-sleeved cotton shirt he wore looked worse for wear, too. But what alarmed her most were the many fresh cuts adorning his large fingers. Eyes narrowing, she pointed to his right hand.

"It looks like you tangled with some brush and lava today?"

Dev shrugged it off. "All part of climbing, right?" He held up his hand. "Hey, I promised you dinner at the Princeton Hotel. Best food on the island. I charmed your address out of your office manager and I thought I'd pick you up on the way there, get cleaned up in a hurry at my suite and then take you to dinner at the nice little Italian café in the hotel. What do you say?" Never had Dev wanted a woman to say yes more than Kulani.

He saw her hesitate. His heart plummeted with fear of rejection. "Listen, you come the way you are. That sarong looks damn good on you." Good, hell. She looked delicious enough to devour. When he saw Kulani flush, he wondered why.

"For your information, our island sarongs are worn with nothing beneath them." Kulani saw his thick brows arch with surprise, and then a hungry gleam come to his eyes as he absorbed the information. The resulting feeling was good, exciting and a little scary for Kulani. She perused the huge bouquet, which she knew had cost him a lot of money. Should she go to dinner with Jack? After all, she hadn't been honest with him, and he deserved that much from her.

"Okay," Kulani said, stepping aside and ushering him into the bungalow. "If you can give me ten minutes, I'll put on something more acceptable for dinner at that five-star hotel. The maître d' would have a stroke if I showed up in a sarong. Anyway, I owe you an explanation for the way I behaved last night."

Dev shoved his hands into the pockets of his dirty jeans and grinned wolfishly. "You just made me the happiest guy in the world. And I don't need any explanations, Kulani. This dinner's on me and it will have a happy ending." As she walked toward the kitchen, he admired the sway of her slender hips. She was tall and lean, like the graceful palms that adorned her yard. The entire hill was cultivated with ginger, bougainvillea and other tropical flowers. It was as if he'd driven up the dirt road to an enchanted kingdom, and she was the Hawaiian princess who oversaw this lovely, mystical palace.

"I'll be back in a little bit," Kulani promised breathlessly, giving Jack one more glance across her bare shoulder. Just the way he stood made her heart pound. He was so ruggedly handsome! Like a magazine model come to life. And that boyish and charming grin of his was her undoing. That and the burning light in his dark green eyes, which made her heart yearn eagerly for more of his unexpected, tender touches.

Kulani's hand shook a little as she placed the blossoms in a large, pale orange vase. She was remembering how Jack had looked to her when she opened the door. His hair wasn't combed but tossed by the wind, and she had had the maddening urge to thread her fingers through the strands and tame them—and him. Yes, there was a wildness and freedom to Jack that she'd never seen in another man. It beckoned her. He was dangerous to her heart, her safe little stable world, Kulani decided, quickly moving to her bedroom. From her closet, she chose a pale apricot, silk dress that had a scoop neck and elbow-length sleeves. It was a simple gown, but one that wrapped lovingly about her body to show off her best attributes. She placed a gold hibiscus on a simple chain around her neck and delicate earrings of the same design in her earlobes.

Reaching for her favorite perfume, Piki Piki, she sprayed some lightly on her hair and then brushed the strands until they shone like the wing of a raven in sunlight. Kulani was suddenly looking forward to having dinner with Jack! The gloom she'd felt all day was miraculously lifting. In its place was…hope. It was a feeling she thought had died with Stephen.

Kulani knew she shouldn't be going out with Jack. He was a mountain climber, too. And judging from the way he looked, he'd had a rough day of it. How close had he come to falling to his death? The question unnerved Kulani. She stood there in front of her bathroom mirror in anguish. Did she have the guts to tell him the truth? She had to.

"I have a confession to make," Kulani began, once they'd ordered a bottle of burgundy wine. She sat at a small, square table opposite him in the Italian café, which had one of the most desirable views on Kauai, overlooking the huge, bowl-shaped and very shallow Hanalei Bay. Opening her hands nervously, before Jack could speak, Kulani said, "I feel awful about this and I'm not good at withholding the truth. It's about my past, Jack, and my reaction to your mountain climbing here on Kauai."

Breathlessly, she went on, snagged by the brilliant dark green of his eyes. "I was engaged to be married to Stephen McQuarrie, a fellow climber. I hadn't intended on falling in love.... Anyway, I'd just come off an assign—uh, a difficult job, and needed some downtime, so I'd gone climbing the day I met him." Her voice softened. "Stephen was a lot like you, but not quite as brash and derring-do," she said, smiling up at Jack. "He was a geologist who worked for the state of Hawaii. He loved rocks. He loved climbing them. They were so alive to him, filled with personality and incredible beauty. No one loved rocks more than Stephen...." She rubbed her hands together, then tucked them nervously into her lap beneath the pale pink linen tablecloth.

"After that, we often climbed the steep valleys of the Na Pali Coast. One day, a week before our wedding, we decided to climb down into the Kalalau Valley from the ridge top. It was a dangerous climb because, during the day, it rains almost constantly. There's a lot of lichen and moss living on the black lava. The handholds

are there, but they're slippery because of the moss and
lichen. We used pitons, we would belay with lines, but
it was still dangerous.''

Dev watched as her expression became anguished.
Automatically, he reached across the table and captured
her hand. Last night, he'd devoured the personnel file
on Kulani that Morgan had sent with him. And now he
knew why she had reacted so violently to his casual
admittance that he was going to descend into the Kalalau Valley. He felt small now because he had to pretend he really didn't know about her past. ''What happened?'' he asked gently.

Swallowing hard, Kulani found herself unable to say
the words. Shutting her eyes tightly, she struggled to
find the courage to speak. It was the squeeze of Jack's
hand that made her open her eyes and look at him
through sudden tears. ''He fell to his death on that
climb.''

''I'm sorry,'' Dev rasped, squeezing her hand more
firmly. And he was. More than she would ever know.
He felt like a hypocrite in that moment. The suffering
in her eyes tore at his heart. She was trying valiantly to
fight back the tears he saw sparkling in her midnight
eyes.

''That's why,'' Kulani said in a choked voice, ''I
went ballistic on you yesterday. And why, on the helo
ride, I got uptight about your questions about the valley.
I try and get around the north end of Kauai and away
from the Na Pali Coast as soon as I can.''

''I understand now.'' Grimly, Dev began to understand very clearly her reaction on the helo ride, the tension and the strain in her face. No wonder. ''Damn,''
he muttered, ''I'm really sorry, Kulani.'' He was literally pouring salt in her still-open wound from losing the

man she loved. Obliquely, Dev wondered what it would be like to have a woman like Kulani love him with such a fierce, undying passion. He found himself jealous of Stephen, of what they had shared, because he certainly hadn't found it in his marriage to Susan.

Kulani pulled her hand free and dug in her small leather purse for a tissue. Not wanting to cry, she blew her nose instead. It was the tenderness burning in Jack's eyes that caught and held her heart gently in sway. He was sorry. The apology, his voice raw with sympathy, riffled through her like the tide that moved the mighty Pacific, visible out their window.

The waiter brought an opened bottle of burgundy wine that had been allowed to breathe for a while. He poured Dev a small amount in the crystal glass. Dev took a sip and nodded. After the waiter had left, he saw Kulani take a good, bracing drink from her own glass. He didn't blame her.

Setting the glass aside, Kulani went on, wanting Jack to know the whole truth. "When Stephen died, I quit my job. I just couldn't work. I couldn't do much of anything. My old boss flew in and helped me start picking up the pieces of my life." Kulani smiled brokenly and held his gaze. "He even gave me a loan to buy my beautiful Aerostar helicopter."

Surprised, Dev leaned back. He knew Morgan was generous. And from the looks of things, Kulani was more than paying back her loan to him, considering that her flights were booked five days a week. His conscience ate at him—big time. He had to come clean with her about who he was. Leaning forward, his hands around the delicate stem of the wineglass, he said, "Kulani, I have my own confession to make to you."

She frowned and looked up. "What do you mean?"

"I'm feeling pretty badly about this," Dev muttered. His brows knitted and he forced himself to hold her confused gaze. "My name is not Jack Carson. It's Dev Hunter. And I'm a merc. I work for Morgan Trayhern and Perseus. I came here to the island telling Morgan I didn't need a climbing partner to fulfill the mission he sent me on." Helplessly, he opened his hands and gave Kulani a pleading look. "I hope you believe me. I didn't know I'd like you so much or how well we'd get along…and I didn't want to string this charade out any longer than necessary. I'm sorry. I really am."

He saw shock in her eyes, before they narrowed with a fury that he knew he had coming.

"You *lied* to me!" The words came out low and grating.

Dev held up his hands in a plea for peace. "Yes, I did. Morgan ordered me to meet you and try and get you to come on board for the mission. I was just moving through the paces to satisfy him. And then…I met you.…" His voice dropped. He looked out at the bay, which was on fire with gold, red and dark blue hues, then back at Kulani. "I didn't think I'd like you. You were an ex-merc. You know how it is."

Her fists tightened in her lap. Tension sizzled through Kulani. She saw the guilt in Dev's eyes. "Why did you think you had to lie to me in the first place?" she demanded. "I'd already turned Morgan down. You must have known that!"

Smarting beneath her attack, he nodded. "Yes, I knew everything. But he'd warned me that you wouldn't work with me and that I'd need certain information about the climb that only you could provide. I figured if I told you who I really was, and you'd heard my name when you'd worked at Perseus, you'd know I'd been sent by Morgan and you'd shut me down.''

''You could have come clean! You could have been honest!'' Her nostrils flared. Hurt wove through her with the shock of his admittance. She didn't want to accept his reasoning for the alias, but if she'd been in his shoes, she'd probably have taken an alias, too. That took a little sting out of his trickery—but just a little. The memory of his melting and powerful kiss tunneled through Kulani, as it had all day. Was *that* a lie, too? She felt her heart tearing within her breast.

''I tried to find an opening last night, but…we strayed off into personal territory—my life, the loss of my baby daughter—and I just didn't have anything left to work with after that,'' he pleaded hoarsely. ''I was feeling pretty bad at that point, Kulani. I know it's not a good excuse. I can only tell you where I was at. There's something about you…you just sort of pull things out of me, whether I want them to come out or not.'' He gave her a sad smile.

Kulani took a fortifying gulp of the wine. ''I'm really hurt and confused by you, Dev. How do I know you are who you say you are?''

He reached into the pocket of his blue blazer and pulled out his small cell phone. ''You know Morgan's home number. Call him and verify it.''

Stung, she glared at him. ''I want to go home. This is just too much to take.'' She stabbed at him with her index finger. ''Morgan told me about the Kalalau Valley. What he suspected.'' Purposely, Kulani lowered her voice for fear other patrons might overhear their conversation. Leaning forward, she said tightly, ''And if you think you can do this by yourself, you're crazy.'' Glancing at his hands, she whispered savagely, ''Your hands look like ground-up hamburger. My guess is you tried to go down the side of that lava cliff, didn't you? And you got into trouble. That's why you're so cut up. Admit it, dammit.''

Kulani wanted to tell herself she didn't give a damn about Dev Hunter—or whoever he was. Just looking at his hands brought back a flood of awful, gut-wrenching pictures of Stephen's hands after he'd died. She was frightened of getting involved with Dev in any way. He was a man who willingly put himself in death's path! And the damn fool was going on this mission no matter what she said. She couldn't let him do that either. Torn, Kulani could only stare at him in confusion, hurt, anger and terror.

"Calm down," he pleaded. "There's more to this than you realize." Dev hunched forward until his head was almost touching hers. "Please, let's go outside. What I have to tell you can't be said in here." He begged her with his eyes.

Her face was contorted with barely contained rage. Dev knew he deserved her fury.

Rising, he moved around to her chair. "Please…" he pleaded near her ear.

She didn't want anything to do with him. But when Kulani felt the brush of his fingers against her shoulder as he pulled the chair back for her to rise, she left the restaurant with him as quickly as possible. Moving down the steps of the palatial Princeton, Kulani headed directly for his Mercedes in the side parking lot. She was immune to the beauty of the fiery gold-and-red sunset. Her heart was hammering with hurt, with betrayal. Her mind was spinning with questions. Had Morgan set him up to do this? Or was this Hunter's decision? Either way, she was angry as hell.

At the Mercedes, she whirled around to find Dev not two steps behind her. His face was dark, his expression grave. She wrapped her arms against her chest. "All right," she rasped angrily, "what *else* do you have to tell me? And it had better damn well be the *truth!*"

Hanging his head, Dev jammed his hands into the pockets of his trousers. Grimacing, he forced out the words in a low, taut voice. "What you don't know is that Stephen was murdered. He didn't slip on the cliff that day when he was climbing." Dev looked up as he heard Kulani give a cry.

Shock roared through Kulani. She reared back as if struck. "What are you talking about? What!"

Reaching out, Dev gripped her wrist and held it firmly, though not hurtfully. "Morgan had an autopsy performed on your fiancé, Kulani. He never told you about it because of the top-secret nature of the mission. The lab found traces of a fast-acting poison. Not only that, they found the puncture needle mark in the back of his thigh. Someone from down below was firing up at you two as you descended the face of that cliff. Morgan's guess is that it was the professor and Black Dawn mercenaries protecting their territory. The lab had been in place for quite sometime before Morgan discovered the location. Apparently you two were too close to the actual lab facility. The terrorists had to do something to get you out of there and keep anyone from discovering the lab, which I'm sure was not directly below where you were climbing or someone would have spotted it sooner. You were probably in the vicinity and the terrorists felt you were too close for comfort. By killing Stephen, they scared anyone else off climbing in that area for some time to come, didn't they? You never went back there, did you?" He saw tears splatter down her drawn, pale cheeks. His gut twisted. He didn't want to hurt her like this. Nostrils flaring, he took a deep breath.

Kulani tried to pull free of his grip. "No. Listen to me," he growled. "I'm sorry to have to tell you like this, but I have to. It will explain, in part, why I didn't reveal who I was right off the bat. Morgan gave me permission to tell you about Stephen only if absolutely necessary. He feels bad about witholding this information from you for so long, but put yourself in his shoes. He was trying to hunt down a bioterrorist making anthrax on a highly populated island. My apologizing for him isn't enough, but it's the best I can do under the circumstances. That's something you have to settle with him in person after this mission is over. Right now, I need you to know that I didn't go on making you think I was someone else for the hell of it. This is a deadly serious business, Kulani. I was up on that ridge today. And yes, I got a little too close to the edge during a rainstorm, and I slipped. I would have fallen off over that damn cliff if I hadn't grabbed for a bush growing on the rim."

Kulani sobbed. She pressed her hand against her mouth. "I want to go home," she murmured, clearly rattled. "I want out of here." The powerful impact of the news that Stephen had been murdered rippled through her in widening waves of anguish, followed by shock.

Dev nodded and slowly flexed his fingers on her slender wrist. Guilt roared through him. All he'd ever done since meeting her was hurt her more and more. What kind of a heartless bastard was he? He saw the look in her eyes; it was the same look Susan had given him when he was about to leave for a mission—a look of absolute betrayal and boiling fury. "I'll take you home. I want to be with you. To talk through the rest of this."

Chapter Six

"You lied to me!" Kulani said, her anger flowing freely once more now that she was in the privacy of her home. Her voice echoed oddly through her bungalow as Dev followed her inside. His shoulders were no longer thrown back with pride. Instead, he had a hangdog expression on his face, and his lips were compressed. He looked very much ashamed of himself. Kulani dropped her purse on the bamboo couch as he quietly closed the door behind him. She was shaking with anger, with grief, and she wanted to lash out at him.

"I didn't want to," Dev muttered as he turned around and faced her. Opening his hands, he added, "You're the last person I ever want to lie to, Kulani." Would she believe him? He saw the tears glittering dangerously in her black eyes, saw the incredible pain in her gaze. He felt her pain himself. No woman had ever affected him like this. Swallowing hard, his voice raspy, he said, "I screwed up. I shouldn't have told you about Stephen being murdered like that—outside the restaurant. It was lousy timing. I'm sorry."

Kulani sat down, closing her fists in her lap. "Oh, and I suppose it would have been better if you had added that little piece of information just at the right time to manipulate me into helping you?" The sarcasm in her voice was strong, but she didn't care. This man who'd seemed almost to be a natural part of her, who had held such tenderness toward her, was a sham. "I can't stand liars!"

Frustrated, Dev lowered himself down on one knee next to where Kulani sat rigidly, her eyes flashing with fury. "I have a mission, Kulani. You know it's not unusual for us to go undercover, assume a new identity. That's all I was doing." Desperation leaked into his deep voice. "I told Morgan I'd go on this mountain climbing expedition alone. I didn't feel I needed a partner. He disagreed. I told him at least I'd look you up, which I did. I wanted information on the climb, that was all."

She looked at him sharply. Her heart still warred with the news of Stephen's murder, on top of that, she was worried over Dev's upcoming climb. Now as he knelt so close to her, looking so damned male, she hungered for him. Even after his lie. Right now all Kulani wanted was to be held, because grief was tearing her apart. "Why would you want to try that climb by yourself?"

"I just do things alone, that's all."

She studied him. "Because?"

"What do you mean, because?"

Her lips tightened. "There's got to be a reason why you refuse a climbing partner." Kulani suspected his refusal was because of his ex-wife and the fact she had not reached out to him, not even during her greatest hour of need. Dev had armored himself against needing anyone after that terrible event. Kulani could understand it, but she couldn't accept it.

"I just don't like relying on any but my own skills," he muttered, defiance in his voice.

Kulani saw his pride—the dangerous type that got a person in a lot of trouble eventually. His pride was keeping him from leaning on anyone ever again. He'd rather scale a dangerous mountain than rely on another human! "You *can't* make that climb down there by yourself," she warned him in fury. "That's a recipe for disaster if I ever heard one, a really stupid move. People climb in teams. What would happen if the tangos started firing at you?"

Dev smiled hesitantly. "First of all, I'm not going to climb down that cliff face during the day. I'll do it at night."

"That doesn't guarantee they won't have infrared and spot your body heat."

He nodded. "That's true, but that's our—I mean, my option. Daylight is too risky." His eyes narrowed thoughtfully. For a second, he saw her anger ripped away, felt her care for him. It wrapped around him, startlingly warm and wonderful. How much of that feeling had he destroyed in their relationship? Dev ached to reach out, touch her hand and try to give her solace from the pain she was trapped within. But he didn't. He didn't dare under the circumstances.

"Nighttime means it's harder to see those handholds and place those pitons," she warned him, bitterness in her voice.

"I'll wear night goggles. They gather the light that's

available, so that I'll be able to see fairly well under the circumstances. Enough, at least, to place pitons into the wall. Besides, there's a full moon tomorrow night. I figure if all goes well, I can make it down in two nights.''

"Oh? And what are you going to do during daylight hours? Hang on the side of that cliff unnoticed? Not only that, Kauai is expecting a tropical storm to hit tonight. That means a day of god-awful rain drenching us off and on, if it doesn't move on like anticipated. You might have night goggles, but your full moon will be wiped out if this storm hangs around the island a day longer than what the weather forecasters are saying. It will be very dangerous under those circumstances.''

He shrugged. "I have a detailed topographical map. I'm hoping to find a place to hole up. I know the brush will hide me to a certain extent. The weather is something I'll have to endure. The night goggles will work, regardless, although not as well.''

Eyes flashing, Kulani shot to her feet. She went into the kitchen. Grabbing a rarely used brandy bottle from the pantry, she located a shot glass from the cupboard and poured herself some of the fragrant apricot liquor. Dev followed her soundlessly. He leaned tensely against the door jamb and watched her, his hands stuffed into the pockets of his slacks. Why did he have to be so damned handsome? So self-assured, when she felt like she was falling apart? Putting the glass to her lips, she opened her mouth, tipped her head and slugged the brandy down the back of her throat.

Fire burned in the path of the brandy and miraculously began to unknot her stomach. She set the glass on the drain board a little harder than she intended, and glared at Dev. "I'm calling Morgan, right now. He owes me an explanation."

Nodding, Dev whispered, "I understand." He took a hand out of his pocket. "Do you mind if I stick around after you've called him?"

Kulani wanted to scream, *No!* To her surprise, she heard herself say, "I don't care what you do, Dev or Jack or whoever the hell you are." She moved past him and left him standing in the kitchen. As she walked down the shining teak hall, Kulani felt like sobbing, but she pressed her fist against her mouth. She couldn't cry. At least, not yet. She had to hold herself together long enough to talk to Morgan.

Sitting on her queen-size bed, with its black silk coverlet decorated with bird-of-paradise in oranges, purples and greens, she shakily picked up her phone. Kulani knew Morgan's home number by heart. When she heard his growling voice at the other end, her heart sank with real grief.

"Morgan, this is Kulani. I'm sorry to be calling you so late, but we have to talk."

"Sure. How are you? Have you met up with Dev Hunter yet?"

She closed her eyes. Well, at least Dev was his real name. "Yes—yes, I have." Kulani leaned forward, pressing her hand against her eyes. Her voice became wobbly. "Morgan, how could you? Dev said Stephen was murdered. That his fall wasn't an accident. Is it true? Oh God, if it is, why didn't you tell me this before?"

There was silence at the other end of the phone.

Kulani began to sob. Hot, unwilling tears fell from her eyes and ran down her taut cheeks. "Morgan? You owe me an explanation. Why didn't you tell me the truth when Stephen died? Why did I have to learn it secondhand like this?''

"I'm sorry, Kulani. On a hunch, I ordered an autopsy performed on Stephen without your knowing about it. I suspected foul play and unfortunately, my gut hunch proved out. When they found that fast-acting poison, we suspected a bioterrorist lab. It immediately became top secret and I couldn't tell you a thing. God knows, I wanted to, but my hands were tied. And I'm deeply sorry Dev Hunter had to take that step and let you know. I was planning, after this mission was over, to fly over to see you, sit down with you and tell you everything. Damn, I didn't mean to make you cry. You're like a daughter to me...you must know that.''

"I do," Kulani whispered brokenly, "and that's what makes this even more painful, Morgan.''

His voice grew deeper and filled with remorse. "I'm sorry you had to find out like this. I wanted to tell you myself and I was planning on doing that.''

"I'd rather have known!" Kulani cried. "Damn the top secret stuff!" Sniffing, she reached for a tissue and blew her nose.

There was another long silence on the phone. "Hindsight is always twenty-twenty," he said heavily. "I made a command decision. Maybe it was the wrong one. And I'm the one to blame for that. Not Dev Hunter. He was just the messenger. In fact, I told him not to tell you unless really necessary because of the danger of this top event mission. I didn't want you going off half-cocked down that cliff." Apology was in his voice. "I'm truly sorry. Damn. Is there anything I can do to help you over this?''

Wiping her eyes, Kulani felt all the anger in her dissipate like a balloon losing air. "No." All she wanted now was to be held. Just held. Dev Hunter's face loomed before her tightly shut eyes. Why would she want him to hold her? He'd lied to her. He'd set her up.

"That's why I wanted you to go on this mission. I knew Dev would probably have had to give you all the details about Stephen's murder. I wanted someone I trusted implicitly to tell you, if I couldn't tell you myself. Dev is reliable and he's the only merc for this job. You were the other...."

Shaking her head, Kulani murmured, "Morgan, you're putting me into such a horrible position. No matter what I do, it's terrible."

"What are you talking about?"

"Dev said he's going on this mission solo. Hell, he can't descend down into that valley alone. He doesn't know the terrain. He almost fell to his death today when he was out there scouting along the edge of the ridge. And to top it off, we've got a tropical storm bearing down on us. The forecasters are saying it will be over by the time of the climb, but that's no guarantee. If this storm hangs around, Dev will be in big trouble." Kulani opened her hand, helplessness in her voice. "And if I don't go with him, he'll die. And if the professor has his lab down there, they are going to be looking for climbers." In her heart, Kulani knew without a doubt Dev needed her. But he was trying to pretend he needed no one. Was her decision to let him go alone just as foolhardy as his risky desire to do so?

"Damn his stiff-necked pride," Morgan muttered, anger in his voice. "He was *ordered* to take you along. I never authorized him to take on this mission alone. That's sheer suicide. I was worried his pride would get in the way of his better judgment."

"Pride is right," Kulani said. "He's got this attitude, this belief he doesn't need anyone at any time."

Sighing heavily, Morgan rasped, "Maybe with two trained mercs making the climb the outcome would be different, Kulani. You know this climb better than anyone—that's a big advantage. And the inclement weather will cover any noise you're making placing pitons as you descend that cliff."

"Yes, that's true," she whispered, wiping her eyes with trembling fingers. "But the only way to make this climb is at night. That is so dangerous, Morgan. Dev doesn't know the terrain. He doesn't know the moods of the Na Pali Coast, and with this tropical storm bearing down on us, he's really going to need a partner."

"I know that," he answered heavily. "Now can you understand why I chose you?"

Bitterly, she nodded and sniffed. Grabbing another tissue, Kulani said, "It's very clear to me."

"And Dev is going in alone because you won't go. Is that right?"

"Dev made it clear he was doing this alone, but there's no way this is a one-person job." It hurt to admit that because it made her feel guilty, Kulani thought, watching the light shining from the hall into her darkened bedroom. That was how she felt—trapped in a hellish darkness. And yet, as she sat there on the edge of her bed, moonlight flooding in the floor-to-ceiling windows through the gauzy curtain that wafted gently in a breeze, she craved Dev's closeness.

Her grieving heart wanted Dev. Wanted his strong arms around her to hold her, to rock her as if she were the hurt child she felt like presently. Had he left? Was he waiting for her? She hoped he was still there...or at least a part of her did. "And I'm still angry over Dev keeping his cover until tonight. I don't like lies, Morgan.''

''Dev probably felt it was time to tell you who he was. That's up to him. So, he said he's still going alone?''

Kulani nodded and whispered, ''Yes.''

''He'll die, then.''

Her heart squeezed violently with pain. With a surprising sense of loss. Vividly, Kulani recalled Dev's kiss. How warm and melting it had been! Oh, an hour hadn't gone by in her day when she hadn't thought of that reckless kiss of abandon he'd shared with her. Her heart warred with her head.

''I don't want him to die, Morgan.''

''Then,'' he warned sadly, ''you're the only person that can stop that from happening. I know it puts your life in danger, too. You can see why I wanted two of you, don't you?''

She heard the hope in his voice. ''Yes…''

''Listen, this has been a rough night for you. Go take care of yourself. Get a good hot bath and just go to bed. Talk to Dev tomorrow when you're in a better place. He has orders to go down that cliff either tomorrow or the next day. We're out of time, Kulani. We know the professor is making genetically engineered anthrax. We've got to verify it and stop the production. I'm not going to try and trap you into going with Dev. I respect your decision, whatever it may be.''

''Okay…'' Kulani said, her voice washed out, her spirit beaten. ''You're right—I need to sleep on this in order to make a decision. Goodbye.''

''Goodbye, Kulani. Stay in touch, all right? I'm really sorry.…''

As she gently placed the phone back into its cradle,

Kulani could still hear the raw regret in Morgan's voice. She couldn't fault him on his decision. He'd made the best one he could, even though she'd rather have known the truth at the time of Stephen's death. Sitting there in the quiet of her bedroom, her mind and heart in tumult, Kulani lifted her chin. Dev? Was he still out there in the living room? She didn't want to need him, but she did.

Pushing herself to her feet, she moved down the hall. The living room had one corner lamp glowing. As she looked around, she saw that Dev was gone. Her heart fell. Hard. Well, she'd given him a choice, hadn't she? Moving weakly out to the kitchen, she was going to make herself a pot of tea when she saw a hand-scrawled note on the bamboo-and-glass table, set up against a small yellow vase that held several pink-and-white cymbidium orchids.

Frowning, Kulani moved to the table and picked up the note. Her heart squeezed as she read it:

Kulani...I don't know how you can even begin to forgive me. I'm sorry. If I can make it up to you, please call me at the Princeton. I'm in suite 105. Right now, I wish I could hold you because you need it.

Dev

"Damn you, Dev Hunter...." Her words echoed hollowly in the pale pink kitchen. Darkly, Kulani stared out the windows over the sink. It was black outside except for the moonlight touching the swaying palms that danced to the ever-present trade winds. Dev was like sunlight to her. She hadn't laughed so much, or felt so alive in the past year and a half as she had over the past two days. And she knew it was because of Dev.

Turning, she went through the motions of making herself some jasmine tea. Should she go on the mission? If she didn't, she was sure Dev Hunter would die, one way or another. And yet the terror of just having to look down that black lava wall falling two thousand feet to the valley below instantly made her stomach knot. She'd have to relive Stephen's murder. Murder, not an accident... That shook her to her soul in a way nothing else ever could.

She picked up the pale rose china teapot from the cupboard and set it on the drain board. Setting the teakettle on the stove, she turned on the gas. The flame, blue and yellow, licked to life beneath the copper container. Leaning against the counter, Kulani covered her face with her hands.

Stephen had been cold-bloodedly murdered. *My God.* He'd been shot with a dart filled with swift-acting poison. Allowing her hands to fall to her sides, Kulani watched the teakettle almost in a stupor. So, he hadn't slipped to his death. After the accident, Kulani had gone over every inch of their climbing gear and the placement of the pitons, investigating whether one of the pitons had failed them, or if one of the ropes had. She'd ruthlessly searched the harnesses inch by inch for any indication of wear. She'd found one frayed rope—the one that supposedly led to Stephen's plunge to his death. It was very possible that another bullet or dart had struck his line and frayed it; no one would have known what had caused it.

Thinking through it all, Kulani remembered that at the time Stephen was killed, a thunderstorm had suddenly built across the valley, as thunderstorms often did on the Na Pali Coast. The wind had howled and lightning had crackled all around them, sending thunder rolling relentlessly along the walls of the valley. They wouldn't have heard bullets or darts being fired from below. As it was, they'd been in a very dangerous place on the cliff, with little brush to hold on to or utilize. The wind had been gusting sixty miles an hour and buffeting them cruelly. The lava was slippery from the rain. No, neither of them would have heard a rifle being fired.

Rubbing her wrinkled brow, Kulani turned her thoughts to the present. If that lab was down there—and they didn't know that for sure—Black Dawn would more than likely see them climbing down the cliff. Morgan was probably right about the climb being safer for two mercs who knew the score. Partners who knew what they were descending into would have certain advantages on their side—maybe even the element of surprise. The approach of that tropical storm bothered her greatly. No mountain climber in his right mind would descend into that valley during those perilous conditions. And there was no telling what the whimsical weather would do; on Kauai conditions could change at the snap of a person's fingers. It would be a deadly unknown in this climb.

Again Kulani closed her eyes, and instantly, Dev's strong, shadowed face appeared. She felt her heart long for him as she pictured his dark green eyes, so warm and filled with humor. He made her laugh. He was so confident in himself as a man. She'd never met anyone quite like him. If he only weren't so damned proud. Opening her eyes, she whispered, "Damn you, Dev Hunter. You deserve to get your comeuppance, but I can't let you climb alone."

Turning, Kulani took the boiling water off the stove and poured it into the awaiting teapot. She needed a good night's sleep on this before she made any decisions. Fear warred with her worry and anger. Anxiety riffled through her. Kulani was afraid of climbing, but knowing that Stephen had died by the hands of men filled her with a desire for revenge. Tomorrow morning, when she got up, she'd know what to do. She hoped.

Something nagged at her. Without thinking about it, she picked up the wall phone and dialed the number of her climbing mentor and friend, Cappy Martinez.

"Cappy? This is Kulani."

"How are you, my dear?"

She felt her fears dissolving instantly at the sound of his rough voice. Cappy was seventy-two years old and a world-class mountain climber of international fame. He had taught her how to climb when she was only nine years old, on the walls of the infamous Kalalau Valley. "I'm not doing real well, Cappy. That's why I called. I need your help—your advice."

"You're going to climb again, aren't you, child?"

Choking back a sob, she answered, "Y-yes. I don't want to, but I have to." Kulani pressed the heel of her hand against her brow. A headache was lapping at her temples. "Can you come over now? I know it's short notice...and I don't want to say anything on the phone."

"Ah, stealth stuff." Cappy chuckled. "Of course, child. I'll be right over. Hang on...."

Kulani hung up the phone. She felt relief flushing through her knotted stomach, though she was far from at peace. Moving dully out to the living room, she looked around.

"What have I done?" she muttered as she clasped her hands and sat down tensely to wait. Thank God for Cappy. Her old, wise friend had replaced her parents in many respects after they had died so suddenly. She looked to the old man, who was half-Portuguese and half-Hawaiian, as she would a beloved grandfather. He himself was a kahuna, and had known and revered her mother. Since that time, and especially since Stephen's death, he'd become irreplaceable to her. Kulani wrung her sweaty hands. Oh, if only Cappy were here. She desperately needed him. If she could talk out her fears, they wouldn't hold her in such a death grip.

Right now, her heart was centered on Dev. On losing him. She had no right to feel that way, but she didn't try to suppress the feelings. Dev made her feel good. He made her feel like living once again—something she hadn't felt since Stephen plummeted to his death. And now Dev was going to try the impossible, under the same dangerous circumstances as Stephen. Only this time, Kulani bitterly reminded herself, they knew of the danger below.

"Hurry, Cappy, please hurry...." she whispered into the silent night.

"Come here, child," Cappy said when he arrived a little while later. He held out long arms that had been tanned a dark brown by the equatorial sun.

With a sob, Kulani stepped into them. Cappy was lean and built like steel cable. He wasn't much taller than she, and as his arms slid around her waist, she laid her head on his narrow shoulder. "Oh, Cappy..."

"Hush, hush, child." He chuckled softly and laid long, large-knuckled fingers across the crown of her head. "It's all right, my girl. That's it, just breathe through it. You'll be fine in a few moments...."

Miraculously, in a few minutes Kulani did feel better. Lifting her head, she smiled weakly up into Cappy's shining brown eyes. His face was horselike, deeply wrinkled and tobacco-brown from all the time he'd spent under the sun while mountain climbing in harsh elements all over the world. He was dressed in a loose gray T-shirt and baggy dark blue jeans and wore open-toed sandals on his callused feet, though he usually went barefoot.

Cappy reminded her of a venerable old lion with a silver mane. He took great pride in his thick, curled locks, now gathered up in a ponytail at the back of his head. His nose was long and narrow. His thin mouth was set in a gentle smile. When she saw the curiosity in his warm brown eyes, Kulani moved aside to let him into the bungalow.

"Thanks for coming over on such short notice," she said. Cappy lived a mile down the road from her. Often he'd come over to tend her herb garden and do the landscaping around the house. Kulani paid him monthly for his help. He was a military veteran from the Korean War and had never held a job long enough to gather a pension. So he did odd jobs for people to make enough to buy climbing rope, a new set of boots, pitons or whatever he needed to scale the next mountain that grabbed his passionate heart and soul. Cappy lived by his heart only, as all good kahunas learned to do. Life was to be lived, to be felt fully—the pain as well as the joy—grabbed and fully embraced without flinching.

Stepping into the kitchen, Cappy reached for the coffeemaker. He always made himself at home when he was at her house. "Sit down," he told her as he worked at the drain board. "And tell me what's going on."

Kulani sat. Just having Cappy here helped soothe her shredded emotional state. Without preamble, she told him everything. She couldn't leave anything out, not even the part that was top secret. Cappy was completely trustworthy, and besides, he needed to know everything in order to make an informed decision about what she planned to ask of him. When she finished, he was leaning his narrow hips against the counter, his large-knuckled hands resting on the drain board, his eyes thoughtful.

"What I want to do is help Dev. I have to go down there with him."

"Or," Cappy said as he poured steaming hot coffee into colorful ceramic mugs, "I could go down with him instead of you."

With a shake of her head, Kulani said, "No, I can't let you do that." She gratefully took one mug after Cappy poured a jigger of brandy into it. A little liquor at this point would help unknot her gut, and he seemed to sense that. "Thanks…"

"Strictly medicinal, you understand," he replied as he sat down with a grin that exposed the missing front teeth he'd lost in a fall last year and never had replaced.

She managed a one-sided lift of her lips and took a sip of the liquor-laced coffee. "Right…medicinal."

"Well, if you don't want me goin' down the side of the mountain with 'im, then do you want me on top to belay ropes and other stuff to you?"

Nodding, Kulani placed the mug on the glass surface of the table. "Yes. I trust you with my life, Cappy. This isn't a two-person mission. It's really three. We're going to need hundreds of feet of rope as we get farther and farther down the cliff. I'll need you at the top with a static belay. Once I get the pitons in place, you'd have less to do. But I'd want you on top to monitor us all the way down, even if your job with the lines is done.''

"You are going to need food, dry clothes and sleeping bags. We're in for a tropical storm. At least, that's what my nose tells me. The forecasters are wrong on this weather. The winds are already up to forty miles an hour, and the weather bureau on Kauai is saying it might develop into a hurricane tomorrow night—just when you're supposed to start that descent.'' He shook his head. "Man alive, this really sucks, but I see the wisdom of going down the wall instead of trying to hike back up into the canyon. Chances are they've got motion sensors planted all over the place in front of 'em. They won't have any up on the walls of the canyon.''

"Right. Another reason to descend,'' she agreed quietly. Cappy had been an army ranger during the Korean War. Some said he was crazy when he returned from Korea, but Kulani knew it was post-traumatic-stress disorder that made Cappy live his life the way he had since then. She saw his mouth twist. "What?''

"When you spoke of Hunter, your voice went real soft.'' He eyed her, humor dancing deep in his dark brown eyes. "This guy grab your heart, Kulani? Sure looks like it from where I'm sitting.'' He grinned broadly.

Flushing, the heat rolling up her cheeks, Kulani avoided Cappy's laughter-filled look. "Oh, Cap, don't be ridiculous! You can't know someone for two days and have that happen.''

"Really?'' He patted her hand in a fatherly way. "Child, your voice goes soft, your eyes go soft...why, you're the soft-boiled egg and he's your shell, your protector, the guy who holds you with his arms and his heart.''

"I'm an egghead for even thinking this guy means *anything* to me," Kulani growled, a faint smile crossing her compressed lips.

Chuckling loudly, Cappy sipped his coffee. "Child, it's about time somethin' good happened to you. Now, this Dev Hunter fellow seems to have only one fault, from where I sit. He's got a lot of pride and thinks he can descend that cliff alone. No one can. Not even him. You were right to call me. And it will take the three of us to pull this off." Reaching over, he gripped her hand and squeezed it. "You did right when you called me. I'm the right person to be a part of your team."

Relieved, Kulani said, "Then I need to call Dev and tell him what's up."

"Good idea, child."

Kulani dialed his room at the Princeton Hotel. She was anxious to connect with Dev. Why wasn't he answering? An operator came on the line, and she left her name and phone number and a message that it was urgent that he return her call her the moment he got in. Reluctantly hanging up the phone, Kulani walked slowly back into the kitchen.

Cappy looked up. "He might be down at the Sunset Cliffs store, checking out climbing gear. He's gonna need a helluva lotta coiled rope for that descent."

Nodding and trying to hide her worry, Kulani sat down. "Sammy probably has that much nylon rope on hand?"

"I'm sure he will," Cappy said with a snort. "He can completely outfit Hunter for this climb, if that's what he wants. Or maybe Hunter brought all his equipment with him. Who knows?"

Raising her eyebrows, Kulani said, "God, I hope he doesn't go out to that ridge point by himself before we can get to him."

"He's bound to go back to the hotel sometime tonight." Patting her hand, Cappy said, "You worry like a lovesick girl."

"Oh, Cappy!"

Chortling, he released her hand. "One thing I know about you, Kulani, is when you blush, you're in love. Saw that," he said, taking a long, delicious sip of his coffee, "when I climbed with you and Stephen. He made you blush all the time." Pointing at her reddened cheeks, he said, "Now this feller, Dev Hunter, holds your heart. I feel it's good for you. No one should be alone, you know?"

She gave him a skeptical look. "You're alone," she retorted defensively.

"Me? The ole mountain goat of Kauai? Why, child, no woman in her right state of mind would have me around her." He touched his silvered temple. "I'm crazier than a dingy cormorant, remember?" And he cackled.

"Oh, sure you are." Kulani laughed with him. His wife of fifty years, Elena, had died a year ago. Kulani had seen Cappy's utter devastation at the loss. They'd been deeply in love. His hair had been shiny black with just a touch of silver at his temples before she'd passed on. Afterward, he'd turned gray almost overnight. He was a shadow of his former self. Elena had understood the wounded war vet. With her, Cappy had found safety and love. Without her, he would have been lost had it not been for Kulani. She'd lost Stephen six months before, and knew the pain of loss, too. She'd saved Cappy from holding a gun to his own head and putting himself out of his grief-stricken misery. Since then, she and Cappy had been closer than ever. He was like a foster father to her, and she, the daughter he'd never had, but always wished for.

"Tell me more about this Hunter fella. Since we'll be meetin' up tomorrow, I'd like to understand as much as I can about 'im."

Sighing, Kulani said, "He's got your eyes, Cappy. Not the same color, but the same mirth and humor in their depths. When he looks at me, I feel his laughter. He's not laughing at me, but has that impish, Irish blarney look. Like he knows something I don't." She waved her hand gracefully. "Or maybe he knows the inside joke and I don't."

"I'll bet the twinkle in that young fella's eyes is about the joy of getting to lay 'em on the likes of you. You're beautiful. A wild ginger growing in the midst of a green jungle, untouched and unearthly. I'll betcha he thinks he's died and gone to heaven." Cackling, Cappy waved his bony finger at her. "And don't sit there and spit and sputter in denial, child. You are one of the most beautiful women I've ever laid on eyes, 'cept for my 'Lana."

Lowering her lashes, Kulani absorbed Cappy's passionate statement. "Mama always said real beauty was in the heart. That's what I strive for, Cappy. My outer looks will fade and change with age. I want my real looks, my inner attractiveness, to shine through like the lighthouse beacon at Secret Beach."

"Believe me, you're like a radiant sun. Never mind that lighthouse, child. If Hunter is half the man I sense he is, he'll think you're more valuable to him than any amount of money, gold or gems. Believe me, I feel it here, in my heart." He pressed his fist against his bony chest. "And my senses tell me that Hunter isn't any ordinary run-of-the-mill fella, either. But then, all I gotta do is look into your eyes and see the stars shinin' in 'em, and I know he's one helluva man where you're concerned." Rubbing his hands together, he said, "Nope, I can hardly wait to meet this gent."

Chapter Seven

Sunset along the ridge overlooking the steep lava walls of the Kalalau Valley was turning a bloodred color as the last light of day peeked between layers of prominent storm clouds. Dev was leaning over, making last-minute adjustments to the harness he was going to strap into when, to his utter surprise, he saw Kulani and a thin, wizened man appear at the top of the steep trail above him.

Freezing momentarily, he studied Kulani's deeply shadowed face as she, too, hesitated. Her shoulders were packed with black nylon climbing ropes, he noted. Anguish and fear etched her face. But he also saw resolve there, in the way her soft mouth was compressed.

Slowly straightening, Dev put the nylon leg harness aside and met Kulani as she carefully made her way down the vertical path. It was muddy and slippery from a rain shower, the first of many to come with the tropical storm, which had arrived less than an hour before. The old man waited at the top as she descended.

"What are you doing here?" Dev demanded as he gripped Kulani's outstretched hand and helped her down to the ledge where he stood.

"You never returned my call last night. I was going to tell you that I'd climb with you."

His eyes widened momentarily. "I never got the message," he told her in apology. "Maybe it got lost or something? If I'd have known you called, I would have returned it, believe me. But, you don't have to climb with me. I told you, I don't need anyone."

Anger surged through Kulani. She halted inches from him. "You are stubborn as a mule, Dev! I talked to Morgan last night. He said you are *not* to go on this mission alone. Are you in the habit of disobeying orders, too?" She jabbed her finger toward the lip of the cliff, where they would begin their descent. In the west, the clouds thickened and shut off the weak stream of sunlight, reminding her that the tropical storm had not moved on. In fact, it was forecasted to hit Kauai full force this evening—just when they were starting their climb.

"Well," Dev muttered defiantly, checking his harness, "I told Morgan I could do this alone."

She stood there, breathing hard, and looked from him to the lip of the cliff. Fear rose higher, along with hurt and hope. Kulani realized in that moment that *she* needed to make this climb, regardless. Cappy was right: she had to face her fears.

She captured Dev's hand in hers, and in a ragged voice, she pleaded, "Look, I'm really hurting right now. I *need* you in order to make this climb down that face. I'm afraid. I keep having flashbacks from the past. I'm going down there with you or without you. You can't stop me from coming, but it would be better if you agreed to let me come along. That way, if I needed you, you'd be nearby, Dev.'' Her throat closed off with tears as she watched his eyes soften with her admission. "Please...I *need* you on this descent, Dev. Will you be there for me?''

His conscience railed at him. The vulnerability, the raw truth she was sharing with him moved him as nothing else ever had. Kulani needed him. How long had it been since someone had really needed him? Susan— when she'd lost their baby; that was when. But she hadn't reached out. Not to him. Not like this. Mouth tightening, he stopped fiddling with his ropes and harness. The tears glimmering in Kulani's eyes were his undoing.

"You need me?''

"I said it, didn't I? Do you think I'm lying to you?'

"No...no, I don't.'' He knew she wasn't lying just by the look on her face. Kulani was incapable of such a lie. He tried to grapple with her quavering request because it was tearing his heavily guarded heart wide open. The feelings pouring through him were wild, untrammeled, filled with hope, with desire—for her alone. Swallowing hard, Dev motioned to the coils of rope. "I was a little busy last night getting all the equipment to climb with, and I didn't have much time to think things through. Maybe I could use a little help, after all, on this descent.''

Kulani accepted his explanation, and relief tunneled through her. There was a lot of business to attend to shortly before a climb. "We're here to help,'' she said tightly as she released his warm hand. "But first, I want to you to meet Cappy Martinez.''

Dev narrowed his eyes at the old man who was now descending gingerly down the trail. Then his eyes widened with shock. Cappy was a legend in his own time. Anyone who was serious about mountain climbing knew of Cappy Martinez.

The old man moved agilely toward them. "These belay lines are damned heavy, young man. Help me get them over to your static belay point," he said, pointing to where Dev had already set up a block and tackle around a huge, gnarled umbrella or schefflera tree that stood near the ledge where he was going to begin his descent.

Dumbfounded, Dev did as he was ordered. In no time, almost five hundred feet of nylon line lay in neat, orderly piles near the trunk of the tree. When he was through he noticed that Kulani was dressed for climbing. She wore dull black, clinging material from head to toe beneath her jeans and white, long-sleeved shirt. Around her neck was a set of night goggles.

"Just in case you had any thoughts on this topic, you ain't climbin' alone, young feller." Cappy pointed his finger toward the valley behind where Dev stood. "Kulani told me everything. I know of only two kinds of climbers, son—those that live and those that die. Now…with the info she gave me, I'd say you're gonna be in the dead column real quick. So I'm glad you decided to let her come along with you." He jabbed his thumb across his narrow shoulder. "She's the right partner to have. She's climbed these valleys all her life. I taught her to climb them when she was only nine years old." And he smiled proudly at Kulani, who was standing tensely, the nylon harness she was going to wear in her hands.

Scowling, Dev swung his attention to Kulani. She

had plaited her hair into two long, thick braids, which lay across her shoulders. Long hair was a detriment in climbing, particularly as the winds swept up a cliff. The strands could blind the person, or worse, get tangled in the equipment and cause even more problems. With her ebony hair in braids against her golden skin, she looked very Native American.

"It's time to face my fears, Cappy," Kulani said.

Without saying anything, Cappy glanced significantly at Dev Hunter and then nodded to her. "Yes," he told her softly, "it is. And it's a good thing. I think this young lone wolf can be there to help you if you get in trouble, too."

She made sure her harness was turned inside out so that the wide nylon webbing would not be kinked or twisted when weight was placed into it, and then rapidly began to unbutton her blouse. She stepped out of her jeans, folding them along with her white shirt and putting them into a plastic bag to keep dry.

Dev saw the terror in her expression as she readied herself. Her hands were trembling. She was afraid. And she needed him. The thought buoyed him. It made him feel good in a way he hadn't experienced in a long, long time. Kulani was counting on him to help her if she got into trouble while facing her deep fears. And he found he wanted to be there for her.

Cappy stepped forward and waved his finger in Dev's face. "Kulani said you were a man to be counted on in an emergency." He grinned a little as he looked up, tilting his head slightly like a bird looking at something. "Are you?"

Dev stared down at Cappy and then over at Kulani, who stood poised and waiting for his answer. "It's been a long time since I was needed by anyone...."

Cappy chuckled. "Well, she needs you, so how about that?" He gave Dev a satisfied smile. "You're important in her life. To her." He looked around at the darkening landscape, at the swollen rain clouds approaching. "It's a good thing you're going down as a team. If one of you gets in trouble, no helicopter pilot in his or her right mind is gonna come for you. Not with this storm on top of us." He shook his head. "No way. Not with the winds screamin' up these walls from the Pacific. You'll have each other. That will be enough. You made the right decision to let her come along with you."

Chastened, Dev swallowed his usual arrogant reply. When he saw the way Cappy was looking at him, the old man's thin mouth twisted into a knowing grin, he replied, "Yeah, well, I was worried for Kulani...." Dev waved his hand in her direction. "I care about her. I didn't want to have her jeopardized on this assignment...but if she needs me, I'm willing to go along with everything."

Rubbing his bristly gray chin, Cappy grinned a little more widely. "You care about her, young feller?" He chuckled indulgently and turned to Kulani. "See? I told you so. He likes you. I knew this figured into his reasoning for not wanting you to come along."

As heat pummeled her neck and cheeks, Kulani bent down and pretended to busy herself with the thin, protective black flak jackets she'd brought along for both of them to wear—just in case. "Hunter would say anything to keep me from coming along," she retorted. When she straightened and stared defiantly across at Dev, she saw that her words had hurt him. "Oh, hell," she muttered, "I'm sorry. I didn't mean that."

"Love is never smooth sailin'," Cappy said with a chuckle.

Kulani's breath hitched. "Love?" The word came out strangled. That was impossible! She couldn't love this arrogant man!

"You're crazy, old man," Dev breathed savagely. He moved over to the new coils of nylon rope and bent to inspect them. His heart pounded at Cappy's unexpected statement. Love? No, the old man was nuts. Dev liked Kulani, but love didn't happen like this. Or did it? Dev was unsure. All he knew was that, as he prepared his gear for the descent, he'd spent one guilty, sleepless night because of how he'd mistreated Kulani.

Cappy moved carefully over the slick, red clay, heading to where Dev stood. "Ah, to be young again," he said wistfully, "with all the pain and joy that comes with it." Bending over the coils, he announced, "There's enough line here to get you three hundred feet down the cliff. Where're your pitons? I wanna check 'em out."

Dev pointed to several leather sacks clipped to carabiners, which would eventually be snapped onto the climbing belt around his waist. Carabiners were oval shaped rings of smooth metal that the nylon rope was strung through. The line was the best money could buy, but Cappy ran his roughened, experienced fingers down the smooth, nylon length anyway, and out of habit, tested it here and there. He also checked it for any signs of wear, any rough spots or possible nicks and tears. A mountain climber always checked out his gear carefully before a climb.

Cappy grunted his approval after testing, poking and studying the gear. "And after three hundred feet, what did you have in mind? Pitons hammered in every hundred feet?"

"Yes," Dev said.

Cappy grunted his approval once more as he checked the static belay. The line had been circled around the tree on a block and tackle assembly. The tree was the anchor point for the initial descent over the cliff.

"I'll belay you the line you need, when you need it," Cappy said, patting the pile of ropes in approval. "You'll just use the same lines over and over again, every three hundred feet of your descent. That way, you aren't carrying too much weight on your shoulders or hips. Too much would tire you out too soon, and you two have a long descent ahead of you." He stared over at Dev. "In case you've never been around lava walls before, they cut into nylon line. If that happens—" he patted his belt, where a cell phone was attached "—I'll be putting a call in to Sammy's and we'll get more line out here to you. Once a rope has a knick in it, don't use it. When climbing a wall like this, we throw away any rope that's in any way flawed. It's too risky to use it again." Cappy studied the different types of carabiners that Dev had chosen for the climb. Holding a couple of them up, he said, "You've got to make sure your carabiners keep that line away from the rock face at all costs. Lava is infamous for rubbing a line raw so it breaks."

Dev nodded. "This will be my first time climbing lava. I appreciate your input." He felt Kulani's approach. She had that kind of effect on him; there was a peacefulness, a sweet longing that filled him every time she came near. She was the eye of his hurricane. He realized now that life—his life—was always in chaos exactly like a hurricane—or had been until she'd unexpectedly stepped into it.

"Have you heard the latest weather report?" Kulani

asked as she knotted some of the line that she'd be using to lower herself down the wall.

"Yeah," Dev muttered, "the tropical storm didn't move on. It's hanging around Kauai's north coast and intensifying." Looking up at the heavy clouds scudding over them, he added, "And it looks like we're about to get our share of it pretty soon."

"Yep," Cappy chortled, "It's right on time." He pointed to the bloodred-and-gold sunset to the west. "All those clouds are gonna thicken in a helluva hurry, young man. And if I don't miss my guess, in another hour the rains are comin'. You ever climbed in a tropical storm?"

Dev shook his head. "No. I've climbed in blizzards and rain, but nothing continuous like a tropical storm."

"Right. It's different. You're gonna get wet and cold goin' down that wall. The winds will cut at you like a knife as they move inland and strike the rear wall where you're gonna be climbin'. Your hands are gonna get slow when you use your hammer to pound those pitons into the rock. The hammer handle is gonna get real slippery. So will the handholds in that lava. The chances of you slippin' or fallin' are real good. The only thing between you and the ground is your equipment and your partner." He gave Dev an imperious look.

Pointing his finger at Kulani, he said, "That's why, young feller, when you begin your descent, I'm sending Kulani down first. She knows this wall like the back of her hand. She knows where the dibits are at, where the handholds are, what bushes you can rely on not to tear away from the wall when you grab onto 'em." Cappy moved within inches of Dev, his face serious and dark. "You listen to her, son. Don't *not* listen. Put your testosterone and ego on the shelf. They don't belong here, tonight, on this descent. They could cause your death and hers. Now, I don't care about you dyin', to tell you the truth, but her?'' Cappy smiled benignly at Kulani. ''She's my godchild. She means everything to me. So, if you don't listen to her, you'll have me climbin' down your case like the fired-up mountain goat that I am. Besides, she needs you. You read me loud and clear on priorities regardin' this climb, son?''

Dev got it. ''Yeah,'' he muttered. ''I still think I should go first. If we're detected and they start firing up at us, Kulani will take the bullet first and you know it.''

Cappy took off his frayed, dark blue knit cap, which had seen better days. ''We'll be in touch by walkie-talkies. You'll each have a cell phone. If stuff happens, I'll be up here and we'll do what's necessary to help you. I know it's dicey. But having a greenhorn climber like you at the end and not knowing the ins and outs of these lava walls is sure as hell asking for big-time trouble. Kulani leads. You follow.''

Dev noticed the mantle of night quickly moving upon them. ''It's time to get in our harnesses,'' he told Kulani in a growling voice. He, too, had worn a form-hugging, black nylon bodysuit. When she handed him a flak jacket of the same color, their fingertips met. For a moment, he saw the raw need in her, for whatever he could give her to help her conquer her fear on this climb. He managed a crooked smile meant to buoy her. Her eyes turned soft momentarily in acknowledgment as their fingertips eased apart. He shrugged into the piece of equipment, noticing how achingly beautiful Kulani was in the way she carried herself. Her body was slender and strong looking as she placed her legs through the harness that she'd wear for the duration of the climb. All of her motions were those of an experienced climber; there was no waste, no hesitation as she hooked up the harness to the tinkling sound of ten carabiners hanging around her waist. Snapping the leather bags containing the lifesaving pitons on the right side of her waist, she made sure her hammer was securely anchored in the leather holster farther down on her hip. Dev motioned to two rifles he'd brought along for the climb. He handed one to Kulani. She nodded her thanks. They would each carry a rifle strapped to their backs along with their knapsacks. ''They've got tranquilizer darts in them instead of bullets,'' he told her. ''Morgan wants those terrorists taken alive if possible.'' Dev glanced down at his pistol. ''And if we can't do that, we're authorized to use bullets instead.''

Kulani nodded. ''Understood.'' She made a special knot—a bowline—because she was the lead climber. Dev would make a butterfly knot because he was the second climber.

Tension lined Kulani's set lips and her eyes were narrowed, her mind focused on the job before them. Moving to his own harness, Dev made quick work of climbing into it and fashioning a butterfly knot. Cappy handed him the belt he'd wear, which contained ten carabiners, several sacks of pitons, a military knife with a jagged, ugly-looking blade, a cell phone, a walkie-talkie no larger than his hand, a Beretta 9 mm pistol, several shock grenades, a canteen filled with water and several cartridge pouches filled with replacement bullets should he need them.

As Kulani screwed the carabiners closed around the line that would take her down the cliff, Dev saw a marked change in her. No longer was she a soft, compelling woman. Now, as she stood near the lip of the

wall, surrounded by damp ferns that hid the actual
jump-off spot, she looked like a capable warrior. Her
face was set. Her eyes were dark and unreadable. Each
movement she made was swift and steady. No longer
could he detect any trembling of her fingers as she
worked the knapsack over her shoulders. He saw that
her piton hammer had a thick leather strap at the end
of it, which she would wrap securely around her wrist
as she used it on her way down. That way, she couldn't
accidentally drop it. The leather was like a lifeline, because without the mallet-type implement, the pitons
couldn't be placed into the lava.

"Now, listen to me, young 'uns," Cappy said as he
gestured for them to come and stand close to him. "I
got helpers comin' at timed intervals. There will be
other friends of ours a'comin' shortly to help belay the
line as you need it. If you get in trouble and need to
ascend, then I'm gonna need raw muscle to pull you up
the cliff and to safety."

Dev nodded. He saw no need to question Cappy's
choice of people. The old man was a world-famous
climber. Dev also knew Cappy had written a book of
poetry more than thirty years ago on the mountains he'd
tamed, including Mount Everest. Dev cherished that
book, his copy dog-eared from so many readings. "If
we get fired upon, you need to call—"

"I already told him," Kulani said. "Morgan gave me
the SOP—standard operating procedures—for this mission. Cappy will initiate what we need, when we need
it, so it's taken care of."

Nodding, Dev felt guilt eat at him. Kulani was silhouetted against the coming night, her body tall, proud
and strong looking. Never had he wanted to love a
woman more than her. She made him go hot with long-

ing. She made him want to forget about this mission. He hoped at some point he'd get a chance to tell her he was sorry—that he wanted to start all over with her. Judging from the glint of challenge in her eyes, Dev wondered if she would ever forgive—or forget—his deception.

"Now," Cappy said, "a thousand feet below is a cave. It ain't much, but by the time you reach it, you'll be damned glad it's there. No social amenities. The floor is rough but serviceable. You can sit up in it, but you can't stand up. Your objective tonight is to reach it, understand? You'll sleep there during the daylight hours and it will be your jump-off point for the second night or day, depending on how long the first part of the climb takes."

Surprised, Dev said, "A cave? Halfway down?"

Kulani gave him a bored look. "Yes. If you'd have trusted me, if you'd have asked me to look at the map and the climbing course, I could have told you about it. But you didn't ask and you didn't want me in the loop, according to Morgan." In light of Dev's past, Kulani understood his earlier decision, but now he was going to learn that he needed her as much as she needed him.

Shamed, Dev nodded. "Okay, I get the point." He met her defiant gaze. Right now she looked like a warrior out of the pages of history, either Hawaiian or Native American. She was confident looking, her thighs firm and her arms well muscled in a sleek kind of way. It was how Kulani held herself, with incredible self-esteem and pride, that made Dev feel good about the mission. Kulani had the right stuff. In his heart, he knew it.

"About a hundred feet from the bottom of the box canyon wall you'll be descending down into," Cappy said, "is a ledge. Again, not much, but better than nothin'. That's your second night's objective, depending on the speed of your descent down that wall. You can use that second ledge to get some shut-eye, or as a jumping-off point into the valley, which is only about two hundred feet below it. Now, the walls get testy the second thousand feet of the descent. They're a lot rougher and sharper. You got climbing gloves and you need to wear 'em at all times. You each got a first aid kit, and believe me, you'll be using it to wrap your fingers from all the cuts you're gonna receive."

That was good news about the ledge. Dev said, "I saw the notch indicated on the map as a possible ledge. So it's wide enough, stable enough for two people to sleep on?"

"Yes, and what's even nicer is that there's an over-hang," Kulani offered. "That overhang will act like a roof over our heads so we can at least, at the end of the night, get out of the constant wind and rain and try to dry off a little."

Cackling, Cappy said, "The only way you two will begin to dry out is to sleep in one another's arms and let your bodies generate enough heat to do so. Otherwise, you've got two miserable days and nights of teeth-chattering rain, wind and cold. This ain't gonna be easy. If you could delay this climb, I'd sure as hell do it, but I understand the urgency of it, so you two will have to weather the storm *and* descend safely down this wall."

Dev thrust his hand toward Cappy. "I want to thank you for coming, for helping. It means a lot...."

Gripping his hand, Cappy looked meaningfully at Kulani, who stood apart from them, her climbing gloves on as she held the line that would take her down the wall. "Young man, the one to thank is her, not me."

Releasing his hand, Dev grinned rakishly and turned. "I'm damned if I'm going to go down this wall without mending some fences." Looking at her beautiful face, the hint of vulnerability still there in her eyes, Dev felt a surge of warmth. She needed him. The feeling was like an ongoing tidal wave within his chest. His heart felt like it was expanding with an incredible joy he'd never felt before. And it had to do with Kulani, with her need of him. He knew this meant that she trusted him. And it had been a long time since a woman had trusted him. Savoring the feeling, Dev felt almost intoxicated by it. He'd be damned if he'd let Kulani down.

Kulani's eyes widened as Dev loomed over her. Before she could do or say anything, he slid his arms around her waist and drew her hard against his powerful, masculine body. His fingers slid beneath her neck and he positioned her so that he could kiss her. Her lips parting in a soft gasp, Kulani lifted her arms automatically and dug her fingers into his hard upper arms. The glint in his eyes was feral; he was the predator, she, his quarry.

The world spun to a halt in those split seconds. Suddenly, all her fear, her anguish, was erased. Kulani saw him smile boldly down at her as he leaned over to capture her mouth. She felt his strength as she stood balanced within his arms. She felt the movement of his muscles, felt his hot, moist breath across her face, and then his mouth descended on hers. This wasn't a tender kiss. This was a kiss of claiming her as his woman. His mouth was warm, cherishing, taking and giving. Her heart lurched. Kulani moaned as her lashes swept downward across her cheeks. His breath was hot against the coolness of the coming night and his mouth wreaked havoc within her body, her stunned emotions. Never had she been kissed like this! Kulani's world spun out of control. She'd not expected this. Not this sweet assault.

His mouth was cajoling as it slid across her wet lips. It was so easy to relax within his steely grip, to allow him to take her full weight, to know that he would protect her and keep her safe within his embrace. There was such incredible confidence communicated between them. She felt the glory, the joy of him kissing her, and reveled in all that she was as a woman. His fingers caressed her hair as he deepened their contact. Kulani moaned again, only this time it was a moan of raw need. Dev was so masculine. Brutally fashioned out of rock and steel. Yet he was a man with a heart. She felt the tenderness of his mouth as he eased away slightly and began to worship her lips. He tasted of coffee and she smiled to herself. Without thinking, she eased her fingers up across his broad shoulders, following the line of his thickly corded neck, and tunneled them into his short, dark hair.

Dev trembled violently beneath her ministrations. How good it felt to be needed once again! He had expected Kulani to back away, to fight him, to push him out of her life. Not that he didn't deserve it, but he couldn't help himself where Kulani was concerned. His need for her overrode his fear of rejection by her. And now her fingers were sliding through his hair in adoration, and she was leaning against him, her mouth hungrily taking his as he was taking hers. Heat erupted through him. He felt like a primal animal; she was his and he would give his life to keep her safe. The sweetness of her mouth did nothing but accentuate her beauty, and desire sizzled through him as her hands caressed his face.

Groaning, Dev felt the massive control he held over himself dissolving. Kulani's mouth was wreaking havoc through him like a volcano exploding with red-hot lava. The violence of his need for her shook him. No. He had to stop. He didn't want to, but he had to. There was a mission to undertake. There were lives hanging in the balance. Their lives. He wanted to survive this with her if only to explore all the promise of her sweet, sweet kiss. As he broke contact with her glistening mouth, he drowned in her sultry, half-opened eyes. Shaken by the emotion he thought he saw there, and unwilling to believe it, Dev eased her back on her feet. He kept his arms around her until he was satisfied she could stand on her own once again.

Kulani's hands rested firmly against his upper arms. She was gripping him hard, as if she were dizzy. Dev studied her in the building, heated silence that swirled around them. He never wanted to let her go. She looked dazed. Had his kiss impacted her *that* much? His mouth lifted in a slight grin.

"Pretty good, huh?" He rejoiced over the fact that his kissing her meant something good and clean was happening between them. Maybe, just maybe, he had a chance to atone after all for all the mistakes he'd made with Kulani. Judging from the drowsy look in her eyes, the soft parting of her lips and the rose hue staining her cheeks, the answer was yes. His heart soared like an unshackled eagle in that moment of yearning. But behind that surge of joy was fear. Fear of losing Kulani, of losing whatever they had before he had a chance to explore it with her.

This mission was dangerous. They could easily die.

But Dev fought his fear. Gripping her arms firmly, he stepped away from her. "Okay now?"

The rasp of his dark voice flowed through her like cooling water spilling across hot, boiling lava. Her lower body felt scalded, aching and in need of Dev in all ways. Shaken, Kulani released her hands from his heavily muscled arms. "Y- yes, I'm fine now…I really am…." *Liar.* She was anything but fine. She saw the pleased look in Dev's deeply shadowed face. His eyes glinted with arrogant confidence. He was primal. And she thirsted for him in ways that she'd never thirsted for another man.

Pushing a few loose tendrils away from her temple, Kulani tried to get ahold of herself, of the joy thrumming through her heart and soul. She saw Cappy smiling in a fatherly fashion at the two of them. He looked like he knew something they didn't.

"C'mon, kids, time to descend," he urged them quietly as he came up and put a hand on each of them. "And I want you to take your time. You got too much to lose if you don't. Let's get on with it…."

Fear ripped through Kulani. She glanced up sharply. Dev's dark green eyes glittered with a burning look that made her feel simultaneously protected and hungered for. His kiss had been galvanizing and unexpected. But then, there was little to this man that was predictable, Kulani decided. He was surprising—all the time. She saw the look in Dev's eyes soften. Her heart thumped once as he moved over to her.

The darkness was descending on them in earnest. "I'm just going to check your gear," he told her in a low tone, his hands moving methodically, expertly, across her harness, the lines and their attachments.

Kulani trembled. His touch was brisk and professional. Nothing like moments before. "I can't figure you out," she whispered unsteadily. She watched him as he continued to lean over her, double-checking the harness system.

He chuckled and slowly raised his head. There were inches separating them. He could smell the fragrance of her skin. The taste of Kulani lay on his mouth like honey. He wanted her. All of her. "Me? I'm hard to figure out? I thought I was pretty forthcoming."

Kulani stepped away when he was done. "My turn," she said, and began to check his harness.

Grinning recklessly, he held up his arms so she could lean from one side to the other as she gave him one last safety check. "Far be it for me to stop you."

"You're impossible, Hunter."

"Yes," he agreed with a grin, "and you like me for it." *And you need me.*

"I forgot to add egotistical to the growing list." Kulani stepped away. It was so easy to be in his powerful, sunlike radiance. Far too easy, Kulani warned herself. She couldn't ignore the pulse fluttering at her throat. Dev's presence was enticing. Promising. He offered her hope when she'd had none.

Glancing over the ledge, which was covered with knee-high ferns, Kulani smiled a little. "Hunter, you're like all the rest. Once this mission is done, you'll be outta here like a shot. I know your type."

He saw the challenge in her eyes and the mirthful grin on her lips as she made sure the fine, thin leather gloves fitted her tightly. Her fingers were long and beautiful. In a few minutes, he knew they would become bloodied. The thought of anything cutting into her golden flesh made him flinch. Dev wished that Kulani wouldn't come along, but he knew it was too late to throw up an argument to stop her. She'd asked for his help and that was the one thing he couldn't refuse her. Somehow, she'd found his Achilles' heel when she'd said she needed him.

"Well," he said in a silken tone as laid his hand on her shoulder, "I enjoy proving people wrong. You think you're going to get rid of me, Ms. Dawson?"

His fingers sent tiny ripples of pleasure across her shoulder and Kulani savored his touch. His eyes were bright with laughter and challenge, and she saw the playfulness in them. "I didn't say I wanted to get rid of you. All I said was that you'd leave the instant this mission is accomplished, that's all."

Gently, he ran his fingers down one of her long, thick braids. "I'm going to enjoy proving you wrong. Again."

Her scalp tingled wildly. Dev had barely grazed her hair and yet his touch created a delicious ripple that moved all the way to her heart. Dev was so alive. So virile and strikingly handsome. That heart-stopping smile of his charmed her. "You should be paid to sell things," Kulani said, "because you have a way of making people believe whatever you say."

If he didn't step away, he was going to kiss her again. This was not the time or place, as much as Dev wished it were. He allowed his gloved hand to fall to his side as Cappy walked over to them.

"Just remember that last kiss," Dev murmured darkly, and then gave her a devastating smile meant only for her.

Kulani nodded to Cappy as the old man placed his hand on her back. It was time.

"You okay?" he demanded gruffly.

"As okay as I'm going to be," she said. She positioned the night goggles over her eyes. Wrapping her gloved hands around the black nylon line, Kulani tested it against the block and tackle around the tree twenty feet away. It felt strong and solid. Cappy walked her to the ledge, the wet ferns swatting around their legs.

"Okay, take it *easy* on the descent. You know what you have to do—make your way down through the brush and ferns living on the sides of this slick, moldy wall. *Feel* your way, Kulani. Just remember, if you lose your balance or something breaks free and you start a free fall, I'll be up here. We'll stop you. You just hang on." His fingers dug deeply into her shoulder. "I know you're afraid. I know you're remembering the last climb with Stephen."

Kulani nodded. She could barely see the edge of the wall, but she could feel it with the heel of her boots. The surface was wet and slippery. Above them, the clouds were churning darkly and she knew they carried the bad news that more rain could hit at any time now. "I'm ready, Cappy."

"Good luck." He stepped away as she took the line in hand and moved the rest of it through her harness.

At the last moment, Kulani looked up. Up into the face of Dev Hunter, who stood tensely just behind Cappy. His face was shadowed, but she saw worry in his eyes. Worry for her. It was a good thing he didn't know she was more worried about him than herself. Taking a deep breath and then releasing it, Kulani eased first one foot and then the other against the lava wall. Everything held as she stood suspended over the twenty-two-hundred-foot cliff, with nothing but a nylon line and her own experience keeping her from falling to her death.

Chapter Eight

Dev cursed richly. The tropical storm, which would come in bands of pouring rain, struck just as he shoved off from the lip of the ledge. Below him, Kulani struggled through bushes that grew out of the lava wall and ranged from three to ten feet wide. Because of the large sizes, some could not be avoided. He heard Kulani pounding a piton into the wall and knew she would then place a carabiner on it and slide the line through it. After carefully lowering herself another hundred feet, she would place the next piton and begin the process all over again. In this way, they would inch down the wall. As Dev descended, he found out quickly how important the bushes were as handholds when there were none to be found on the slick, moldy walls of the canyon. Dev knew hammering pitons in the growing darkness was challenging. The night-vision goggles helped tremendously. One miss and Kulani's hand would be injured.

It would require her complete concentration to place each wedge safely into the rock. But the brunt of this work rested on Kulani, who was suspended a hundred feet below him, leading the way. He had the easy part— just following the line down the cliff that she was putting in place with the pitons and carabiners.

Minutes after the storm struck, the rain slashed almost horizontally at Dev. The darkness was complete now. They did not dare use any form of light to make it easier to see where their next handhold might be. Everything must be done by touch and night goggles. His senses became quickly oriented by his grasping, searching hands. The rain was cold and jarring. The sleek black nylon uniform he wore repelled a lot of the water, but not all of it. All too soon, Dev felt raw moisture seeping in above his turtleneck, chilling his skin.

Wind came in breath-stealing gusts, howling up the long, narrow canyon and sounding like a banshee wailing out her grief. The gusts pounded him savagely, like a giant's fists pummeling his suspended body. He was repeatedly swung this way and that by the brutal wind, batted around like a rag doll at the whim of the weather. Worse, the rain made his fingers slick and it became difficult to hunt for the next stabilizing piton and carabiner that Kulani had placed earlier.

As he ran his line through the next carabiner and continued to descend, he had to pull his line above him through the one overhead. Because the line was wet, it would drop heavily toward him. Then the wind would rip it out of his hands, and it took precious minutes to gather it all back up in a coil so that he could hang it on one of the snaps from his belt to use later. The whole process was painstakingly slow.

They each wore a headset with battery power packs

snugly fitted into their belts so they could communicate when necessary. Grunting, Dev twisted around. Sheets of rain pummeled his face and he couldn't see anything. The cloying blackness of the night made him feel like a blind man. Through his headset, he heard Kulani gasping abruptly.

"You okay?"

"Yeah…everything's slicker than hell…."

He heard her hammering and knew she was placing another piton in some narrow crack in the lava's surface. Grimacing, he searched around for another toehold to place the tip of his boot in. The brush was thick. He couldn't find purchase. "This damned wall is something else," he grunted, and heard Kulani give a choked laugh.

"Right now I'll bet El Capitan looks like a walk in the park?"

He chuckled and allowed her husky tone to flow through him. "This is work. Real work. Now I see why it's going to take us all night to drop a thousand feet."

"Yeah…slow going. And you can't hurry," she huffed. "If I don't find a deep enough crevice or crack to place the piton in, it'll work loose and we'll be in trouble. Trying to find them at night like this is taking more time than I care to give it."

Dev knew he had to keep communications to a minimum. Cappy also had a headset and was monitoring their every move from above. In this kind of precarious situation, Dev was very glad to have an old hand like him involved.

The wind and rain grew more fierce. Dev wiped the night goggles with his fingers. Fortunately, the goggles not only aided him in seeing the glistening cliff but protected his eyes from the slashing water. Mouth open, he gasped for air as he hunted with his fingers for a good, solid bush that would hold him as he continued edging, inches at a time, down the wall to the next piton and carabiner. With his other hand, Dev followed the trail of line created by Kulani. Her expertise was undeniable, and Dev no longer was sorry she was along. Without her, he admitted, he could never have accomplished this climb. He intended to tell her that once they reached that cave, which seemed a million miles away right now. Kulani was right: this wall was slicker than goose droppings on a rainy day. He grinned tightly as he wrapped his bloody fingers around the roughened trunk of a bush. Giving it a good yank to make sure it would hold him, he released a few inches of his line. This was going to be a painfully long job.

"You okay?" he demanded of Kulani when he heard her grunt.

"Yeah…fine…just tore open my hand is all. No big deal. Off belay. Let me get it bandaged. I'll let you know when I'm ready to belay on."

Damn. The last thing he wanted was Kulani injured. "Off belay" meant "stop." He cringed, thinking of her beautiful golden skin being ripped open by the piton hammer. He could feel warmth flowing over a number of his own fingertips and knew they were bleeding profusely. The leather gloves he wore protected all but the fingertips, which were left open to seek out and feel the grip of the next handhold on a slippery rock. Climbers couldn't find good purchase if their fingers were encased in leather. He had to be able to tell a good handhold from a bad one, otherwise the risk of plummetting to his death was too real. Fingers always bled—just part of the dues paid when challenging a mountain.

He hung on the side of the wall, his back turned to

the weather, gripping a bush on either side of himself to stabilize his body so he wouldn't swing out and away from the rock. He heard Kulani breathing erratically.

"Got it dressed?"

"Yeah, almost… Damn, this weather is bad!"

"You need to talk to your gods and goddesses about this."

Chuckling darkly, Kulani said, "But it provides us the perfect cover. There's no way they can spot us descending in this stuff."

Dev nodded. Again he wiped his fingers against the goggles that protected his eyes. Cold rain dripped in rivulets across his face, following the line of his jaw. "Damn, I'm cold. How are you doing?"

"So far, so good. I'm chilled, but not shivering."

He worried now about a new threat to them: hypothermia. It wasn't something to be taken lightly, either. Hypothermia was a cunning killer. It began its subtle assault on an unsuspecting victim with shivering. And then the mind began to be affected, causing poor judgments to be made—and the wrong decision on this wall could kill them. A person's reflexes began to worsen over time as well.

Glaring out into the darkness and the unrelenting rain, Dev knew without a doubt that hypothermia was now their number one enemy on this descent. A tropical storm was in fact a small hurricane, with winds below seventy-five miles an hour. Swathes of rain clouds would sweep over them like ocean tides. This first onslaught would probably last an hour, maximum, there would be a lull of an hour or two, and then the second swath would hit. Mentally he calculated that it would take them until dawn, or seven hours, to reach the safety of the cave. That meant they would be soaked three times tonight, with the rains getting colder as the temperature declined.

There was no way to protect themselves against the rain and cold, either, apart from a thin fabric of nylon, a flak jacket and the knapsack each carried. That was it. *Damn.* As if they didn't have enough against them! The wind chill was their worst threat. He estimated the gusts to be at fifty to sixty miles an hour as the wind hit the rear wall of Kalalau Valley, then roared straight up the canyon at them.

"Okay!" Kulani gasped, "I'm ready. Belay on?"

"Belay on," he told her. In climber's vernacular, that meant "ready to resume climbing." Just hearing her voice made him feel better. "You let me know if you start shivering, okay?"

She laughed shortly. "Testing." She jerked the line to indicate the direction in which the pull would occur. "Yeah, right. What are you going to do? Come down and hold me? Dry me off?"

Grinning into the slashing rain, Dev said, "Ready to climb," he told her. "I'll do more than that. When we get to that cave, I'm gonna hold you at my side and warm you up."

Kulani laughed a little. "Descending. Stop talking, Hunter. I need to focus on where the hell I'm going."

Chastened, he said, "Down rope."

"Twenty-five feet," she rasped.

Where was the cave? Kulani was exhausted. A bare hint of grayness was touching the horizon, and as her weary hands and sliced fingers searched for the next bush, and her boots moved to find the next steadying niche, she yearned to escape the icy coldness that had held her in its grip the last two hours. She had hypothermia. She knew it. But she hadn't said anything to Dev. He would break radio silence every fifteen minutes and inquire as to her health, but she lied every time. There was nothing he could do to help her, anyway. Right now she had to draw on all her experience to get them out of this dangerous situation.

The last of the rain had ended an hour ago, and for that, Kulani was grateful. But where was the cave? She pushed away from the cliff and leaned out from the cliff wall to search the darkness. There! She thought she saw it to her left. Their descent down the wall hadn't been vertical; they had had to move left and right to make it around massive bushes. Her fingers were numb from the cold and from hammering pitons. She was shivering violently. Her teeth were chattering and she couldn't stop them.

"Check in," Dev ordered.

Kulani gulped. She tried to force her teeth to stop chattering. She couldn't. "I think I see the cave. H-hold on…" she stammered. Twisting her body, Kulani pushed herself away from the wall once again with her booted feet. She swung a good ten feet outward.

"Y-yes!" she crowed triumphantly. "It *is* the cave!"

"Your teeth are chattering."

Kulani heard the worry in Dev's voice. Her feet landed back against the wall and she absorbed the shock by flexing her knees deeply. "I'm okay. The cave's just below me, maybe fifteen feet. I'll make it. Don't worry."

Her hands slipped on the line. For an instant, Kulani dangled limply. Struggling, her movements now sluggish, she hung helplessly in the darkness of space. Exhausted, she calmed herself. It was so hard to think straight! She knew what she had to do. Twisting her body again, she thrust out her hand. Her fingers grazed a bush. There! Instantly, she grabbed at it, but her fingers weren't working well and she missed. Now she sailed off the wall in a slow-motion semicircle. Cursing softly to herself, she tried to relax. She knew she would hit the wall with her body this time and not her boots. *Damn.* Preparing for the inevitable collision, Kulani sucked in a breath, and shut her eyes and waited.

Her body swung hard into the wall. A sharp breath of air exploded from her lips. The jarring motion moved up into her head and jolted gratingly across her hips. Momentary pain serrated her entire back. Making a grab, Kulani found and clung to a nearby bush, then sucked in several breaths of air. She was badly hypothermic, she knew. She had to think! She had to plan her next moves carefully or she could die. Dev was descending and she didn't dare remain static too long. For safety, they had to maintain at least fifty feet of clearance between them. If they got their lines tangled with one another, it could be deadly.

"Kulani?"

It was Dev again. This time there was real worry in his tone.

"I'm okay!" she snapped. "Stop talking to me."

Struggling wildly, Kulani used the bush to aim her in the direction of the cave, which wasn't far away. The last ten feet were hellish for her. Everything went in agonizing slow motion. Each time Kulani lifted her arm, she felt like she was moving it through molasses. It took a horrific toll on her bankrupted reserves. Breathing hard, her legs dangling precariously, Kulani finally felt the opening to the cave with the toes of her boots. At last! Just a few feet to go.

Her lungs ached and her breath was fast and chaotic.

Hands slipping dangerously on the wet line, Kulani lowered herself quickly onto what she thought was the lip of the cave. Her boots slammed into the rock below her. Out of instinct, she buckled her knees and pitched to the right to roll in order to absorb the shock of her fall. The rock was cold, hard and wet. Kulani let out a gasp as she hit and rolled. The line tangled around her, but again her experience counted. She threw out her legs and arms and came to a stop. Lying flat on her belly, with huge sobs shaking her chest, she realized she'd made it to the entrance of the cave.

Before she could move, rocks and pebbles from above pelted down on her. Dev was descending fast! Trying to move out of the way, Kulani cursed her hypothermic condition. Staggering to her feet, she pulled herself into the cave and jerked the nylon line away from the lip.

"Dev?"

"Almost there. I see it!"

His voice soothed her panic. Kulani felt the hours of strain and stress catching up to her. She sat against the cave wall, her head bowed against her knees, which she'd brought up against her chest in an effort to try and conserve her dwindling body heat. Shaking badly now, she knew she should get the knapsack off her shoulders. It was waterproof, thank goodness. There was a dry uniform inside it, along with blankets. She could become warm if she could just get herself to move. Gasping, she realized it was impossible—all she could do was sit there, trembling violently.

In the grayness of the coming dawn, Dev saw the mouth of the cave. He allowed the line to sing through his gloved hand. Landing on his feet, he heard the sound of his arrival echo back from the dark opening. Anxiously, he looked around as he straightened up. There! Kulani was sitting just inside the cave, her arms around her drawn-up knees, her head resting against them.

"Kulani?" There was a raw edge in his voice. Dev quickly unbuckled his harness and threw it aside. As he knelt down, his hands went instantly to Kulani's shoulders.

"You're shaking," he whispered fiercely. "Damn… hypothermia…why didn't you tell me?" He got up and rapidly shrugged out of his knapsack. Taking a penlight, he flashed it around the cave. It was larger than he'd expected. The rear of the cave was dry and protected from the ragged wind that continued to bluster up through the canyon.

"Hang on," he pleaded with Kulani, "I'll get some blankets out. I'll get you warmed up." Right now, his whole awareness was focused on her. She was dangerously close to losing consciousness. Her body temperature had plummeted in this grueling weather. He'd been able to handle the violent temperature change better because he wasn't acclimated to the island as she was. His blood was thicker and therefore able to combat the temperature variance better.

Once he was in the rear of the cave, Dev ripped open the top of his knapsack and quickly spread out the four dry blankets. Moving to his feet, he had to bend over so his head wouldn't hit the roof of the cave. As he approached Kulani, the gray light was strengthening. He saw a white dressing on her left hand. That must be where she'd injured herself earlier, he thought.

Jerking off his headset, Dev threw it aside. He knelt in front of Kulani. "Okay, sweetheart, you're mine. Come on, I'm going to get you to the rear of the cave where it's warmer." He wrapped his fingers strongly around Kulani's biceps and pulled her forward into his arms. She was shaking violently. He heard her teeth chattering nonstop. Quickly, Dev slipped the knapsack from her damp back and arms. Her every movement was sluggish and stiff, warning him of the depth of hypothermia she was experiencing.

"Come on," he whispered harshly as he put his arm around her waist and helped her stand. "Just lean on me."

Kulani had no options. Dev's strength was wonderful. When her damp body came into contact with his, she moaned. Her head dropped forward on her chest. She could barely move. "I—feel like a baby—I can't coordinate...."

"I know," Dev grunted. Lowering her onto the blankets, he quickly removed the flak jacket with the help of the penlight. Going back for her knapsack, he retrieved four more dry blankets. Kneeling down beside her, he began to strip her out of the wet nylon suit. "Sorry, but this has gotta go...."

In protest, Kulani tried to stop him. She wore nothing beneath the suit! Absolutely nothing. Panic ate at her. She didn't want Dev to see her naked, but she felt helpless...like a baby in his arms. Her arm flopped outward in uncoordinated protest as he turned her around and positioned her across the blankets. In the dim light, she saw the apology in his eyes. Care radiated from him like a beacon. Kulani had never experienced the rush of relief she felt now as he began to rapidly strip off the wet material from her shoulders. The sensation shocked her. Automatically, she tried to push his hand away before he could expose her breasts.

"No..."

"Dammit, Kulani," he breathed near her ear, "just

take it easy. You're hypothermic. Your skin feels like ice. Don't fight me...."

The impatience in his tone struck her full force. Her body simply wouldn't follow the commands of her mind, which seemed to be shorting out. Her fingers relaxed over his hand, which held the material just above her breasts.

"I'm okay!" she muttered in slurred tones.

He grinned tightly as he unsheathed the material from her breasts. "Sure you are. You're past the point of being able to shiver. You've got a failing level of consciousness and you can't even control your muscle movements." Dev made sure he kept his gaze on the job at hand and not on her exposed breasts. Sure, he'd wanted to see her naked—but not like this. Feeling badly for her, he continued stripping the suit off her. Reaching over, he grabbed the first blanket and brought it around her, covering her shoulders and breasts. There. She couldn't take umbrage with him now. Moving to her legs, he tugged off the last of the chilled, wet material. Kulani had remarkable legs and dainty feet. Wrapping her lower body in a second blanket, Dev took the other two and placed them around her as she lay in a fetal position on her right side.

Sitting down beside her, he scooped her back into his arms. He heard her mew of protest. "Just be patient," he rasped as her head rested against his jaw. Placing his hand on the outermost blanket, Dev began to rub her shoulders and back with fierce, rapid motions designed to draw the heat that was held deep in her organs back out to the external surfaces of her body.

Kulani moaned as she surrendered to his superior strength. Her mind was mush. She couldn't think two thoughts coherently. His hands were firm and brisk against her skin as he created a warming friction across her icy flesh.

"That's it," Dev coaxed against her ear, "just give in and let me help you. Damn, but you're a stubborn woman."

Kulani sighed. She lay curled up within his embrace, her knees pressed against his massive thigh. Dev Hunter was hard. Hard as the lava wall she had fought all night long. When his hand moved to her arms and he began the same brisk ministrations, she felt slightly better. Her back already glowed with returning warmth.

"Sleep…" she murmured. "I want to sleep, Dev…."

"Go ahead," he grunted as he moved his hand in small, circular motions down her hip and thigh. "I'll hold you and keep you safe, sweetheart. Go ahead and sleep. When you wake up, you'll be warm again…."

Sunlight streamed in brightly and momentarily blinded Kulani. Blinking, her mind slushy, she lay there feeling marvelously warm and safe. It was only moments later, as she felt her sleepiness dissolving, that she realized Dev was stretched out beside her and she was lying fully against him beneath the blankets, her head in the crook of his shoulder and her left arm wrapped around his torso. As she lifted her gaze, she saw his naked shoulder. And then Kulani realized with alarm that her hips flowed against his, and her leg was tangled intimately between his.

Shocking awareness plunged through her. She was naked, too. She could feel the scratchy quality of the lightweight but warming blankets against her bare skin. Was Dev completely naked? Kulani wasn't sure. Her heart was pounding—not with dread, but with anticipation. As she slowly eased herself from the shelter of his embrace, she felt Dev suddenly tense. Instantly, his dark green eyes opened. His pupils were large and black, filled with drowsiness for just a moment before he became fully awake.

His arm around her waist tensed and Kulani was trapped. There was no barrier between their naked forms. Panic ate at her. How easy it would be to simply fall back into his arms, against his warm, hard body, and love him. But Kulani knew this was not the time or place. Her panic increased because she couldn't trust herself, her response, if Dev asked her to come back into his arms.

"Everything's all right," she told him in a husky tone. "I just woke up. I've got to get up."

Dev gazed at her drowsy features. Her braided hair had come loose in tiny tendrils that needed taming. Her ebony eyes were huge and burned with life once more. Smiling lopsidedly, he said, "And I suppose you want me to let you go?"

She smiled a little uncertainly. "Please?" Hunter removed his arm from around her waist, and Kulani immediately felt bereft of the powerful care and sense of safety he always bestowed upon her.

"I was having one hell of a dream about you and me," he teased as he watched her move into a sitting position, the blankets pressed to her breasts for modesty's sake. "Want to hear about it?"

Kulani reached for her pack and drew out the second nylon suit. "Do I want to, Hunter?"

He raised up just enough to place his hand beneath his head. Right now, Kulani looked delicious. "If I were in your shoes, yes, I would."

"Turn over so I can get dressed."

Dev nodded and reluctantly obeyed. Outside the cave,

there was a thin piece of blue sky sandwiched between dark, rain-swollen clouds. "Looks like our tropical storm is still with us," he growled unhappily. His ears caught the sound of the blankets falling away from her as she stood up. The rustle of nylon came next. The temptation to turn over and appreciate her nakedness nearly overwhelmed him. Dev resisted—barely.

Kulani glanced out the opening as she balanced herself on one foot. The rear of the cave did not allow her to straighten to her full height. She gripped the rocky wall for support as she pulled her pants on. "Cappy said it would be two days."

"Too bad," Dev said, scowling. The cave was warm and dry and he was apprehensive about Kulani facing the elements again. "That was a close call you had last night. Why didn't you tell me you were going hypothermic?"

Kulani knelt on the pile of soft blankets and pulled up the skintight outfit. "What good would it have done? You couldn't have helped me while we were descending. I just had to gut it out. You can turn around now." She sat down and pulled on the thick, warm socks. Her stomach growled and Kulani rummaged through her knapsack and found an MRE—a meal ready to eat. She was famished. But one look at Dev as he slowly rolled over and sat up, and she forgot her physical hunger. The dark brown blanket fell away to expose his darkly haired and powerful chest. He wasn't wearing anything. She had slept on that chest. Feeling heat rush up her neck and into her face, she gave him a lame look. "Are you hungry?"

Hunter grinned wolfishly. "Depends on what you had in mind."

Kulani rolled her eyes. And then she burst into laughter. This man had saved her life last night. Reaching over, she trailed her fingers down his large, muscled arm and caught his rough, swollen fingers, careful not to squeeze them. "For food, so get that look out of your eyes, Hunter. You're about as obvious as a Mac truck, do you know that?" She sobered. "And I owe you for saving my life. Thank you."

He saw the seriousness in her dark eyes. Just the way she tenderly caressed his arm and held his fingers in her own was more of a gift than he ever thought she'd give him. He'd stolen two kisses from her. Experience had taught him not to take another. If she wanted to kiss him, she had to initiate it this time. Humor lurked at the corners of his mouth. "So, how are you going to repay me, Ms. Dawson?"

Chortling, Kulani eased her fingers from his. She sat down very near him, her legs crossed and her knee brushing his blanket-clad thigh. "Ohh, I've got a feeling that in that steel trap mind of yours, Hunter, you've got a wish list of how I might thank you."

His grin widened into a devastating smile. Reaching for his knapsack, he said primly, "Well, Ms. Dawson, I'll let you think of a way to thank me. Fair enough?"

With a shake of her head, Kulani busied herself making the MRE edible. She took out a magnesium heating tab and it sparked to life. Setting a small aluminum pan that she filled with water over the white-hot flame, she said, "In all seriousness, I was pretty much out of it. Did I give you a hard time after you dropped into the cave and realized what was happening?"

Dev pulled out his clean black uniform. "Yeah, you were a little hellion under the circumstances. You tried to give me a black eye, but I ducked real fast."

"Oh, I did not!" Kulani watched the water come to

a boil. There was enough water in the pan for two MREs, so she said, "Choose your poison. I'll put water in your meal, too." Holding her hand toward him, she saw him study it intently.

Dev saw the multitude of cuts and lacerations on her fingers and across her palm. Her fingertips were just as badly swollen as his. Drawing one of the packaged meals from the knapsack, he opened it and handed it to her.

"Don't look," he warned her as he swiftly got to his feet.

Kulani choked and quickly looked away, but not before catching a glimpse. Dev Hunter was completely naked. He had a beautiful, sculpted body that only climbing mountains could give a man. "Geez, Dev, a few seconds warning would have been nice," Kulani muttered as she concentrated on pouring water into the MREs.

"You're pretty when you blush, you know that?" he teased as he shoved first one foot and then the other into his clean, dry suit. He saw her jerk her face away from him.

"You're impossible!" she said as she set down the pan.

"But you like me anyway?" he bantered as he turned toward her and sat down only inches away. Outside, thunder rumbled warningly. Dev noticed the sun and blue sky had been chased away. The cave darkened slightly as the thunderstorm moved across the width of the valley.

Chapter Nine

After their fortifying meal, Dev got up and moved behind Kulani, his thighs spread wide to encompass her sitting form. "Let me look at your injury," he murmured as he placed his arms around her and gently captured her right hand. For an instant Kulani resisted, but then, to his delight, she leaned back against him.

"Good, you're finally learning you can trust me," he joked as he picked up a nearby first aid kit and opened it. The desire to be needed filled him with a powerful warmth throughout his chest. His heart hammered briefly at the realization.

Kulani felt mildly drowsy after eating the hearty meal. She nestled contentedly against his strong body. "I shouldn't trust you at all."

"No," Dev murmured as he leaned over her, his arms moving around her proud shoulders, "you shouldn't, but you have a good heart and you'll give a bastard like me a second chance, I know." And then he risked everything by saying, "Besides, you said up on top that you needed me."

A mirthless smile raced across her lips. Kulani was too exhausted to fight Dev's concern. Besides, she craved his attentiveness and wanted his closeness, whether she admitted it to him or not. "You're so arrogant, Hunter." She saw the uncertainty in his eyes as she looked up at him. "Yes," she whispered softly, "I do need you. And I'm glad you're here for me. I couldn't have gone this far without you." And she couldn't have.

Chortling, he examined her fingers closely. "Yes, and you like me for it, don't you?" He scowled as he saw the raw condition of her fingertips. Kulani had cut her fingernails very short, but he saw the nails were chipped here and there from trying to find purchase on that unforgiving lava wall.

There were many bruises on her hand as well, revealing how many times she'd missed the piton and smashed the hammer into her hand, instead. It hurt him to think how much pain that had caused her. She was so damned brave under the circumstances.

With a slight shrug, Kulani said, "You're like a bad cold. Can't get rid of it or you." He was so arrogant and sure of her feelings for him. She felt a little afraid of admitting much because of his boldness.

"Now, you don't mean that, do you?" He grinned as he opened a jar of ointment. "This is calendula. My brother Ty knows a homeopath in Sedona, Arizona, and she told him what to carry for first aid situations." Taking a bit of it and spreading it on a sterile gauze pad, he added, "This is great for healing cuts and lacerations in half the time. And," he whispered, his mouth less than an inch from her delicate ear, "this won't hurt at all...."

Just being cared for by Dev sent warm waves of emotion through Kulani as he applied the ointment to her fingers. He was right, there was no stinging sensation. How tender he was as he took each of her aching fingers and gently covered all the tiny cuts she'd gotten thus far from the climb.

There wasn't anything weak about Dev. Kulani closed her eyes and absorbed him, the marvelous heat of his body. "You should have been a nurse, not a merc," she whispered with a sigh.

"Is that a compliment?" Dev asked. Susan had never allowed him to minister to her like this. Kulani's vulnerability, her total trust in him, made his heart soar as never before. She honestly *did* need him. What an incredible gift she was giving him, he realized.

One corner of her mouth lifted. "You know it is."

"So," Dev said lightly as he turned his attention to her left hand, where she'd haphazardly wrapped a dressing around her wrist, "tell me about your dreams, beautiful and ancient Hawaiian goddess or princess, or whoever you really are...."

Dev's voice was deep and lulling. Her heart mushroomed with an incredible hunger and joy until those feelings filled her chest. Without opening her eyes, Kulani relaxed in his arms, his body her sole support. There was nothing sexual in his ministrations. She relished his nurturance, sensed his need to somehow sustain her through her recovery from her bout of hypothermia.

"Is that how you see me? A mystery?"

Carefully unknotting the dressing on her wrist, Dev laid her arm along the hard surface of his thigh to examine the injury more fully. "From the moment Morgan showed me that color photo of you dancing the hula, yeah, that's how I saw you. A mysterious woman with an ancient past and a magnificent, courageous heart." He glanced down at her. She was incredibly beautiful, her lips slightly parted, her thick, black lashes resting against her high, flushed cheekbones. Dev noted the shadows beneath her eyes and saw the tension still in her features from last night's near brush with death. Hypothermia was a silent, ruthless killer. He'd seen more than one man succumb to it on high-altitude, snow-covered slopes.

Kulani could have died last night and Dev knew it. That thought sent a paroxysm of terror through him. It also made him talk about things he would never normally bring up. "So, what are your dreams? Is flying a helo all you want to do for the rest of your life?"

The teasing in his tone took away some of the pain Kulani felt as he examined the deep cut she'd sustained on the inside of her wrist. A lava outcropping she couldn't see in the darkness had opened her flesh in seconds like a razor blade. She felt him apply some of the calendula ointment around the edges of the two-inch-long wound.

She found it easy to speak to Dev. "No...after Stephen died I wanted to stay home, sink my roots here. At the time, I was working on the mainland and flying in on weekends to be with Stephen. After his death, I wanted to make my life more into what my mother's had been. She was a kahuna, a healer, and she knew so much about herbs. I grew up at her knee and she taught me all about them." Kulani felt Dev place a new dressing over her wound. His touch was excruciatingly gentle and patient. She greedily absorbed his strength each time he touched her. Her mind was lulled, and hazily she wondered if he would cradle a baby in the same manner. Her instincts told her he would.

"You want to become an herbalist then?" Dev smiled to himself. Talking to Kulani was like capturing the gentle trade winds. Her soft, husky tone seemed to filter through his body like sunlight and release a sense of joy he'd never felt before. Completing the dressing around her wrist, Dev deliberately slowed his ministrations because he wanted to keep her in his arms like this forever. That wasn't possible right now, but he was enough of a beggar to make every second with her count, because tonight, when they made it to the floor of the valley, one or both of them could die in an instant. No, he didn't take life lightly. Every breath he drew while she lay trustingly in his arms was a gift, he realized, as he inhaled her special gingerlike fragrance.

Kulani rolled her head slightly from side to side. Beneath her hair she could feel the solid beat of Dev's heart. "No...I don't pretend to want to be a kahuna like Mom was. What I do want to do is write down the knowledge she's passed on to me over all those years. I've got lots of notes lying around here and there. The kahunas have no written history—it's passed down through word of mouth. I want to put my mother's knowledge into a book as a lasting tribute to her."

"Sounds like a good project," Dev said as he picked up her fingers. "What do you want to do after that goal is met?"

"You'll laugh."

His brows arched. "Me? Laugh at you? I don't think so. Give me a try."

Sighing, Kulani barely whispered, "I'd like to have a family. Children. I'm thirty now. I want to settle down and have a real life, not a mercenary life-or-death kind of life, you know? I want to sink my fingers into the deep, rich volcanic soil here and grow herbs. I want a man who will honor my needs, my ways of being creative and being connected to this island and its ancient spirits. I dream of a man who will love becoming a father and doting on the children as much as I'm going to...."

His hands froze momentarily as he heard the deep, welling emotion in Kulani's halting voice. He felt her tremble slightly as she spoke the passionate words that revealed the inner longings of her heart. "Kids, huh?"

"Yes."

"How many of the little critters?"

She smiled, enjoying the touch of his fingers. "Maybe three if we can afford them."

"And you found that man in Stephen?"

Kulani barely opened her eyes. Oddly, with Dev here she no longer felt the keen grief of Stephen's loss. "Yes...we'd talked about it. Stephen would have made a good father." And then she raised her head and looked up at Dev. How close he was! She drowned in the dark green of his glittering eyes as he studied her thoughtfully in the silence. "You'd make a wonderful father."

Kulani saw surprise and then pleasure in his gaze. She watched as Dev's mouth curved wryly. There was something so endearingly boyish about him that she ached to raise her fingers and tame some of those dark strands dipping over his brow.

"Me? A dad? No way. I'm a loner."

"Even loners need family. Why not you? Look how you care for me. How you cradle and hold me. Why wouldn't I think that you'd hold a baby just as tenderly?''

Her insight into his vulnerable heart was startling. With Kulani, however, Dev didn't feel panic as he had with his wife. His instincts had always warned him that Susan could not be trusted with his inner heart. Kulani was different and he didn't try to defend himself. ''I think hypothermia has addled your brain,'' he admitted, scowling.

Kulani repositioned herself against him, a sense of rightness overwhelming her. This was a man to be trusted with her heart and soul, she realized. Kulani had thought that, with Stephen's death, she could never love again. Dev was so easy to open up to, to invite into her wounded heart. He held her like she was a precious and cherished gift. ''Do you ever want to get married again?'' Holding her breath against the possible answer, Kulani couldn't wipe away the vision lingering before her closed eyes. She saw Dev holding their baby daughter in his large, scarred hands, his expression a mixture of awe and incredible joy over the little miracle he held.

Sometimes Kulani had flashes of insight into the future. It was nothing she could trigger or control. The images had occurred often enough to tell her they might come true. The night before the fateful climb with Stephen, she'd had a nightmare in which she saw him fall to his death. She was sorry she hadn't stopped the climb the next day. Ordinarily, Kulani never talked of these visions. Her mother, who was known to have the ''sight,'' the ability to see into the future, had passed on some of her genes to her, Kulani had realized long ago.

''Marriage?'' Dev said as he eased the unguent across

her fingertips. "No...once burned, twice learned. Remember that old saying?"

"And children?"

"I told you—I'm not cut out to be a father." And he wasn't. He couldn't even be there for Susan. He hadn't been there for his baby daughter. No, he would never be a father. He was better off as a loner.

Kulani said gently, "I would think losing your first baby would make you a little gun-shy of wanting another one?"

With a shrug, Dev finished his ministrations. Reluctantly, he eased away and began to minister to his own cuts before he methodically repacked the first aid kit. Kulani was treading on the open wound in his heart. Suddenly, Dev didn't want to keep protecting that wound, hiding it from her. His hands stilled as he looked up, holding her soft, ebony gaze. "Yeah, I have a lot of fear around that. I know people don't think men feel, that when a woman loses a baby, she feels the loss more than the man."

"But that's not true?" Kulani suggested quietly. He would make a wonderful father. He just didn't want to admit it. She saw raw grief etched in his shadowed features. Outside, the wind was beginning to gust once again and the sunlight was snuffed out. In its place was a rapidly approaching rainstorm.

"No." Dev's voice was unsteady. He avoided the velvet look in her eyes. What he felt for her in that moment was warming and hopeful. And frightening. He could lose her on this mission. There could be no tomorrows for them. Each second with Kulani was precious, and he absorbed her compassionate expression. Opening his hands, he rasped, "Children are the future. But I'm not cut out to have them or be a father. I'm a big kid at heart, though...." His voice trailed off for a moment. "Our parents were professionals, but that didn't stop them from having four of us. Growing up in Colorado, I can remember the long conversations at the dinner table every night. I can still hear the laughter and joking." Dev smiled a little as he drowned in the splendor of her midnight eyes, which shone with stars in their depths.

"Is there anything different you'd do this second time around if you found the right woman?"

"Plenty," he said with a sigh. Opening his large, scarred hands, he studied them ruthlessly. "But that just isn't going to happen."

"Marriages fall apart from lack of repair, from what I've seen," Kulani interjected softly. She saw the anguish in Dev's features. With her, he was an open book, so very readable and easy to access. Her instincts told her he wasn't that way with many people, and the moment became even more special to her. She looked up to see that the rain was beginning to wash the canyon once again. The lip of the cave gleamed as water rushed down the lava wall.

"You nailed it," Dev said with a sigh. Taking the calendula ointment, he reopened the lid.

"Let me...." Kulani stretched forward and captured the small plastic jar from him. She smiled a little up into his surprised eyes. "It's the least I can do. You nursed me. Now it's my turn to help you."

Dev didn't hesitate. Starving for her touch, no matter what the reason, he opened his hand to her. When she placed it on her knee, a ripple of need feathered through him. He watched, mesmerized, as she dipped her index finger into the golden-colored ointment and drew out just enough to lavish his fingertips with. Her flesh was warm and soft. Tiny trickles of fire licked up his hand and into his lower arm as she gently applied the unguent to each of his fingers.

"Looks like you had some major scrapes up there last night," she told him seriously as she studied the many abrasions and cuts. Kulani gloried in holding Dev's hand. She felt the inherent power of him. His was a hand that could kill, but it was a hand that could heal her and her suffering heart. Her voice lowered to a whisper. "I don't know what to make of you, Dev. You crashed into my life. You scared the hell out of me. I knew intuitively you weren't who you said you were, yet I ignored my knowing. I got all mixed up inside because your smile touched me so. It's like the rainbows here on Kauai, like the sunlight that turns the world twenty shades of green after the five-minute rainstorms that pop up all the time over the northern end of the island." Kulani looked up and smiled tenderly at him. Now his face was peaceful as opposed to tense. But it was the hunger burning in his eyes for her that gave her the courage to go on.

"I was so angry at Morgan for using you to manipulate me into helping you. I don't like being anyone's pawn. I understand what he did and why he did it." She finished with Dev's right hand and removed it from her knee. He held out his left. Smiling a little as she drowned in the forest-green of his eyes, she added, "Now, for whatever reason, I'm glad it happened, in a perverse kind of way." What she didn't admit was her growing fear of losing him now that she had opened her heart to him. Another realization struck her: since Stephen's death she had only been going through the motions of living—until now. Until Dev crashed into her life. He was making her feel once more. He was making her want to really live life, with a passion she'd had before Stephen had been murdered.

"Why are you glad?" Dev felt his heart thumping hard in his chest. Heat pooled in his lower body with each light stroke of her hand upon his. How badly he wanted to capture her, kiss her and love her until she cried out in raw, utter pleasure. He knew he could give her pleasure. That made him feel good and strong. He knew he could give Kulani all that she had dreamed of. The future looked bright. But then, the present was not guaranteed for either of them. Her life could be snuffed out just a quickly as Stephen's had been. Or his own...

"Promise you won't take advantage of anything I share with you?" she said with a smile, her teeth white against her golden skin as she met his mirthless gaze.

"Oh," Dev teased, "I probably will, but go ahead, confide in me. I did in you. And you can always hold what I've told you as a threat over my head should I try."

Chuckling, Kulani dipped her finger into the calendula ointment once again. "I'm glad you came into my life because you make me happy." She risked a glance at him. The surprise was glaringly evident in his gaze. Chancing everything, Kulani rushed on. "I'll probably be sorry as hell for sharing this with you, knowing your bruising male ego like I do, but I like you. I like being around you. When you're nearby I feel safe. I know that sounds stupid, because no one can give you a sense of safety like the one you get from inside yourself. But *you* do...."

He sat very still. He wanted to confess that he'd never seen Susan as a partner in his life—but he certainly saw Kulani in that role. Kulani was an utterly capable woman, strong and resourceful, who, when the chips were down, would figure things out and do what she had to do—family or no family. Fear ate at him as he admitted it to himself, for that meant Kulani had snared his heart. Oh, she held him gently, there was no question. Susan hadn't been able to open up to him when he was her husband; even in her time of grief and need she had turned to her family, not him. And it had driven him away. Dev had been unnecessary to her. Unneeded. Kulani was the opposite. She allowed him into her life and heart. She reached out to him in her time of need. And she was able to lean on him for help and solace.

"Okay," he offered huskily, "it's put up or shut up time with me, too." When Kulani stopped her ministrations, lifted her head and looked up, Dev felt an incredible sheet of warmth flow through him. Just the way she looked at him, the starry shine in her eyes, that understanding and compassion that radiated from her like light from a full moon made him swallow hard. The words came out choked. "I like you more than a little bit. And I'm scared to death. Scared I'll lose you, because we have so much to lose. Time is..." He looked up at the black lava ceiling of the cave. "Time *isn't* on our side. I'm afraid I'll lose you to a bullet, to a fall.... What happened this morning—that was too damned close for comfort. I didn't know how much trouble you were really in. When I got into the cave and realized how bad your hypothermia was, I was never so scared, sweetheart."

Risking everything, Dev got to his knees, cupped her face and made her look directly into his eyes. "And more than anything, I've been wanting to kiss you breathless. Having you lie at my side shivering, your legs tangled with mine, feeling your breasts pressed against my chest and sensing the courage of your heart beating in time with mine…" He leaned down because he wanted to tell her his feelings in another language— one he was much better at.

Never had Kulani looked forward to a kiss more than right now. Automatically, she lifted her chin and met and melded with Dev's descending mouth. This was a mutual kiss, one that was begging desperately to be taken and given. His lips plundered hers. Opening her mouth more, she welcomed him inside. Simultaneously, she felt his strong hands move in a caressing motion from her face, down her neck to follow the line of her shoulders. As his hands cupped her breasts, Kulani moaned recklessly. She felt him smile and she leaned into his hands, welcoming him, asking him to explore her even more.

Dev felt the precious gift being given to him as he caressed the beauty of her breasts beneath the skintight fabric. Her nipples grew hard and insistent as he grazed them in a provocative motion with his thumbs. Groaning, he felt her arms go around his neck, and she moved wantonly against him. There was such sweetness, such hunger in her clinging, searching lips. Her hands moved of their own accord, caressing the nape of his neck, tangling in the short growth of hair at the back of his head, and finally, ranging downward across his tense shoulders.

Their breathing grew stormy. The thunder caromed throughout the valley and matched the power of their heated, melting kisses as they clung hungrily to one another's mouths. She was bold and yet delicate, pleasuring him with her questing lips. He liked her boldness, her taking what she needed of him to give herself pleasure. The mutual exploration detonated minor and major explosions throughout his taut body. The moment her hand ranged down across his chest toward his hips, Dev knew that if he didn't stop her now, he never would. The mission, the danger, the urgency of their situation pounded through him.

Tearing his mouth from her wet, glistening lips, he gripped her firmly by the shoulders. ''No...not yet...not now. I'm sorry...damn, I want to take you right here, Kulani. I want to spread you like hot honey over me, lie with you and take you and make you mine....''

His dark, husky words vibrated through her sensitized being. As he grazed her breasts one last time, Kulani moaned. It was a moan of understanding, of loss, because right now, she wanted him just as desperately. The mission came first, her head shrieked. The hammering of her heart in her breast delivered another, equally urgent message. A part of her—the woman, not the mercenary—wanted to make love with Dev right now, no matter what the cost. He could die tonight. So could she. Kulani wanted to remember the feel of him deep inside her, wanted the branding memory of his body, his heart and spirit, loving her fully and completely.

''Damn,'' Dev rasped as he forced himself away from Kulani. He saw the ripe flush across her cheeks, the brilliance in her eyes, the desire for him alone written in every nuance of her soft, haunting features. Moving his hands in a trembling motion across her hair, he whispered, ''I'm sorry. I shouldn't have gotten carried away.''

Shivering with need as he withdrew his arms, Kulani whispered, ''I'm not sorry at all for anything we did, Dev. Not now, not ever....'' And she wasn't afraid of living, for the first time since Stephen's death. This man made her feel alive once again. Licking her lips, she went on in a halting voice. "I was carrying my grief and memories around like a good friend, Dev. And then you walked in, and all of a sudden, I didn't feel as bad as before. Every time you came around, my load of grief lightened. I don't know what it all means, I just want you to know what's going on inside me."

He clung to her impassioned gaze. The roaring of thunder and sizzling lightning continued to dance in the sky above them as they remained dry and safe at the rear of the cave. He saw the pulse fluttering softly along the line of her slender neck. His mouth tingled hotly with the memory of her boldness and neediness; his lower body throbbed with raw need of her. Dev understood as never before that honesty between them was necessary. The next twenty-four hours could kill one or both of them. His fear of the past—of not being good enough to be a father—and his belief that he would never find a woman who could love him, warred with his desire for Kulani.

Looking at her tender expression, the way her lips were breathlessly parted, her cheeks stained a rose color, he could think of no other woman who could fulfill him as much as she already had—and they weren't even lovers! Could a person really fall in love this fast? He wanted desperately to speak of these things with her but knew it wasn't the right time or place.

Instead, he opened his hands toward her. "I've had this dream all my life and I want to share it with you," he began quietly. "I told Susan about it, but it didn't inspire much of a response from her." With a shrug of his shoulder, he hesitated before baring it all.

"Dreams and visions are important," Kulani coaxed. "Share yours with me?"

She was sincere. Emboldened by her support, he

grinned nervously and waved his hand toward the opening of the cave. "Ever since I was knee-high to a grasshopper, I used to dream of owning a small horse ranch. I can remember, when I was as young as eight, I used to sit around and draw the ranch with crayons. I knew what it would look like, the color the house would be painted, the number of corrals and all that stuff. I used to wait until my mom and dad came home at night, and at the dinner table, after eating, I'd pass my artwork around to my three brothers and my parents."

Dev laughed, but it was a strained sound. He looked up at the rugged lava ceiling above them. "My brothers always heckled the hell out of me over those pictures. They made fun of my stick horses and stuff. My parents, though, encouraged me. They praised my efforts and asked me questions about this crazy dream I had. We lived on a ranch, but it was never really a working one because my mother was a medical doctor in town and my father a professor at a university in Denver. I liked where we lived. I used to daydream by the hour out in the fields where the alfalfa had once grown, and imagine working the land as if it were a real ranch. I'd sit out there with pen and paper and sketch the scenes I saw in my daydreams. I'd pretend there were cowboys, horses and cattle instead of just a lot of weeds growing."

Kulani smiled. "It sounds like a great dream."

"Well, I took it even further than that. I drew pictures of this black-haired woman who would one day be my wife. I drew the three kids I'd imagine we'd have—two girls and a boy. The ranch was alive and busy. I was working full time in the saddle—and I was so happy...."

The wistfulness in his deep voice caught and held

her. She saw the dream in Dev's shining green gaze. She heard it in his voice. Reaching over, she pressed her palm gently against his powerful chest, over his heart. "Sometimes we're blessed with a dream or vision like you've held. It's a wonderful one. It's one you shouldn't ever give up on. In life, anything's possible."

Sliding his hand beneath hers, Dev closed his fingers and gripped it softly. Sitting in silence as the rain poured down in unrelenting sheets, the wind gusted, and the low rumble of thunder echoed throughout the valley, Dev realized even more how much he wanted Kulani to be a part of that dream.

"Have you ever considered leaving your island?"

She shook her head. "No...my heart, my spirit, is here. Kauai has helped heal me, Dev. I want to pick up where my mother left off with her herbal lore and knowledge. I want to tend that herb garden of hers and someday soon begin selling fresh herbs locally to the people who can use them to help themselves toward health."

Stroking his fingers across the top of hers, he said, "I understand." And he did. Reluctantly, he released her hand. Dev saw the mix of emotions cross her face— the desire for him, the hunger and the fear. Why fear? Maybe from the past, he mused. And didn't his own past war with the present? Didn't it keep him from seeing Kulani as an integral part of his life?

Right now, life was too tenuous. Death could be as quick as taking in a breath of air. Frowning, he muttered, "I wish we could go on talking like this, exploring...."

Kulani nodded and looked at her watch. It was 2:00 p.m. "I know—me, too. But we need to check in with Cappy."

"Right," Dev said, already grieving over the loss of intimacy they'd established so easily moments ago. Back to business. Back to trying to survive this nearly impossible mission.

Chapter Ten

"Are you ready?" Dev peered through narrowed eyes at the view from the ledge where they'd stayed after the second night's arduous descent. They had made it to the rocky lip in the very early morning and had managed to grab a few hours sleep before the turbid dawn approached. In the gray half-light of morning, they were going to disappear into the jungle below and try to locate the professor and his team.

Kulani nodded. "Are you?" The rock ledge where they'd stayed was small—no more than a ten-foot break in the cliff wall—but the black lava overhang effectively sheltered them. The ledge floor was narrow and had been hard to land on this morning. Dev had taken a spill just as he'd descended the last thirty feet. One of the lines holding him had been sliced through and he'd fallen to the hard rock ledge right in front of her. At first Kulani had thought Dev was dead. Luckily, he'd only had the air knocked out of him. However, his left shoulder had taken the brunt of the fall. He was favoring it now and Kulani knew it still bothered him.

"Yeah," he muttered as he locked and loaded the special rifle that would be used for the hunt. Morgan wanted the Black Dawn members to be brought down with specially made tranquilizer darts if possible. Morgan's goal was to keep them all alive for interrogation. It was a good plan but it left Dev and Kulani at a distinct disadvantage, because the bioterrorists wouldn't be firing darts back at them if they got within range. No, they would be using bullets, with the intent to kill. However, Kulani and Dev also had standard issue pistols that shot bullets. And if push came to shove, Morgan had authorized shooting at Black Dawn members in self-protection if Dev or Kulani thought the darts were too risky.

Kulani inserted a tranquilizer dart into the breech of her rifle. They were both sleep deprived, but adrenaline was keeping them wide awake and hyperalert. They planned to leave their packs behind on the ledge and had stripped down to their black nylon suits and flak jackets. Each had painted the other's face with thick dark camouflage paint so their skin wouldn't stand out in the dark green jungle. They each wore headsets, the microphone against their lips so that they could communicate in little more than a whisper, if necessary. Cappy, far above them, would monitor them and send anything they said via satcom link directly to Morgan's facility and to the FBI headquarters in Washington, D.C. From there, the federal agencies involved would receive a blow-by-blow account of their reconnaissance of the area.

Looking at Dev, who knelt on one knee near the edge

of the rock shelf, Kulani shivered. They hadn't any time left. How badly she wanted to discuss so many other things about herself—and Dev. Neither knew what lay down in the darkness under that jungle canopy. Looking up, Kulani saw that the tropical storm was pretty much over. It had rained only once last night, thank goodness, and she'd handled the descent much better. This time, she'd been able to throw off the hypothermia on her own.

Hunter's sharp profile was etched against the gray light. From their vantage point on the canyon wall, Kulani could look out across the jungle treetops to the far-off Pacific, where clouds caught the colors of dawn. She felt momentarily unnerved by the crimson glow. Was it a sign? Of blood? Whose? Their own? Was it a signal of impending death for one or both of them? They had no idea if the professor was down there or not. This was going to be high-risk reconnaissance, Kulani knew. All her military training would take over.

Dev had been a Navy SEAL, and he was perfectly equipped for this mission. Kulani knew she was the weak link in their team. She prayed to her ancestors to give her the courage and guile needed to keep her and Dev from being exposed to enemy fire. Although they carried loaded 9 mm Berettas at their sides, Kulani knew that in thick jungle, where trees grew so close together, no one would get a straight shot for very long. No, bullets would ricochet wildly off the trees.

That meant they'd have to get very close, no more than a hundred feet away from their intended target. She didn't feel any safer with the tranquilizer rifles. While Black Dawn would be firing at them with real bullets, they were supposed to attempt to fight back with a dart designed to render a human being incapacitated for two hours. It wasn't a fair fight, Kulani thought as she moved soundlessly to Dev's side.

"Ready?" There was so much Dev wanted to say to Kulani. He knew their communications were being monitored, so he said nothing.

"Yes."

He heard the grimness in her low tone. Reaching out, he gripped her hand momentarily and gave it a firm squeeze. When she lifted her chin to look up at him, he winked at her and gave her a devastating smile.

"For luck," he told her.

Kulani's heartbeat quickened. Not from the fear that ate at her, but from the incredible tenderness she saw in Dev's eyes as he held her fingers in his large, warm, roughened hand. She saw the smoldering desire banked in his eyes and knew he wanted to kiss her. She felt it in his touch. Instantly, her body and heart responded to his nonverbal communication. Kulani squeezed his hand back and gave him a broken smile. "Yes, luck..." she whispered.

Releasing her hand, Dev moved quickly and quietly down the pile of lava that had fallen and shattered over the centuries, creating an incline of loose rock that led to the jungle four hundred yards away. He rapidly negotiated the boulders as well as the gravel and made it to the tree line. Turning, he motioned for Kulani to come down. He was on full alert now, his hearing accentuated. Gripping the rifle in his right hand, he watched her careful progress down the treacherous slope. Even now, she was graceful. He grinned as she reached for his outstretched hand, and met her fingers, stabilizing her as he drew her into the surrounding jungle. Good, now they could move with more ease. Being out in the open was dangerous.

The soft plop of rainwater falling from leaf to leaf sounded above them. Ferns, the main plants to grow beneath the jungle canopy of guava, umbrella and palm trees, swatted at them.

Tree ferns, reaching thirty feet above them, provided them with excellent cover, as did Amau ferns, two to five feet tall. If they had to, they could literally squat or flatten out on the ground and the thick ferns would completely hide them from an enemy. The older fern fronds were a healthy green color, the younger ones a bright, contrasting red. To Dev, it looked like a Christmas land as they continued more deeply into the jungle.

The ground beneath them was unstable and dangerous because colorful lichens covering the rocks held moisture and made conditions slippery. For the most part, the black and gray stones were sharp-edged lava. Dev took each step carefully to test the stability of the rock where he placed his booted feet. He felt Kulani close behind him. A few times they tripped and almost fell. The terrain was wet, slick and unforgiving.

For an hour, they moved almost soundlessly among the trees, hugging the lava wall at the rear of the valley. If Professor Valdemar and his team were around, Kulani wasn't sensing them. She knew this Black Dawn operation was small. And probably well camouflaged.

Voices!

Instantly, Kulani dropped to her knees, to be swallowed up by the surrounding ferns as Dev ducked against a tree. Her heart pounded wildly in her chest. She saw Hunter's face turn stony and emotionless as he held the rifle in readiness. Her mouth went dry. Yes, there it was again! Laughter this time. Two men were joking as they walked along, oblivious of their presence. Kulani couldn't see them; she could only hear them.

Gulping, she hugged the ground, the sharp points of the rocks pressing into her body. It was damned uncomfortable, but she didn't want to risk being detected. The voices were coming their way.

Suddenly, from behind them, rifles cracked once, twice, three times.

Gasping, Kulani saw wood from the trunk of the tree where Dev was standing explode into a hundred needle-like projectiles. Rolling over on her back, she raised into a sitting position. There! Two men in camouflauge fatigues were standing no more than a hundred yards behind them, in the opposite direction from the voices they'd heard. The men's faces were darkened with greasepaint, their rifles aimed directly at Dev.

Kulani heard a sudden groan. Dev! Twisting to look across her shoulder, she saw him crash to the ground. Blood was spurting out of his right forearm. *Oh, no!* Without thinking, Kulani fired back at the two men. They ducked behind the trees.

"I'm hit...."

Hunter's muttered words sent a wild chill through Kulani. Scrambling to her feet, she lunged toward Dev as he lay at the base of the trunk, hidden by thick fern fronds.

"Come on!" She slipped her arm beneath his.

The roar of the military rifles boomed around them. Bullets pinged. She yanked Dev upright, her adrenaline flowing. Gripping the rifle in her left hand, Kulani pushed him ahead of her. He staggered, caught himself and pushed on.

No one knew, Kulani hoped, about a hidden cave here in the Kalalau Valley—a secret cave along the edge of this jungle, not that far away.

"Run!" she gasped at Dev. He was gripping his left

hand across his right forearm. Bright red blood was spurting from between his fingers. He moved brokenly. Stumbled. Fell. Kulani raced up to him and looped her arm beneath his once again.

"Follow me!" she rasped when he was on his feet.

It would do no good to fire back at the Black Dawn terrorists. Kulani continued to move swiftly. She heard Dev sucking in breaths ladened with pain. She heard the rasp of agony in each explosive gasp. How badly was he hit? Would he die? Bleed to death? Her mind swung in a hundred directions simultaneously. First, they had to outwit the terrorists on their heels. Up ahead, the understory ferns of the jungle grew even more thickly. More bullets ricocheted around them. Kulani jerked a look over her shoulder. Dev was right on her heels. She had lost sight of the terrorists. *Good!*

Breathing hard, her mouth open, as she gasped for breath, Kulani plowed wildly through the heavy barrier of ferns. The cave wasn't far ahead, if her memory served her correctly. *Come on! Come on! Where are you? Where?!*

There! Kulani skidded to a halt. In one movement, she twisted around, grabbed Dev by the shoulder and savagely shoved him downward.

"Get in there!" she ordered breathlessly as she dropped to her knees. Now they were completely protected by the overhead ferns.

"What?" Dev gasped, on his hands and knees among the damp, lichen-covered rocks.

"There!" Kulani jabbed her finger in front of him. "Get in there!"

He saw it—a dark hole in the earth, not more than four feet across. He realized through the haze of pain that it was a ground cave. Instantly, he powered himself down into the maw of darkness. Once inside, the rocks disappeared and his knees met a floor of sand and pebbles. Breathing raggedly, Dev plunged headlong into the darkness. He slammed repeatedly into the sides of the tight, confining tunnel. Up ahead, he began to see grayness. *Light!* What was this place? Kulani knew of it. Did the terrorists? His mind spun between survival and pain.

He heard Kulani scrambling behind him on all fours. She was barreling through the tunnel at a high rate of speed. Trying to steady his raw breathing, Dev shoved on toward the gray light ahead. The entire floor of the cave was composed of fine, black sand, he noted, making movement swift and easy. Within moments, Dev reached a small, oval room—a womb-shaped cave about twenty feet in diameter. Far above him, a shaft of light could be seen, mostly blocked by leafy green fronds covering the opening. The gray, filtered light illuminated the cave dimly.

Kulani dove from the restrictive tunnel and tumbled forward. She landed heavily on her shoulder and rolled past him, her boots clipping his left arm. Once inside the cave, she scrambled to her knees, put her rifle aside and turned all her attention to Dev. As she tried to steady her breathing, she saw him sitting with his back against the wall, fumbling for a dressing from his belt, without much luck.

"Here, let me...." Kulani whispered raggedly. Hands shaking violently, she ripped the nylon away to expose the bloody wound. A bullet had gone completely through his right forearm. It was bleeding in spurts.

"Apply direct pressure until I can get a dressing on it," she whispered as she fumbled for the first aid kit on her waist belt.

Dev warily kept watching the tunnel. ''Will they know where we are? Where this cave is?''

She shook her head as she quickly doused the dressing with antibiotic. ''I don't think so. Only the old Hawaiians, the kahunas, know of it. Lift your hand....''

He watched gratefully as Kulani tightened the dressing around his wound. The bleeding had been staunched. He knew that most artery injuries would close off on their own in two or three minutes. Thankfully, the artery hadn't been severed at a flat angle, or he'd have eventually bled to death. Another sensation flowed across him: the realization that he wasn't such a loner after all—that he needed Kulani just as much as she needed him. Only together could they finish this mission. Only together could they survive it.

They heard the terrorists nearby. Sounds of their running footsteps, of rocks being dislodged by their heavy combat boots, echoed eerily through the tunnel entrance. Dev held his breath. He tensed as the voices got much clearer and closer. Kulani didn't seem to care one way or another. She continued fixing the dressing around his arm with more supplies from her waist belt. Drawing out a syringe of antibiotics, she unceremoniously lifted a pinch of his skin below the wound and expertly slid the needle into it. Hunter barely felt the prick, his attention fixed on the entrance of the cave.

Capping the used syringe and needle, Kulani placed it back into the pouch on her belt. She saw Dev tensely watching the tunnel mouth.

''They won't find us,'' she whispered so only he could hear. ''Just relax. They'll never find the opening.''

He wanted to believe her but didn't. Reaching for his rifle with his left hand now that his right arm was useless, Dev was glad he'd trained with the SEALs, who insisted that all team members become ambidextrous. Kulani signaled for him to put the rifle down. She sat near him, her mouth open so that she could breathe more easily and quietly. Her face was tense and her eyes narrowed and assessing.

Voices drifted into the tunnel. They seemed farther away this time. Dev looked over at Kulani. She'd just saved his life. Reaching with his left hand, he closed his fingers over hers momentarily. Her head snapped up and her eyes widened.

He winked at her and gave her a pain-filled smile of thanks for what she'd just done. Right now, they couldn't talk. The chance of discovery was too real. His mind revolved back to their dilemma. How would they get out of this? Cappy had to be called, but not right now.

Dev's breath eased a bit as the voices floated away, indicating that the terrorists were leaving the area. Rubbing his furrowed brow, Dev shot another glance at Kulani, who hovered protectively at his side. He saw the fear in her eyes. As she turned her head and met his gaze, she managed a broken smile.

"They're leaving," she whispered. "They'll think we escaped and they'll mount a search party for us somewhere else." Sitting down, her legs crossed, she faced Dev. "How bad is your wound? It looks clean, with no bones involved, but you tell me?"

He lifted his bandaged arm and slowly flexed his bloody fingers. "You're right," he told her in a low tone, "just a muscle injury, no broken bones."

Kulani began to feel shaky. She gripped his left shoulder. "They surprised us. I wonder if they knew we came down, and were waiting for us?"

Dev shook his head. He absorbed her firm, steadying touch. "No, or they'd have picked us off that wall this morning. We'd have been easy targets," he replied, studying her. She looked beautiful in a wild and natural way. The gray light silhouetted her head, the tendrils of hair, frizzy in the dampness of the cave, framing her face. Her cheek was smudged with mud, her lips parted. Dev saw the shock in her eyes. Smiling gamely, he said, "Hey, I'm okay. I'll live. I've got the best doc in the world—you."

Worriedly, Kulani eased her hand down the hard muscles of his left arm. She felt his fingers tangle in hers and she released a broken sigh. "I was so scared, Dev. I wasn't expecting them." She placed her hand against her face and tried to take a deep, stabilizing breath. Just the squeeze of his fingers around hers made her feel better.

"It was a damn good thing you knew about this hideout or we'd be dead right now. Tranquilizer darts aren't any match against the firepower they had. I'm glad you used the real things, the bullets. We'll use the darts if we get a chance, later on."

Kulani nodded in agreement and allowed her hand to fall away as she looked up at Dev. "The big question is what do we do now? We know someone is back here. We haven't confirmed it's Black Dawn yet. Those two guys could have been hunters, not terrorists."

Grunting, Dev said, "They were mercs. They made every shot count. They didn't wildly spray the area like a hunter would. They were mercs hired by Black Dawn, would be my guess. But you're right. We need to confirm it's Black Dawn."

"I think we need to get you to safety," Kulani said. "To hell with Black Dawn right now. Your life is more important.'' When Kulani pulled her satcom phone from her belt, she saw to her surprise that the case was smashed.

"Damn," she muttered, lifting the instrument and examining it. "It's broken." Looking over at his, she said, "Give me yours. We need to check in with Cappy."

Dev nodded and fumbled on the right side of his hip where the satcom phone was. "Well..." he growled, unsnapping it from the carrying case, "look at this." He held it up. A bullet had grazed the black plastic phone and destroyed it.

Kulani gasped. How close Dev had come to dying! If that bullet had not struck the phone, it might have entered his hip and abdomen and he'd have surely died. A chill ran through her. "You got lucky...." she managed to say in a choked voice.

Dev tossed the phone to the floor of the cave. "Yeah," he muttered, "I did." Looking up at her blanched features, he said, "That means that at some point in that firefight, we lost all contact with our people. They don't know whether we're dead or alive. Our walkie-talkies are useless. The rain got to them. I tried them up on the ledge last night. No go. Must have been the moisture that did it. We have no way of contacting Cappy or anyone now." Grimly, Dev stared at the entrance to the cave. "That means Morgan will be forced to hand things over to the FBI. We don't know what the FBI plans are. And they don't know we're still alive...."

He saw the desperation in Kulani's eyes. She was raw and hurting. Her fingers gripped his hard. Dev began to realize how much Kulani really cared for him.

"Look," he said, "we can't blow our cover. I have a plan. Right now, Black Dawn is suspicious. They can't find us so we'll let them guess about us—are we military, or not? They'll probably be shutting down their operation right now and looking to get out before the feds can nail them. My guess is they will be moving out of here very soon. No, we've got to operate on the premise our cover is blown. That means we have to assume those mercs will run back to the professor and tell him what went down. It means we need to finish this mission before the FBI comes barreling in here with guns blazing. They could blow up the anthrax and release it accidentally. We, at least, have a chance to find it, pick off the terrorists and keep that deadly stuff capped and contained.''

Kulani nodded, seeing the wisdom in Dev's speculation. ''To escape, the professor will probably call in that black helicopter that comes and goes into the valley.''

''Bang on,'' Hunter grunted. He looked over at their weapons. ''And that means we go after them before they make their escape.''

Kulani's heart knocked violently in her breast, an icy feeling showering through her. ''You mean—now?''

''No better time,'' Dev said. He flexed the poorly working fingers of his right hand. The soft tissue had swelled, inhibiting his abilities. ''We'll give them an hour. Those mercs will be searching other areas for us, thinking we are still running. That's our ace in the hole. We know that black helo flies in from another island. We don't know which one. The professor will call it in to pick up him and the anthrax. We've got to be at their camp, waiting for that to happen. That's when we take them out with the drug darts. It's the only chance we'll have, Kulani. You know that.'' Dev met and held her grave gaze. He saw the protest on her lips, warring with

the dawning realization of the truth in her widening
eyes.

"Kauai lies a hundred miles from the nearest island,"
Kulani agreed. "And most helos can fly faster than a
hundred miles an hour. It could arrive here in less than
an hour."

"My guess is that the professor and his men aren't
going to call in the helo until they've gathered up everything they need to take with them. That buys us at
least an hour." Dev felt the pain floating up his arm.
"Get me a pain med?" They had to move—quickly.
Or all hell was going to break loose around them. Dev
didn't even want to think about the possibility of Kulani
being killed if that anthrax was released during an FBI
raid. And that could happen all too easily. No, it was
up to them to finish this mission pronto.

Kulani dug into one of the other pockets around her
waist. "Morphine derivative," she told him as she
placed one white, round tablet on his tongue. She
opened the canteen and handed it to him. Watching as
he slugged down several gulps of water, Kulani felt
shaky all over. Dev could have died out there. And this
mission wasn't over yet. As he removed the canteen
from his lips and handed it back to her, she whispered,
"This is a helluva fix, Hunter. I just find a guy that
turns my world upside down and now we're in this
pickle."

Wiping his mouth with the back of his hand, he
grinned a little through the pain. "Yeah, well, you
turned my head from the beginning." Reaching out, he
cupped her cheek. Her skin was damp from perspiration.
"Hang in there, sweetheart. I'm betting on us. Besides—" he grinned a little as he stroked her cheek
"—I'm too damn mean and ornery to die."

Sighing, Kulani pressed her hand against his. She lay her cheek against the palm of his hand and simply absorbed Dev. "You're not mean or ornery. You never have been." Shutting her eyes, she felt tears crowding against them. "Just promise me one thing, Dev. One thing."

"I'll promise you everything," he rasped. He saw the anguish in her face. The tenderness between them was palpable.

"Just promise me you won't do anything stupid out there. We're a team." Kulani took his hand and pressed a kiss against the back of it.

Her kiss tingled up his arm. Looking at her intently, Dev rasped, "We're a team. You saved my hide."

Sniffing, Kulani opened her eyes and self-consciously brushed away the tears. "I was so scared. I'm scared now, Dev." Her lower lip trembled against a wall of emotion that threatened to avalanche her. Kulani knew men didn't like to see women cry. Especially in a situation like this. Dev had to rely on her even more than before. She would carry the brunt of this mission, now. Even though he could shoot with either hand, he would not be as good left-handed as he was right-handed, she knew.

Sliding his arm around her tense shoulders, Dev drew Kulani against the left side of his body. She did not resist his overture and sank gratefully against him, resting her head against his shoulder. He felt her arm slide around his torso. "Mmm, now this is living," Dev sighed as he held her tightly. "This is all I'll ever want. My life is here in my arms, did you know that?" Dev knew he was saying a lot. Right now, the truth was the only thing he wanted on the table with Kulani. "I know I don't deserve somebody like you. Hell, I've run scared from women since my divorce from Susan. I felt like a loser. I couldn't be a father. I couldn't even be a good husband to her. I was gone when she had the baby…when the little tyke died—oh, hell… But I want to be there for you when you need me.'' Pressing a kiss to Kulani's hair, he offered in a roughened tone, ''Somehow it's easier with you. You let me into your heart. You aren't afraid to be vulnerable with me and somehow I'm not afraid to open up to you. It's like a miracle….'' And it was, despite the danger around them.

Kulani tightened her grip around his torso as she heard the undisguised hurt in his deep voice. Tears stung her eyes. She pressed a kiss against the solid cords of his neck. ''It wasn't your fault you lost the baby, Dev. It wasn't. And that's malarkey that you couldn't be a good father. I've never met a man as gentle and tender as you are. You know when to drop those hard, male walls you live behind. You know when to be vulnerable….'' Wiping her eyes, Kulani whispered fiercely, ''So don't you *dare* think you're less of a man! I happen to think you're wonderful, and I'm falling for you….''

Dev heard the hitch in her voice and he held her as tightly as he dared. The words *I love you* were almost ripped from his mouth. He savagely forced them back. Now was not the time to admit anything. He wanted to talk to Kulani about all of this in a place of safety, not in the midst of death. ''Hey, sweetheart, you hold my heart in your hands. Remember that, okay? You have from the start….''

Kulani nodded and pressed her lips together to stop a sob from rasping out of her. She heard Dev's powerful heartbeat, felt his chest expanding and contracting as she lay against it. There was so much life, so much heart in this fearless warrior. Death was stalking them in earnest now and she didn't want Dev to die. Would her ancient ancestors decree they both should die today? She pressed her face upward, sought and found Dev's mouth. With a fierceness she'd never felt before, Kulani kissed him. As her mouth opened beneath his, she felt the returning strength of his lips upon hers. He groaned and the sound reverberated through her like the thunderstorms of yesterday. It was a healing sound. A sound of visceral pleasure—of one primal animal sharing with another.

That was how he made her feel—primal, a part of all things, and especially a part of himself. As she slid her lips against his, drank of his strength and the molten heat he held for her, Kulani knew that she loved Dev Hunter. She'd never thought she would love again, but now life had given her a treasure in this man—a treasure she hadn't believed existed, until now.

Tearing his mouth from hers, his eyes slitted with fire and need, Dev looked down into her innocent, upturned features. How beautiful and wild Kulani looked in that moment, despite the greasepaint. Her lips were parted and so vulnerable to him. Yes, she had given her heart to him in that surprising, heated kiss she'd just initiated. It was as if she were feeding him her strength so he could complete this mission. Easing his hand from her shoulder, he gently touched the crown of her hair.

"You're mine," he growled. "And we've got a lot to talk about after we get through with this mission."

The sweetness of his promise cut through the massive fear Kulani felt. With a nod, she choked back the rest of her tears. "Yes," she whispered brokenly. "Yes..."

Grimly, Dev released her and picked up his rifle. "Let's saddle up. Time isn't on our side, sweetheart. And we've got a mission to finish."

Chapter Eleven

Kulani wondered if the tangos could hear her heart slamming violently against her rib cage. She and Dev had located the lab and now they squatted among the ferns, completely hidden. The lab had been easy to find; they simply followed the path of broken fern fronds the mercs had left when they'd returned to headquarters after their unsuccessful search.

It was just past noon and the sun was burning overhead. Humidity was high and sweat crawled down her temples and ribs. Kulani glanced quickly to her left. Dev's profile was sharp and hard, his mouth thinned. She was seeing his warrior side, the ex-Navy SEAL. There was a different energy around him now, that of a lethal predator. Slowly lifting her hand, she wiped away some of the sweat that threatened to drip into her eyes and make them sting.

Moving her attention back to the anthrax operation,

Kulani was amazed at how small it really was. The lab was simply a dark-green-and-brown camouflage tent set up against the black lava wall, half-hidden by a profusion of guava trees. The area was shaded with green-and-brown netting, making it look like there was a spider web over the whole camp.

Dev motioned swiftly with his good hand. She jerked her attention to the left of the tent. Two mercs emerged out of the jungle—the same two who had nearly killed them. One was red-haired, tall and angry looking, the other blond, shorter and stockier. His voice rang across the area.

"Professor Valdemar?"

Kulani held her breath as they approached the tent. A third merc, a sandy-haired, thinner man who sat stationed nearby, rose to his feet. "He's busy."

The blond-haired man snarled, "Tough. Professor, we got trouble. We need to talk. *Now.*"

Professor Jevon Valdemar emerged from the tent. He was a short, emaciated-looking man with a steel-gray goatee, dressed in camouflage fatigues that were obviously too big for his small, wiry frame. He gave the two mercs an imperious look of expectation. "Well? We heard gunfire. What was it?"

The red-haired one said, "Johnson, here, spotted two tangos. We know they're military operatives by the way they were dressed."

Johnson added, "Yeah, and Campbell here put a bullet into one of 'em. Winged him. They got away, boss. They disappeared on us," he said, snapping his fingers to underscore the point.

Valdemar snorted violently. "You fools! You let them get away? I'm paying you Americans good money to do your job." His voice rose to a screech of disbelief.

"We must leave at once!" He turned to the third merc. "Stuart, put a call in for the helicopter. Pronto." Glaring at the other two mercs, he snarled, "You two get everything packed up in one hell of a hurry."

"Boss," Johnson said, holding up his hand, "we wounded one of them. If anything, they're long gone."

"That's precisely the problem. I'm sure they have satcom links." Valdemar peered through his gold-rimmed glasses toward the blue sky, which was now clouding over with an approaching rain shower. "They'll be coming in with guns blazing. We don't have much time." He swung his attention to Stuart, who was on the radio. "Come, I need to get the anthrax into that special carrying case!" He jerked back the tent flap and disappeared inside.

Kulani let out a long, slow breath. Her heart was still pounding. She knew what had to be done. Looking over at Dev, she saw him slowly turn his head in her direction. His dark green eyes were slits. The intent was there.

Kulani's stomach knotted. This was the side of Dev that she'd always known had existed. The warrior side. Now the stakes were high. Deadly. It was two against four. She was glad for the protection of the flak jacket covering the vital parts of her body.

Dev made a signal for her to pull back from their position. She nodded and followed him silently and slowly. Waving fern fronds would give away their presence. It began to rain, fat drops hitting the trees above them and drips splattering on the ferns. Water began to soak into her nylon suit as they moved farther away.

Finally, Dev slipped behind the thick, tangled roots of a huge octopus tree, which shielded them completely. Kulani crawled next to where he was crouched. Here they could talk in a whisper and not be overheard. The rainstorm intensified. All that could be heard now was the rustling sound of water striking the canopy far above them. It would be a good cover for their movements.

Placing the butt of her rifle on her thigh, Kulani sat against the trunk, her shoulder touching Dev's. She leaned near, her voice low.

"That helo will be here in less than an hour."

Nodding, Hunter said, "That will be when we'll take them."

She frowned. "Because they'll be diverted by the helo landing?"

"Yes." Dev pointed behind him. "Did you see that cleared area near the wall? Where the trees were cut down?"

Nodding, Kulani said, "That's where the helo's been landing and taking off from. Although—" she frowned and looked in that direction "—that's one helluva landing place. The pilot has to be good, setting down next to that lava wall. He's got about a fifty-foot clearance before his blades start taking chunks out of the rock."

"I estimate about the same amount of clearance on the other side, too," Dev said. He flexed his right arm. The pain was bearable, but to his consternation, he could barely move his fingers. Swelling was now setting in around the gunshot wound, clearly inhibiting his ability to use the arm effectively.

Kulani saw the tightness in his face. "How's the wound?"

"Okay."

She grinned a little. "Liar. Want me to try that again? How's your wound?"

He smiled briefly. "Hurts a little. I'm worried that I

don't have the reflex I want.'' He held up his fingers. ''I can barely use them.''

''The swelling,'' Kulani said. Biting her lower lip, she said, ''Listen, I have a plan. It's risky, but you need medical help now, not later.''

''I'm listening,'' Dev said. There was no doubt she looked like a warrior in this moment. And even now, he thought she was incredibly beautiful. When the chips were down, Kulani was there. She was strong, and her thinking was clear despite the chaotic action surrounding them.

He saw the fear and dread in her dark eyes, though. He was scared, too, but now they were a well-oiled, functioning team. They needed one another. And they worked well together because they had put their trust fully in each other. Dev hadn't thought he'd ever see something like this happen to him. Thanks to Kulani's trust, her need for him, his heart had opened. Even more amazing was his realization that he needed her just as much as she needed him.

Rubbing her brow, Kulani said, ''Let the helo land and the pilot throttle her back to idle pitch. I know he won't shut off the engine—he'll keep those blades turning. I think we should attack at that moment. If you can take out the mercs first, reducing our chances of getting hit with bullets, I'll go for the pilot. I want to get into that cockpit, yank him out of there, and get you and the professor, along with that anthrax case of his, on board.'' She gave him a triumphant look. ''I'll *fly* us out of here. That way, I can get you to the nearest hospital and Valdemar to the authorities all at once. What do you think?''

Hunter sat there digesting her plan. ''If I don't take out the mercs, we're in trouble.''

"Can you do it left-handed? I know you're ambidextrous." She pointed to his right fingers. "You said you can barely flex them. Will you be able to use them to pull the trigger on your rifle? You're the firearms expert, I'm not. I'm good, but not like you."

Understanding Kulani's logic, Dev sighed. "All I can do is try. Those tranquilizer darts are powerful enough to drop a bull elephant, so once those mercs are down, they're out. If I can't get close enough to take them down with the darts, I'll take them out with the bullets."

"If you use darts to incapacitate them, we can leave them behind. All I'm interested in is the professor and his cargo," Kulani said grimly. "I want that son of a bitch."

He heard the grating in her husky voice and saw the glimmer in her eyes. "Okay," he sighed, "it's a good makeshift plan under the circumstances. We've got to get into position. Do you think you can put yourself in the right place to take a shot at the pilot?"

"There's only one way he can land and take off," she said grimly, "and I'll be there. I'll have to get on board and take him out with a dart. There's no way I'm going to shoot a bullet through the canopy. I don't want to risk destroying the control panel." Besides, Kulani didn't want to use her sidearm to kill the pilot, she simply wanted to immobilize him. She had enough nightmares from the Gulf War to last her a lifetime; she didn't want to add to them, if she could help it.

Dev sat there feeling helpless. Kulani's plan placed her in optimum danger. If he couldn't take down the three mercs, her life would be in grave jeopardy. She'd never board the helicopter in time.

"What about the professor?"

Shrugging, Kulani ran her hand across the top of his

hard thigh. She saw he was in pain from the wound. "He's the wild card in all of this. I didn't see a weapon on him. Did you?"

"No. But that doesn't mean the bastard won't have one when it comes time for the helo arrival."

With a shake of her head, Kulani said, "It will be my responsibility to take him down, that's all."

"Him and the pilot." Hunter rolled his eyes.

Grinning tightly, Kulani said, "The price of admission, isn't it? You've got three men to take down, I only have two."

"Yeah, the worst two—and with darts, not bullets. That pilot will be carrying a pistol, for sure. He'll know you're coming on board. That's a high ante."

Kulani felt Dev's concern. She patted his thigh. "I'll be okay. Birds are my specialty."

"If you have to," Dev warned her, "you take them both down with your pistol. Screw the darts. Your life is worth more than theirs ever will be."

The glitter in his eyes made her shiver. He meant it. Her hand stilled on his thigh. "I'll do whatever I have to, Dev. I don't like killing. I'll avoid it if I can, but believe me, I'm not putting myself in jeopardy—or you. Okay?"

He slid his hand over hers. She was so warm and alive. Their mission was hovering like the sword of Damocles over their heads. He could feel the pressure mounting inside his chest and gut. He could taste death in his mouth. Holding her luminous gaze, he rasped, "Dammit, I just found you and the last thing I want is to lose you, Kulani." His fingers gripped hers. "I *want* a chance with you."

Bowing her head because tears smarted in her eyes, she whispered, "So do I, Dev."

Sighing raggedly, Dev felt the water dripping across his hair and down the back of his neck. The storm was easing now. Behind it, he saw another roll of black clouds drifting ominously across the top of the ridge toward them. He wanted to say I love you, but he couldn't. Not now. Did Kulani love him? How had this all happened? Dev's head spun with questions but no answers. His heart, however, was wide open and bleeding with anxiety for Kulani's life. She was the one taking the biggest risk of all, by exposing herself. Him? Well, he'd take out the mercs from the ferns and never be seen. It would be hard to locate him—but not her.

Lifting his hand, he looked at the watch on his wrist. "It's time to go."

The words sent a chill along her spine. Nodding, Kulani moved silently and picked up her rifle. Her heart was pounding with an adrenaline surge. The rain let up just as suddenly as it had started. They would have to be careful getting back to their respective positions or someone might spot fern movement and destroy their surprise plan of attack.

As she got ready to go, she felt Dev's hand on her arm. Turning, she saw his fierce expression.

"Stay safe, you hear me? You mean a lot to me, Kulani. I want the right to explore life with you after this is over."

Shaken, she reached out and touched his hand. "So do I, Dev." In that split second, Kulani realized how much she loved him. She was stunned by the magnitude of her feelings. She loved Dev with all her heart. It was that simple. That horrifyingly complex. Right now, in the next twenty minutes, they could be killed. Her mouth grew dry as she held his glittering green, predatory gaze. "Stay safe, darling...."

The words warmed him like a blanket even though he was chilled and wet from the rainstorm. Their fingers separated. He wanted to cry. He wanted to scream at the gods and goddesses of creation on this island. Life wasn't fair.

Slowly he got to his knees and slung the rifle across his back. Glancing over his shoulder, he saw Kulani disappear among the ferns. She was heading toward the place where she could intercept the helo once it landed. He had to go in the opposite direction. The bitterness coating his mouth grew with each slow, cautious movement he made through the dense jungle. He loved Kulani. Oh, Lord, he loved her. And now he could lose her....

The black helicopter arrived exactly twenty minutes later. It was a twin-engine Agusta, the only type, Kulani guessed, that had the speed and range to make such a quick interisland flight. The aircraft was used by the military for its electronic warfare capabilities. The helicopter could fly at night or in foggy weather. She'd never flown this particular helicopter, but, thankfully, she'd flown military helos in the U.S. Navy. That experience would have to suffice. She knew each helo was a little different, and that put her at a disadvantage, because she didn't know the idiosyncrasies of this aircraft and had no time to learn them. From her vantage point, she watched the huge, black bird slowly begin its descent. It was a very precarious flight operation and her gaze was riveted on the pilot, who was obviously highly skilled. The buffeting wind kicked up by the massive rotor blades shook the entire surrounding jungle. She lay on her belly, the ferns covering her position.

To the left of the helo, she saw all of the professor's

crew, their faces uplifted, watching the aircraft. She knew Dev was in place by now, but she didn't know exactly where he was. The professor stood with his arms wrapped tightly around a silver metal suitcase pressed to his chest. He moved nervously from foot to foot. So did the mercs, who kept swinging their attention from the aircraft to the surrounding trees. Sweat dribbled down her cheeks. The rain began again and she prayed that it would not be a deluge and make targeting their tangos difficult.

Her hands opened and closed nervously around the stock of her rifle. She had six darts in the weapon. She couldn't afford to miss too many shots. All her focus narrowed on the helo. Within moments, it would land. The mercs were in a group to one side. She knew that would make Dev's targeting them easier. Anxiously, she craned her neck to see if there was a copilot. There was not. That was good news. Were there other men inside? That she didn't know. If there were, it would change the game completely.

The instant the pilot throttled down the rotors and the aircraft settled in for a landing, the professor trotted toward it. As he jerked open the door and slid it back, Kulani heard gunfire erupt and saw the first merc go down. She leaped to her feet. She couldn't afford to watch the mercs. Her focus had to be on the helicopter.

As she lunged upward, rifle in hand, she took aim at the professor, who was trying to clamber up into the aircraft. Just as she shot, she saw the pilot come to the door to give him a hand.

The dart missed! Kulani hissed a curse. She swung her rifle to the pilot, who was leaning down, his hand extended to help the professor into the bay. More gunfire erupted. She knew the mercs were shooting at Dev.

Brushing the trigger with her finger, she fired a second dart. Yes! The pilot yelped and instantly released Valdemar. The professor cried out and fell backward. The pilot swatted at the side of his neck, where the dart had sunk deeply into his flesh. Almost instantly, he crumpled to the floor of the helo, unconscious.

Good!

The professor scrambled back up into the helo. He jerked the pistol from the unconscious pilot's holster. His eyes were filled with rage and fear as he jerked his gaze around the area. Kulani knew the moment he spotted her. Instantly, he lifted the pistol in her direction. She dodged behind a tree trunk. Bullets whizzed on either side of her. Breathing hard, she waited a second.

Go! Now! She leaped from behind the tree. Lifting the rifle, she saw the professor crouched in the bay, both hands on his pistol, which was aimed at her.

Kulani had no choice. She had to stand still long enough to take her shot. Spreading her legs, she anchored the butt of the rifle deeply into her shoulder and took aim. Kulani saw the pistol buck in the professor's hands.

Now! She brushed the trigger with her finger. Bullets screamed by her ear. Dropping to the ground, Kulani saw the professor cry out. The dart had struck him a glancing blow along his arm. Angrily, he brushed it out of his flesh as easily as flicking off an annoying fly.

Kulani jerked a look to her left. She saw the third merc crash into the underbrush, unconscious. Breathing hard, she shoved herself to her feet. The professor still had the pistol. He was staggering backward, his gun arm waving wildly in the air. His knees began to buckle.

Leaping awkwardly across the ferns and rocks, Kulani reached the helicopter. Out of the corner of her eye, she saw Dev running toward the unmoving mercs. The professor was on his hands and knees, the silver suitcase to his left. He glared at her as she approached the aircraft. Drool was coming out of both sides of his mouth and he weakly tried to lift the pistol as she leaped up onto the lip of the helo.

Kicking out, Kulani caught the professor's gun hand with her boot. The pistol went flying off toward the cockpit.

"You bitch!" the professor snarled, but the words were slurred! He fell forward, his eyes rolling up into his head as he slumped to the deck.

Kulani pushed by him. She laid the rifle aside and grabbed up the suitcase, taking it forward with her into the cockpit. The helo was shuddering and shaking. The blades were whipping up gusts of wind all around the area, making the jungle foliage quake. Kulani spotted Valdemar's pistol in the copilot's seat. *Hurry!* She settled into the pilot's seat without preamble. There was no time to shrug into the safety harness. She rapidly scanned the instrument panel. Looking up, she saw Dev disabling the mercs by taking their rifles and slinging them across his left shoulder. She could see he was in great pain as he raced drunkenly toward the helo.

The instant he was on board, Kulani wrapped her hands around the cyclic and collective. The helo was shaking and shuddering, the blades whirling faster and faster now as she fed the engine more power. Suddenly, she heard shouts behind her. Jerking a look over her shoulder, she saw the professor lunging upward at Dev.

Dev cursed as Valdemar, whom he thought was unconscious, lunged forward. Already off balance from carrying three rifles, Dev wasn't ready for the attack. Suddenly the professor's enraged features loomed threateningly before him, his hands outstretched like claws. He hit Dev squarely in the chest. With a grunt, Dev lost his footing. The professor jerked at one of the rifles slung across Dev's left shoulder. *No!* Pain arced up through Dev's right arm as he tried to snatch the weapon back, but the bullet wound had weakened him considerably. At the same time, Dev lashed out with his right foot to knock the man away from him.

Too late! Dev cried out as the professor avoided his swinging leg and, using his fist, struck Dev's wounded arm. Dev instantly released the rifle. Valdemar tumbled out of the helicopter, weapon in hand, as Dev dropped to his knees, blackness rimming his vision. With blood spurting from his injury once again, he sank down to the deck, gasping for breath and unable to fight off the unconsciousness stalking him. He'd used up every reserve he'd had, nailing the three mercs, and the run for the chopper had left him greatly weakened. He was losing a lot of blood. Now, as he lay there on the cold steel deck, sucking in breaths of air, he knew they were in trouble. Through his graying vision, he saw the professor running toward the cover of the trees. The son of a bitch would shoot them out of the sky!

Rolling over with a groan, Dev released the other rifles and tried to get up. The jolting motion of the helo beginning to rise threw him off balance. He tumbled backward against some nylon webbing in the rear of the craft. Dev understood what Kulani was doing. She was trying to get up and out of there before the professor could shoot at the engine and bring them down. Dev felt so damned helpless as he rolled to his left side. Blood was all over the deck now, making it too slippery for him to get a good footing. He had to clamp his hand over his arm or he'd bleed to death. As badly as Dev wanted to reach for one of those rifles and shoot at the professor out the open door, he couldn't. He had to stop the wound from taking his life. The escape was up to Kulani.

Kulani cried out Dev's name, though she knew he couldn't hear her. With the door still open, the roar in the helo was loud and grating. She made a life-and-death decision. As Valdemar skittered away, rifle in hand, she pulled up on the cyclic, and the helo, which was at full power now, groaned and broke contact with the earth. She had to get them out of here! It was their only chance. If she sat on the ground, they were sitting ducks for the professor. She saw the horrifying amount of blood on the deck from Dev's wound. Understanding what had occurred, Kulani knew it was the only decision she could make to save his life.

Gasping, she strained to check the clearance on either side of the helo. The blades were frighteningly close to the lava wall! Rain was pouring down in unrelenting sheets. Kulani struggled to estimate the distance between the wall and the rotors. This was flying by the seat of her pants; no instruments could get her out of this—only her long experience could.

To add to her dilemma, the wind was viciously gusting. She had to readjust the controls after each punch from the blast made the helo shudder like a boxer hit squarely in the face. She had to instantly correct for it or crash. Everything was moving so slowly as they cautiously rose.

They were barely at tree level when the windshield in front of her exploded. With a cry, Kulani jerked her head to one side. Valdemar was firing into the cockpit, trying to kill her! *Oh, no!* Her heart rate soared. Her hands gripped the collective and cyclic so hard her knuckles whitened. Rain poured through the jagged opening on the left side of the cockpit, drenching her and the controls.

She heard several more bullets strike the helo. He was trying for the engine!

Hurry! Hurry!

The helo rose above the treetops. Instantly, Kulani brought the bird around. They still weren't safe, but now she had a fighting chance. The craft groaned because of the wind, the rain and the tremendous pull of gravity upon it. More bullets pinged beneath her feet. She cringed and tucked up into herself. A bullet could rip through her. The gusting of the wind continued. The bird trembled violently as an arc of lightning shot across the Kalalau Valley just in front of the aircraft's nose.

Blinded momentarily, Kulani held the aircraft steady; then aimed it toward the sea. Rapidly now, it sped across the narrow expanse of the green valley. Ahead, she could see the blue-green waters of the Pacific. Her heart was pounding. She risked a look back. Dev lay unconscious on the floor, his hand wrapped around his bloody wound. The deck was red with his blood.

Her mind spun. Why was there so much blood? It didn't make sense to Kulani. Panic ate at her. How fast would this aircraft go? Jerking a look at the gauges, Kulani kicked the aircraft into high gear, red-lining the powerful engines. The air-speed needle shot upward, and within moments they were cruising at over two hundred miles an hour.

The aircraft moved swiftly out of the rainstorm. Sunlight blinded her momentarily as she aimed the chopper over the middle of the island, heading straight for the green grass beside the Kukui Hospital, just outside Lihue Airport. Fortunately, she knew this island like the back of her hand. Kulani wasted no time on the radio or trying to find headphones. No, this was going to be a rough ride down to the hospital. Dev was bleeding to death.

He could die! No! I love him. He can't die! Please, don't let him die. I lost one man I loved. I can't lose another!

Tears blinded her. Kulani fought them back. Below her, she saw the pale yellow, stucco walls of Kukui Hospital. Moving her feet and hands rapidly, Kulani brought the helicopter in fast and low. She was breaking every FAA flight rule in the book. But a life was at stake and she didn't care. At the last moment, Kulani wrenched back on the controls. The aircraft groaned from the sudden loss of forward speed. She knew that by lifting the helo's nose high, the belly would provide a soft mattress of air to break the swift landing on the soft, green grass.

Kulani saw a number of white-coated people running toward her as she landed. Instantly, she cut the engines and leaped out of the seat. Fear weakened her knees. She staggered to the open door and violently motioned to two of the men who looked like paramedics, to hurry. The rotors were still spinning overhead and the wind buffeted them as they raced toward her.

Turning, Kulani fell to Dev's side. She rolled him over on his back. He was unconscious. The wound on his arm was spurting bright red arterial blood. She placed her hand over the wound and held it as tightly as she could. When the first man arrived at the door, in his face questioning, she shouted above the roar, "He's bleeding to death. I need to get him to ER. Now!"

Chapter Twelve

"How is he, Kulani?"

At first, Morgan Trayhern's deep voice warmed Kulani as she sat in the lounge on the post-op floor of the hospital. Then she snapped her head up in surprise.

"Morgan!" Kulani rose unsteadily to her feet. She was still wearing her black nylon uniform, the front of her flak jacket open. She smelled of fear. The metallic odor of blood—Dev's blood—curled around her nostrils as she tried to catch her balance.

Instantly, Morgan gripped her upper arm. "You okay?"

His touch was warm and firm. It reminded her a bit of Dev's masculine grasp. "Uh, no...not really." Kulani wasn't going to try and hide anything from this man, her eyes drinking in the welcome sight of him. Morgan was dressed in a dark pinstripe suit, his paisley tie stark against the whiteness of his starched shirt. He always looked official, Kulani thought. Gazing up into his face which showed weariness and strain, she said, "Dev's in surgery."

"I know," Morgan said gruffly. "Come on, sit back down."

"Don't say it," Kulani joked weakly as she sat down on the plastic sofa with Morgan, "I know I look like hell." She wrinkled her nose. "And I smell like it, too." Earlier, she'd gone to the rest room and washed the camouflage greasepaint off her face and chin to clean up a little.

"I'm not going to complain," he said as he unbuttoned the front of his business suit and slowly sat down close to her. "Dev's been in surgery two hours now?"

She gave him a wary look. "Yes. You must have been monitoring us—and our problems?" That would explain how he'd gotten over here so quickly from the mainland.

He nodded and leaned back, his arm going back across the rear of the couch where she sat. "I was in California at the time we lost contact with you. Cappy called me and told me you were suddenly out of touch on both the cell phone and walkie-talkie. He heard gunfire. So he suspected the worst and made a call to me. I had the jet, so we just flew on over."

"I'm glad you're here."

Morgan studied her exhausted features. He saw the anguish in Kulani's darkened eyes. There were shadows beneath them, too. "I brought our emergency physician, Dr. Jennifer Logan. Just in case... At the time we lifted off, we still had no contact with you."

"And you thought the worst?"

He sighed. "It was impossible not to. The last transmission we got from you, all we heard was the sound of rifles. And then we got the call from Cappy and he confirmed it.'' He frowned and held her gaze. ''Tell me what happened?''

Kulani dutifully gave Morgan a report. All the while, she kept her eyes on the bank of elevators. Dev was being operated on in the basement of the hospital, where all surgeries took place. The doctor who was working on him, Gail Derin, had assured her that as soon as she wrapped up her duties, she'd come up and let Kulani know how Dev was.

''Dev suffered *two* wounds, not one?'' Morgan demanded.

She watched his peppered brows draw downward. ''Yeah,'' she said, her voice strained as she rested her elbows on her thighs. Numbing exhaustion stalked her. She desperately needed sleep. Her mind was rummy and wandering, focused only on Dev. ''He'd gotten wounded in the forearm when the mercs hit us the first time. The professor deliberately struck him there when they were fighting in the back of the helo, and it started bleeding heavily. When the professor leaped out of the chopper, he ran for the trees. I was busy up front trying not to run the rotor blades into the jungle or the lava wall as we slowly ascended. When Valdemar started firing at me, it shattered the windshield on the left side of the aircraft. Then the professor started shooting at the helo's engines. I guess that's when Dev was hit again.'' She rubbed her faced tiredly. As she dropped her hands, Kulani muttered, ''When I turned him over after we landed, I saw the second wound in his thigh.''

''What kind of wound?''

''A bad one, Morgan. Dev's femur was sticking out of his thigh.'' Shivering, Kulani whispered, ''He was bleeding like a stuck hog. I—I lost it then. I realized how seriously wounded he was. I didn't want to lose him.'' She turned her head away from Morgan's eagle-like gaze. Her heart wrenched in her breast as she spoke the words she didn't want to give life to.

"A fractured femur can have a lot of complications," Morgan rasped. "I wonder if it tore his femoral artery?"

"I think so," Kulani said as she slowly turned her attention back to Morgan. His mouth was pulled down at the corners. She knew he was upset about the turn of events. "I couldn't understand why there was so much blood on the deck." She lifted her hand, which still had remnants of dried blood on it. "He lost so much blood! If it weren't for the two paramedics who met me at the helo, I don't think he'd be alive now. They did a lot of fast thinking and applied pressure to stop most of the bleeding. All I could do was sit there on the steel deck and cry like a baby. I felt so helpless...."

Gently, Morgan put his arm around her drooping shoulders. "Hey," he whispered, his voice off-key, "you are one of the most courageous people I've ever known. You took an assignment that I shoved on you. You performed flawlessly, Kulani." He tightened his grip around her shoulders and drew her against him. Kulani turned and fell into his awaiting arms, her head pressed against his chest. Morgan felt her struggle not to cry. "It's all right," he said roughly, his other arm going around her. "I should never have made you do this. I was wrong, Kulani. And I'm so damned sorry I did this to you...."

The first sob ripped out of her. It shook her entire body. All she could do was curl up tightly on the couch, in a fetal position, and allow Morgan to hold her with his massive strength and care. Her fingers dug convulsively into Morgan's expensive white shirt. Tears splattered down across the material as she wrestled with her fear and grief.

"Go ahead and cry," he whispered against her hair. "Cry for what I've done to you, and cry because you went through hell...." The fact that Dev had had to spring the news on her that Stephen had been murdered weighed heavily on his conscience, as well. He wanted to make amends as best he could, to take that shocking pain away from her, if possible.

Kulani couldn't stop the flow of hot tears from her eyes. Morgan's gruff care simply aided and abetted her need to let loose with all her fears. "I—I'm not crying for myself," she sobbed, "I'm crying because I love Dev and I'm afraid I'm going to lose him...." More sobs wracked her as she pressed her face against Morgan's solid chest.

Morgan shut his eyes and groaned. As he held Kulani and rocked her like a frightened child in his arms, he understood so much more. What kind of hell had he forced Kulani into? She hadn't been over her grieving and loss of Stephen. Now, somehow, by some miracle, she had fallen in love with Dev. And then she was plunged into a life-and-death mission with him. How had she been able to fly the helicopter out of there with him on board? Morgan had seen the insides of the black helo, which was still parked near the hospital. He'd seen the blood smeared all over the deck. Dev Hunter's blood. Kulani had had to deal with all of that, including her love for the man, and still fly that aircraft. A quiver ran through him as he gently ran his hand across Kulani's shaking shoulders. Her sobs were soft and hurting. He felt like a first-class bastard. He'd made a terrible error in forcing Kulani into this mission. What was wrong with him? He was supposed to look out for his people, not do this to them. Why had he thought this mission would be good for her? Why did he think he could force her out of the quiet, half-mast life she'd been living since Stephen's death? What right did he have to be judge and jury on how Kulani lived?

Morgan sat there a long time as Kulani released her feelings of terror, loss and grief. As she allowed her pain to move through her, he absorbed it and felt the white-hot heat of guilt twisting through him. Kulani was like a daughter to him. Because he loved her, he'd taken advantage of her, of the situation, he realized, and made judgments about her that he shouldn't have.

"I guess," he told her gruffly, "I used our love of you to force you into something that shouldn't have been. I'm sorry, Kulani. Damn, I'm sorry to my soul. I should have told you about Stephen a long time ago, top secret info or not. I made a mistake with you. I'd do anything in the world to make it up to you—and Dev. Just tell me how I can help you."

Lifting her head, Kulani eased out of his arms. With trembling fingers, she tried to wipe her face free of tears. Morgan handed her a white linen handkerchief. She thanked him, her voice raw and trembling. After mopping her face, she looked at the cloth in her hands. It was smeared with Dev's blood, the mud from the jungle and her tears. She closed her fist over it, not wanting any more reminders. She felt Morgan's steadying hand on her shoulder as she tried to take in a deep breath. Opening her eyes, her lashes still wet with tears, Kulani tried to smile at his grave countenance and failed.

"Oh, Morgan," she whispered tremulously, "I don't

blame you for what happened. It's okay. I forgive you. No one is perfect. I make a hundred mistakes a day. How can I be angry with you? We're all flawed humans just stumbling around, making errors. What sets us apart is that we try to learn from our mistakes. If you learn from this one regarding Stephen, then I consider it over and done. If—if you hadn't pushed me into this, I wouldn't have met Dev." She swallowed hard and twisted the handkerchief between her fingers. "The guy is wonderful…. I just sort of fell in love with him. I never thought I'd love again after Stephen…never…."

Morgan sat there, his heart aching with guilt. Kulani's features were pale and strained. The usual softness was gone from her mouth, the corners pulled in with anguish. "It still doesn't relieve me of my choices in this mission, Kulani." He held her tearful stare. "I was wrong to manipulate you into taking the mission. Tell me what I can do to make it up to you?"

She reached out and slid her fingers into his large, scarred hand. "Nothing. You've done it already. You're here. You held me when I needed a good cry on a strong shoulder. That's enough."

Just then, the elevator doors opened and a blond-haired woman in dark blue surgeon's scrubs appeared. When she saw Kulani, she moved over to her immediately.

Kulani's breath hitched. She tensed and stood up. "Dr. Derin?" The words were laced with fear. Anxiously, Kulani searched the older woman's face. "Dev? How is he?"

Morgan stood and put his hand on Kulani's shoulder. The doctor didn't look happy.

Dr. Derin smiled briefly and reached out and gripped Kulani's hand. "He's one tough hombre, Ms. Dawson.'' She looked at Morgan. ''Are you part of Dev Hunter's family?''

Morgan grinned a little. ''You might say that, Doctor.'' He introduced himself.

''How is Dev?'' Kulani demanded breathlessly.

Dr. Derin's smile widened. ''Thanks to Dr. Logan's help in surgery, he's going to make it. As I said, he's tough. He lost two pints of blood and that's a lot. We managed to stabilize him with whole-blood transfusions during the surgery. The bullet wound in his arm was a piece of cake. He's got muscle damage, but with time, that will heal. It's his thigh that was the real problem. The femur was shattered by the bullet. It tore the artery in two. That's why he lost as much blood as he did.'' Dr. Derin gave Kulani a significant look. ''If you hadn't done what you did, landing that helicopter here, he wouldn't be alive today.''

A shiver crawled up Kulani's back. She felt Morgan's hand tighten around her shoulders as she stood in the comfort of his embrace.

''So what does it mean?'' she demanded.

Dr. Derin looked at Morgan. ''If you're expecting Mr. Hunter back to work soon, it won't happen. I had to place metal pins into the bone to reset his femur. He's got a long recuperation ahead of him, and he's going to need a lot of physiotherapy to get back on his feet. We're looking at a year off here, Mr. Trayhern.''

''He's got it,'' Morgan replied. And he glanced down at Kulani. ''Dev will need a place to stay. You want me to rent him a condominium here on Kauai?''

Kulani saw humor lurking in Morgan's eyes. She understood all too clearly what he was hinting. ''No...no, Dev can stay at my bungalow. I've got a second bedroom. We can manage there, I think.''

Morgan's mouth pulled into a smile. "I think you can. With your help and love, my bet is he'll be back on his feet in half the time."

Dr. Derin made a sound of protest. "He might cut off a couple of months of rehab, Mr. Trayhern, but he's going to need help for a long while."

"I'll be there for him, Doctor," Kulani whispered, joy avalanching through her. Dev was going to live! He was going to be staying here, on Kauai, to mend—with her. She felt trepidation. "Well...I mean, if Dev *wants* to stay with me." She glanced at Morgan. "I'll ask him."

"By all means, do." Morgan looked toward the opening elevator doors. "And Shep, his oldest brother, has just arrived. Have you met him yet, Kulani?"

Kulani's gaze went to the bank of elevators. There, standing tensely, was a very tall, powerfully built man in a pair of jeans, a short-sleeved, cranberry-colored shirt and roughout boots. There was nothing soft about this man. Kulani knew of Shep Hunter; his legend had more than preceded him. He had the craggy face of the Rocky Mountains he'd been born in, his body strong and seemingly impervious to anything life might throw at him. She remembered Dev speaking glowingly of Shep, almost as if in awe. Among the Perseus employees, he was known as a rebel with a cause. He was a linchpin mercenary, one who took top event assignments no one in his right mind would even think of taking, because the danger of dying far exceeded the chances of surviving.

Yet, as she gazed at his grim-looking expression, at those narrowed, icy blue eyes, Kulani saw the family resemblance between him and Dev. And Dev was right when he called himself the good-looking one of the bunch.

Her lips parted and the corners of her mouth lifted, "Shep? I'm glad you're here." Kulani moved forward, her hand extended toward him. The tall mercenary stood with his arms across his chest, studying her from beneath those black, thick brows of his. There was no hint of humanity in his face. None at all. Yet, through her exhaustion, Kulani felt Shep's worry for his younger brother—the man she loved.

Shep uncrossed his arms and gripped her hand. "From what I understand, I have you to thank for Dev's life."

His voice was deep and reminded Kulani of the thunder rolling across the valleys of the Na Pali Coast. It was obvious he had to monitor the strength of his fingers upon hers. There was such lethal, tightly wound power in this man. Kulani met and held his frosty gaze. "We got lucky, Shep."

Dr. Derin moved toward them. "Ms. Dawson? Dev's in recovery right now. If all goes well, we'll have him up here on the post-op floor, room 6, in about an hour. I want only one visitor to see him at that time. And I have a feeling it should be you, Kulani." She looked at Morgan and Shep. "You two gentlemen will have to wait a bit."

Gripping the doctor's long, thin hand, Kulani whispered, "Thank you—for everything. I—I didn't think he'd survive."

Laughing a little, Dr. Derin said, "Frankly, we didn't either. But he's a tough buzzard. Where I come from—Arizona—we rarely see a person like Mr. Hunter. He's got a strong will to live and that's what really pulled him through."

Feeling grateful, Kulani released the doctor's hand. Shep moved closer, offered his hand to the surgeon and thanked her, and so did Morgan. After the doctor left, Morgan patted Kulani on the shoulder. "Tell Dev we'll visit him later today? Shep and I have some business to attend to."

"What? The professor? Did the FBI pick him up with the three mercs Dev took down?"

Morgan glanced at Shep, who stood quietly at his side. "The FBI helicoptered in and found the three mercs still unconscious. Right now, they've got a search party looking for Valdemar." He gave her a proud look. "You retrieved the anthrax. That's what *really* counts here. You've saved a lot of lives, the two of you."

"But what about the professor? What if he gets away?"

"He won't," Shep growled.

Morgan nodded. "I'm sending Shep in to track him down."

Just the icy glimmer in Shep's eyes told Kulani about the man's abilities. His last name was Hunter, and she was sure he lived up to it. She had the distinct feeling that Shep was an extraordinary individual with certain skills that few people would ever possess. "Good luck on finding him. He still has a rifle, and I don't know how much ammo he took with him," she warned.

A bare hint of a smile crossed Shep Hunter's thinned mouth. "Doesn't matter, Kulani. He's mine. He just doesn't know it yet."

Kulani saw the look in Morgan's eyes. It was obvious that he highly respected Shep's talents. "Good. Be careful. He's deceptive. You wouldn't think a man of that size would fight so hard, but he did. He's fanatical."

"Listen," Morgan told her, guiding her to the couch,

"just sit here and rest until they bring Dev up. I'm sure he'll be glad to see you when he finds you in his private room, waiting for him."

Kulani nodded. There was nothing more that she wanted right now than to be with Dev. "I'll see you two later."

Shep rubbed his square jaw briefly. "Tell my little brother I've gone hunting. After I find that low-life bastard, I'll come and see him."

Dev hovered between semiconsciousness and waking. As they wheeled him on the gurney into his private room, he saw Kulani standing impatiently near the head of the bed, her arms crossed against her breasts tensely. She was still wearing her black, dirty uniform, her hair in disarray, the thick braids hanging across her shoulders. Never had she looked more beautiful to him. Pain drifted in and out of his body, taking all of his attention for a moment. But he saw her straighten and her arms fall to her sides when the nurses wheeled the gurney closer, and he felt his chest explode with joy. Kulani was safe. She wasn't hurt.

Dev remembered pain erupting through him when he took the second bullet. His last thought had been that they were going to die. And he couldn't stand the thought of Kulani dying.

"Hi, stranger." She greeted him softly when the gurney was parallel to the bed.

He gave her a sloppy, one-sided smile. "They said there was a beautiful Hawaiian goddess waiting for me in my room. I'm a lucky man...."

Tears filled her throat, and Kulani swallowed them. That was her Dev—the charming, teasing man whose smile, even now, made her feel euphoric. She watched as the nurses gently transferred him to the bed and set up the IV drip next to it.

Waiting until they left, Kulani moved to the side of his bed. Dev looked ashen and there was dampness across his furrowed brow as he looked up at her. There was darkness in his green eyes, and Kulani reached out and slid her hand into his.

"You deserve this," she whispered, leaning over the bed and finding his mouth. His lips were cool against her warm ones, but as she clung to his, she felt his returning strength and promise of life. Now she was unable to stop her tears and they ran down her cheeks to their clinging mouths.

Dev was weak. He wanted to claim her soft, gentle kiss and deepen it, but he just didn't have the strength. He tasted the saltiness of her tears. As Kulani lifted her head inches from his and met his eyes, he saw the joy burning in her gaze. "You know what?" he croaked.

"No. What?" Just getting to hold his hand and hear his roughened voice was enough for Kulani.

"I'm the luckiest bastard on the face of this earth. I have you...." He choked back tears as he saw more fall from her large, expressive eyes. She looked incredibly exhausted by the demands of the mission. "Hey...why don't you go home? Get a hot shower, eat some chow and then hit the rack. You look tired...."

Kulani understood the effort it took for Dev to talk. His eyes were cloudy looking from the aftereffects of the anesthesia, and she was sure the pain meds were making him groggy, too. Squeezing his hand, she told him about Morgan and Shep. Dev closed his eyes and sighed raggedly.

"Good...Shep's a lethal hunter. He'll find that son

of a bitch one way or another. No one can track like my big brother can. Morgan was smart to fly him over.''

His last words slurred badly. Leaning back over Dev, Kulani pressed a kiss to his damp brow. ''I'm going home to clean up, but then I'm coming back. You just get your rest, okay?'' How badly she wanted to tell him of her love for him. Did Dev love her? She wasn't at all sure. Still, the driving need to share her feelings with him was almost her undoing. Right now, Dev needed to sleep in order to heal and get rid of the anesthesia.

''Okay...'' he whispered, and dropped off into a deep, healing sleep.

The next time Dev awoke, Kulani was standing beside his bed watching him through her thick, black lashes. It took him a precious moment to realize where he was, what had happened and why. She was dressed, to his delight, in a rayon sarong that was tied behind her neck. Bright red, yellow and pink hibiscus lay on a wine-colored background and lovingly outlined every delicious and feminine curve of her body. He grinned weakly. ''You're not wearing a damn thing under that, are you?''

Laughing softly, Kulani reached out and threaded her fingers through his short, dark hair. ''No. I find it interesting that after coming out of major surgery, your mind, even now, is on things like this. You're incorrigible, Hunter. You really are.''

Dev gave her a tender look. ''But you like me—just a little bit, maybe?'' Closing his eyes, he absorbed the feel of her slender fingers moving gently across his scalp and down his neck. Even now, the tense, tight muscles were loosening beneath her magical touch.

Kulani smiled. ''Just a smidgen, Hunter. I don't want

to feed that big ego of yours any more than I have to.''
And then, as she held his drowsy-looking eyes tenderly,
she said, ''I need you, though. A hundred percent.''

Kulani had headed home, taken a hot shower and
gone straight to bed. Awakening six hours later, she had
grabbed something to eat and hurried back to the hospital. The night sky was bright with twinkling stars, and
on the way over to see Dev, her heart had flown with
joy in her love for him.

''Mmm, I've died and gone to heaven,'' Dev murmured as she continued to lightly massage his head and
neck. ''That feels so good....'' More than anything, her
soft admission that she still needed him, even though
the mission was over, flowed through him like golden
sunlight. He hoped she would need him forever, because he needed her for that long, too.

Heartened, Kulani moved her fingers across his
gowned shoulders, kneading the heavy muscles there.
''I give great foot massages, too, if you're interested.
My mother taught me that by massaging a person's feet,
you stimulate the rest of the body in a very positive
way. Interested?''

Dev barely opened his eyes. ''You can touch me anywhere, anytime. I'm yours.'' And he was. He saw the
laughter come to her sparkling midnight eyes and he
feasted on the sight of her. Kulani had washed her hair,
and it hung straight and full across her shoulders, down
across her small, firm breasts.

''You're easy to please,'' she whispered as she
moved to the end of his bed. His right leg was suspended in a sling. She chose his left one. Taking a bottle
of lotion from the nearby bathroom, she gently pulled
the sheets and blankets away to expose his foot. He
must wear at least a size ten or eleven shoe, she thought

as she squeezed some lotion on her hands and then rubbed it gently across his foot, being very careful not to jar him.

Dev groaned in enjoyment as her slender fingers moved in a slow, sliding motion across the sole of his foot. "Can I get this done every day?"

"Yes, you can," Kulani said. "As a matter of fact, Morgan was going to put you up in a condo here on Kauai for your recuperation, which is going to take almost a year."

Dev opened his eyes. "What?"

"I told him no," Kulani said as she slid her warm fingers across his toes. "I told Morgan that you could come to my place and recover." She held his foot between her hands and looked up at him gravely. "Unless, of course, you don't want to stay at my place?"

His brows shot up. "Your place?"

"Yes. Are you game?"

His mouth pulling into a grin, Dev held her tender expression. "Are you? Do you really need a cripple in your life?"

She gazed at him in the gathering silence, moving her hands down the length of his foot. "You were crippled," she began gently, "thinking that no one needed you. Well, you found out that wasn't true. And as for your leg making you crippled physically? I can handle that with no problem." She smiled. "I make a mean pot of chicken soup, Hunter. And I've got some herbs in my mother's garden that are good for healing broken bones. I can make you a tea from them every day."

His chest grew warm and he felt his heart beating hard in his chest. "You're serious about this, aren't you?"

"Of course I am." Kulani traded a look of humor

with him. "I have a spare bedroom in the bungalow. You'll need a special bed for that broken leg of yours. Morgan will see that you get what you need. All he needs to know is where you're staying to recuperate."

Just the look in her eyes told Dev so much more than ever before. He was weak, but his mind whirled with questions. "Home?" Dev hadn't meant the word to slip out, but it had. He gripped the sheets with his hands momentarily in angst over the faux pas. He couldn't help but see Kulani as his home. His wife. The mother of his children. And Kauai as their home. Love had smitten him. He couldn't look at her any other way because he did love her, and he wanted a home with her...and babies, lots of them....

Hesitating fractionally, Kulani heard the hope, the promise in Dev's voice when he said "home." Carefully replacing the sock on his foot, she looked up and held his anguished gaze. "Yes," she whispered softly, "home, Dev. You're coming home with me...."

Chapter Thirteen

"This is incredibly beautiful," Dev told Kulani as she approached him at a trot after her swim in the ocean. "But not as beautiful as you." He relaxed on the dark red cotton blanket beneath the palms, shaded from the noonday sun on Secret Beach. His mending leg was stretched out in front of him and he was wearing nothing but a set of cutoffs, his chest bared to the sunlight and shadows. He held up a paper cup filled with guava juice in a toast to her.

Glancing at the dark red incision, finally healed, on his thigh, Dev shoved his toes into the warm golden sand. It felt exhilarating to be out of the house and the rehabilitation center. He was getting a little stir-crazy, as he'd told Kulani earlier. She'd suggested going to the beach for lunch and he'd leaped at the idea. The teak cane sat off to one side, a reminder that he still needed physiotherapy on his broken leg and that he

couldn't walk without assistance yet. Still, it was a helluva lot better than that set of crutches he'd had to endure for the first two months of his recovery efforts.

Kulani laughed delightedly at his charming compliment. She stopped just short of the blanket where he
lay propped up on one elbow, and shook the last of the
salty water off her arms before she sat down cross-
legged next to him. "After twelve weeks of rehab, I
figured you'd want a change of pace." Secret Beach
was a hideaway that the locals kept to themselves. The
crescent-shaped bay lay on the north shore of Kauai,
hidden by a range of grass-and-brush-covered hills.
Only a steep climb down a very hard-to-find path
yielded access to the beach. Although Dev did not know
it, Secret Beach was a place for lovers. Through the
decades, it had garnered that reputation because it was
so exceedingly hard to find, nestled lovingly as it was
between white coral rocks on either side. The coral,
long dead, reminded Kulani of huge, misshapen pearls,
their whiteness a stark contrast to the deep blue of the
ocean and the shimmering gold of the sand. The effect
was one of incredible beauty that she never failed to
appreciate.

Snorting, Dev looked up. "I was getting ready to
scream. Anything to get out and get active again." His
fractured thigh was healing surprisingly well, but until
just last week, he hadn't been very mobile at all. As a
matter of fact, Dev ached to get his hands on Kulani,
to love her and make their relationship complete. Since
his wounding, she had divided her time between her job
flying tourists and taking care of him at the bungalow.
She'd cut her flight days in half to make sure he got a
ride to the hospital every other day for long, painful
rehabilitation sessions. His wounded, broken leg was

not as muscular looking as his other one. Healing had come slowly, and Dev looked forward to the day when he could work out hard in a gym.

Sunlight danced beguilingly between the leaves of the overhead palms. The peekaboo shadows moved across them, teased by the breeze. Looking over at Kulani as she sat down, Dev found his body going hot with intense longing for her. Ever since she'd brought him to her bungalow for recovery, they had not made love. Oh, he'd steal a molten kiss from her more and more often, especially of late, but Dev knew in his heart they had needed the last three months to really get acquainted with one another. Never had he laughed so much, felt so happy, as during these last twelve weeks.

He watched through half-closed eyes as Kulani munched enjoyably on a golden-skinned papaya he'd cut up and placed on a paper plate for her for after her swim. Her hair was slick and shining from her recent dip in the cobalt sea. The doctors had told him to wait awhile before swimming in the ocean, as the fractured femur couldn't stand the lashing and pounding of the waves. In another month, he could go swimming in that sparkling blue-and-green water that crashed in foamy froth and champagnelike bubbles along the curve of the sun-gold beach.

"You look delicious," he growled. And she did. She wore a bright red bikini. Her curving breasts, small and firm, were exposed to a large degree, and he enjoyed absorbing her natural beauty into his heart. Tendrils of drying dark hair fluttered around her face, at the whim of the breeze. Kulani looked up and smiled at him, her lips glistening with papaya juice.

"You look kinda tasty yourself," she said and laughed, her heart expanding with a wild kind of joy.

Dev looked absolutely scrumptious in his cutoff jeans. "I always like looking at you, Hunter. You're my dessert."

His grin widened considerably. "You're bold today, Ms. Dawson." More than ever, over the last weeks, Dev realized he no longer needed his pride. Kulani made it easy for him to work on getting rid of it. He liked her in his heart. He liked the fact she needed him in small and large ways, every day, all the time. But he found he needed her in the same ways, too.

Setting the papaya skin aside, Kulani wiped her lips with a dark pink paper napkin. She saw the implike quality dancing in his forest-green eyes as she moved to her knees and eased over to where he lay. Leaning down, she captured his very male, smiling mouth with her own. For a moment, she felt him tense in surprise. Kulani had been careful not to tease Dev during the months he'd been living with her. They'd never made love. They'd never talked about it. Instead, she had a sense that their time together was about discovery of one another, and indeed, it had been.

As she moved her lips along his, she tasted the sweetness of the chocolate bar he'd just consumed. His arm slid around her waist and she eased herself down the length of his tall, powerful body. Breaking the heated kiss, Kulani gazed into his slitted eyes, which held a hot, predatory look in them for her alone. Easing her fingers up his arm and across his shoulder, she whispered, "It's time, Dev. I want you. All of you. I think we've waited long enough?"

His mouth drew into a grin. "I like your brazenness, Kulani Dawson." He threaded his fingers through her very damp hair. "And yes, it's been a long, hellish time waiting for you." She closed her eyes as he gently massaged her scalp with his fingers. "I've missed you in my bed, at my side at night. That's where you belong, you know."

Kulani opened her eyes and drowned in his. Because of his broken leg, there was no way she could sleep at his side, or even make love to him without aggravating the healing bones. They both knew that if his leg didn't heal properly, he'd have ongoing problems with it for the rest of his life, and they had grudgingly accepted the reality of the situation. Kulani sensed that if Dev hadn't broken his leg, they would have loved one another a lot sooner. Still, there was something torturously delicious about waiting, too. Now it was safe to love him. His leg had healed well. As she skimmed the hard line of his jaw, she said softly, "You don't know how many nights I've lain awake, alone in my bed, and wished you were there beside me...."

Untangling some damp, dark strands of hair from behind her delicate ear, he nodded and became serious. "I know, sweetheart, I know...."

She framed his face with her hands and held his burning gaze. The soft trade winds caressed them like the lovers they were going to become shortly. The beach was utterly deserted, and to Kulani, this was a very special place, the place where she wanted to give herself in a sacred way to Dev. Sunlight danced across his form and she was once again reminded how much a part of nature they really were. Animals with a veneer of civilization, really. She thrilled to Dev's touch as he ran his finger in a provocative motion down her cheekbone to her parting lips.

"I've never waited this long to love a woman before," Dev admitted wryly. He saw the returning laughter in her midnight eyes. "And in a perverse kind of way, it was better to wait. It's given us a chance to know one another better, without the pressure of a mission hanging over our heads.''

Somberly, Kulani nodded. She caught his hand and pressed his fingers to her lips. ''I've had a lot of time to think and feel through a lot of issues, Dev. In the past three months, I've been able to let Stephen go…really let him go….'' Quietly, she added, ''I won't ever forget him or what we shared. He's a permanent part of my heart's memories.'' Kulani gazed at him tenderly. ''But so are you….''

''When you love someone, Kulani, it's a process….'' Dev grimaced and recalled the years it took for him to leave his shattered marriage behind him. ''Living with you has helped me let go of my past, too. I lived with a lot of guilt about Susan. About not being there for her when she needed me the most. About…losing our baby daughter….''

Hearing the pain in his voice, Kulani said gently, ''What would you say if I told you I wanted to make love with you, here and now, without any protection? What if I told you I wanted to love you and have your baby?'' Her heart beat a little harder over the admission. ''What if I told you I love you, Devlin Hunter, and I can't conceive of ever not having you in my life, my heart? That I need you every breathing moment?''

Her words flowed moltenly across his expanding heart. Dev understood her courage to speak those truths now. They'd both circumspectly avoided such talk for months, although it was never far from his thoughts or heart at any given hour of the day. He skimmed his hand across her hip and followed the graceful line of her torso. ''My love for you is forever, Kulani,'' he rasped. He saw her eyes instantly grow soft and glimmer with tears. "I've been waiting to say this to you, but you beat me to it." He grinned recklessly. "You're such a brave, brave woman, darling. When the chips were down on that mission, you pulled it off. You saved my worthless hide, to boot. And you've led the way to make it easy for me to shed my past, so I can have a present—and a future—with you." He caressed Kulani's flaming cheek with his roughened hand. "I want everything in that dream of yours. I've lain awake nights, dreaming of loving you…being with you when you had our baby and helping you when it was time to birth it." He looked away self-consciously for a moment and then gazed deeply into her tear-filled eyes. "Loving you here, today, is a commitment, Kulani. It's forever, if that's what you want it to be. And yes, I need and want you for my wife, I want you as the mother of our children, and I want you to be my partner to grow old with here on this magical island of yours. How about it?"

His words were galvanizing. Kulani answered in a choked voice, "Yes, Dev. Yes to all of it, to you…."

Gently moving his hand across her abdomen, he whispered, "And if you happen to get pregnant today, well, I won't be surprised, and frankly, I like the idea. We're old enough to know what we want and don't want. I think we'd make good parents, don't you?"

Wordlessly, she nodded, his hand feeling like a brand against her abdomen. Moving her fingers to the waistband of his cutoffs, she slowly eased the button from the hole. "You're my mate for life," she whispered. "I want you, Dev. In all ways. Love me?" Then she slid her fingers beneath the waistband.

Dev clenched his teeth, unprepared for her molten assault upon him. The cutoffs were removed and he felt

her hand gliding provocatively across his upper thighs,
the fire exploding up through his body. Groaning, he
guided Kulani beside him. She settled next to him and
smiled, a reckless and playful look in her eyes as he
moved first one thin crimson strap of her bikini top and
then the other across her shoulders. It was so easy to
disrobe Kulani. In moments, she lay naked, her golden
body a sensual contrast to the dark red blanket she lay
upon. Her damp hair spread in a dark halo about her
head emphasizing the beauty of her large eyes, which
clung to his. When she parted her lips and raised her
arms toward him, Hunter smiled the smile of a man
taking his woman.

Kulani waited, her breath hitching when she saw the
glitter in his eyes as he leaned down...down to take
her. As her fingers slid across his massive shoulders in
welcome, she felt his lips capture the hardening peak of
her nipple. Sweet, rippling heat caught her and she
moaned, pressing her naked body against his. As he
began to suckle her gently, insistently, his callused
hands moved around her breasts and cupped them in
adoration. At the same time, he ground his hips insistently against hers. There was no doubt he was ready
to take her, and she arched against him, moaning again,
as he lavished her other breast with the same attention.

Her breath coming in gasps, Kulani felt his hand
range down from her breast to her hip and move tan-
talizingly between her thighs. A startled cry of pleasure
erupted from her as his fingers glided silkenly across
her. She felt him growl. It was a sound of primal satisfaction, a growl of the male taking the female and
knowing she was ready to receive him. The sunlight
warmed her flesh; the breeze danced between them. The
ocean pounded along the golden beach, its mighty roar

registered by her flaring senses. As Dev laid her fully on her back and eased his long, hard body over hers, Kulani smiled softly. Nature was a part of them. They were nature.

Opening her thighs to receive him was the most natural thing in the world for her in those shining moments out of time, on this sacred beach where lovers sealed their trust with one another. She opened her eyes and clung to his glittering, dark green gaze. He placed his hands on either side of her head and slowly lowered himself upon her. The instant his steel-like thighs met her soft, firm ones, she moaned and her lashes drifted shut in anticipation. Moving her arms around his thickly corded neck, she felt the dampness upon his flesh, felt his hips grinding hotly against hers. An ache centered in her and she opened her thighs and curled her lower legs around his. It was so easy to raise her hips in invitation to him. So easy, so natural, and she waited anxiously for him to enter her.

The moment he plunged into her slick depths, Kulani cried out in pleasure and arched deeply against his thrusting hips. Her arms tightened convulsively around his shoulders. Breath rushed out of her as he took her hard, took her deeply. He tangled strands of her dark hair in his fists and thrust deeply into her again, taking her, making her his. The crashing ocean waves, the shrill, mournful cry of gulls overhead, the warmth of the sun bathing them and the breeze cooling their heated flesh all melded into one delicious sensation for her. As he rocked forward, she moaned with raw, unfettered pleasure. Her legs tightened around his. She rocked with him, rocked to the tidelike rhythm that bound them, heightened their pleasure and created a lavalike heat building between them.

Leaning down, Dev took her parted lips with a wild urgency. He could taste the sweet papaya on Kulani's mouth, and as he moved his tongue boldly into her warm depths, he smiled to himself. She was sensuous beneath him, her body moving in an ancient rhythm as old as time itself. She was soft and giving, he, hard and demanding. She absorbed each of his deepening thrusts, taking the blunt force of his aggressive urge to mate with her. There was such beauty in drowning in the sweet, hot depths of her mouth, of tasting her smiling lips beneath his. She was bold, giving and taking. As he rocked in unison with her, as their breaths mingled and became one, he felt a massive explosion of fire erupt through his lower body.

In that moment, his breath jammed deep in his lungs. He tore his mouth from hers. His lips drew away from his clenched teeth as he felt the primal power shatter like splintering light through him to her. In that instant, he felt Kulani's legs hold him tightly captive, felt her arch fully against him like a deeply drawn bow. The rush of air from her lungs, her cry of joy, her fingers digging convulsively against his damp shoulders, all combined to make him feel strong and infinitely powerful in that instant. Dev gloried in Kulani's response as he arched fully into her in that molten moment. Somehow, deep in his heart, he knew that a baby would be born out of this incredibly beautiful union on this beach, where the waves lapped against the golden, sandy shore.

Seconds spun beneath hot sun as Kulani felt a volcanic response to his gift to her. Powerful tidal waves of intense pleasure exploded within her, and she gave the gift of herself to Dev. The lightninglike ripples that continued—pleasurable contractions of heat—made her moan and cry out. She felt Dev's arms go around her and he held her as tightly as he could, their bodies melting into one another in that moment of beauty.

Tears streamed from the corners of her eyes as Kulani realized the depth of her love for him. Dev held her length against him, his hand moving in gentle ministrations down her naked back and hips, and she had never felt so loved, so cherished or protected, as now. Clinging to him, she buried her face against the dampened curve of his neck. She could feel his heart thundering in his chest, against her breasts. Their heartbeats galloped wildly together and their breath was coming in gasps.

Her lips parted and she smiled weakly as she caressed his neck and moved her fingers through his short, dark hair. "I love you, Dev Hunter." Her voice trembled with emotion.

Dev eased them apart just enough so that he could look down at her upturned features. Kulani's face glowed with joy, with satiation. Taking his hand, he wiped the tears from her cheeks. "And I love you, my beautiful Hawaiian princess." Her eyes dropped shut as he grazed her full, parted lips with his thumb. Never had anything felt so right. Dev remained within her, their bodies molded into oneness. Only dimly was he aware of the emerald-and-sapphire ocean less than a hundred feet away from them, or the lonely cry of gulls skimming the azure sky above. The warmth of the trade winds cooled his heated flesh as he continued to lovingly stroke Kulani's smooth, golden cheek. He understood the tears she'd shed were tears of joy this time, not of sorrow. Tears celebrating their union. Their love for one another.

Whether he wanted to or not, Dev knew it was time

to ease out of her loving body. She gave a whimper of desertion, and he smiled a little as he sat up and brought her back into the circle of his embrace. Kulani snuggled against him, her arms moving around his torso. Kissing her drying hair, he whispered against her ear, "Something tells me you're very pregnant. Don't you think we should make the baby legal?"

Kulani gazed up at him. There was such tenderness burning in his eyes that she felt her heart open even more widely, if that was possible. Sliding her hand up the expanse of Dev's darkly haired chest, she whispered, "Yes. Any day. Any hour. You just name it."

He met her bold smile with one of his own. "How about today? After we leave this beach where babies are made?"

Kulani saw hope burning in Dev's eyes. It was a hope she'd never seen before, and as she lay there in his embrace, their bodies quickly drying from the trade winds that blew off the ocean, she began to understand the depth of Dev's needs, how he longed for a baby. "I'd like to be married by Cappy. He's a revered kahuna here on the island, and like a grandfather to me. That would honor my mother, and my ancestors. How do you feel about that?"

Dev nodded. He looked across the deserted beach. The colors of the sky, of the water, the white, foamy waves, were like an artist's palette. No one could capture the brightness of all these colors, or how his heart and soul were responding to them right now. Tightening his embrace around her long, sinuous form, he rasped, "That's fine with me. I don't care who marries us. I need you, Kulani. Forever."

She understood. Looking up at the palms above them, their delicate fronds moving with each playful breeze, she said, "Let's call your family first? Let them know? They might want to come over for the wedding on a last-minute flight?"

Dev thought about it. "Do you want to wait a few weeks and have a wedding with family?"

Kulani shook her head. "No, but that's the right thing to do." She caressed his square jaw. Even though Dev had shaved this morning, the dark shadow of his beard was returning, giving him a dangerous and predatory look that made him even more intensely handsome than before.

Chuckling, Dev said, "Listen, my parents would be just as happy to get a phone call from us telling them we're married." He moved his hand across her abdomen. "But whatever you think is best is what we'll do. All I want is to give you—and our child—my name."

Understanding, she eased from his arms. "And you're sure I'm pregnant?"

"Yes."

Shivering with need of him all over again, Kulani reached into the beach bag and drew out her sarong. Standing up, she quickly slipped it around her body and tied the ends behind her neck. Dev loved to see her in sarongs, for obvious reasons. Today she'd chosen a hot pink one with orange-and-purple bird-of-paradise all over it. Kneeling down, she retrieved his cutoffs and handed them to him.

He caught her hand. "I want to promise you something," he told her in a low voice, his gaze locked with hers. "I'm going to quit being a mercenary. My ex-wife was right about one thing—globe-trotting and not being home when she needed me, I'm sure, forced her to rely a lot more than she would have on her family for help. I've got a second chance now, not that I deserve one, and I've been talking to Morgan about taking on a nice, safe nine-to-five desk job so I can be home when it counts. I don't ever want to leave my wife in the lurch again like I did Susan. Deal?''

Tears shimmered in her eyes. Kulani raised his hand and kissed it tenderly. "Deal."

He released her hand and smiled unevenly, tears in his own eyes.

"Then I think we need to get going, don't you?" Kulani laughed joyously, the sound caught on the winds.

A short while after they had returned to the bunga-low, and after they made a few calls to tell everyone of their plans, the doorbell rang. Dev had just placed the phone down after they had talked to his ecstatic parents about the marriage. In two weeks, his parents, two of his brothers, and Morgan and his family would fly over and attend their wedding.

"You expecting anyone?" Dev asked with a frown as she moved toward the door. He'd changed into a white, short-sleeved cotton shirt and a pair of beige Dockers and he held his cane in his left hand. As much as he hated the cane, he knew he'd be forced to use it for at least another month.

Kulani stood in the middle of the living room. "No. You?"

"Nope." Dev opened the door.

"Shep!"

Kulani heard the surprise in Dev's voice. What was Shep doing here? She hurried to the door. Dev had stepped aside to let his oldest brother into the bungalow. Shep was dressed casually in a dark green polo shirt and jeans, which emphasized his powerfully masculine body. His icy blue gaze moved to Kulani.

"Sorry to bust in on you two unannounced."

Kulani smiled. "That's all right, Shep. Come on in. We have some wonderful news to share with you."

Dev closed the door and followed them into the living room. Shep looked tense. Something was going down. It wasn't like his older brother to appear like this, so Dev knew it was serious. That took the edge off his happiness.

"First things first," Dev told Kulani as he walked over and put his arm around her. "Shep, we're getting married in two weeks. We were in the process of calling all the family to tell them, but you're going to get it firsthand. You were the only brother I couldn't reach, so I'm glad to be able to invite you in person."

Shep grinned tightly and held out his hand. "Congratulations, little brother. Kulani, you don't know what you're in for. This guy is a handful. I ought to know— I grew up with him."

Laughing delightedly, Kulani took Shep's hand and his good wishes. "Thanks, Shep. I feel we'll get along just fine."

"Well," Shep said genially as he sat down on the couch, "you're both mountain climbers, so you have that in common." He gave his younger brother a warm look. "And it's about damn time you got her to take your name, brother. I was wondering how long it was going to take you to screw up the courage to ask Kulani."

Dev had the good grace to blush. "Everything is timing, bro. You know that. It wasn't time until now."

Kulani excused herself and went to the kitchen to

make them coffee. Dev slowly sat down in the chair with the help of his cane, opposite Shep.

Shep gestured to his leg. "How is it? You're still lookin' a little gimpy."

Grimacing, Dev muttered, "Let's put it this way—I was on crutches for two months, which I hated. One day I got fed up with them and threw them away. The therapist gave me a cane, instead." He glared down at the cane propped against his chair. "And I'm going to get rid of this damned thing real soon, too."

"So, what's the final word on your leg? Is it going to stop you from doing merc work?"

Dev nodded. "Yes. My right leg is about a quarter of an inch shorter than the other one." He flexed the arm that had been wounded. "And I've got some residual nerve damage. I still don't have feeling in two fingers of this hand. Ty contacted his homeopathic doctor friend, Rachel Donovan-Cunningham, and she sent over a remedy called Hypericum that's really helped in the healing of those nerves. I used to have no feeling in the hand at all, so there's been a lot of progress. The docs are surprised that a homeopathic remedy has helped the serious nerve damage, but they say with therapy and time, I'll probably get full use out of my hand. My leg may always give me trouble, but I'll be glad to be walking again without a cane soon."

"I see," Shep murmured. "I've been away on an assignment until two days ago. Sorry I've been out of contact during your convalescence." He lifted his craggy head and looked toward the entrance to the kitchen. "But I figured you were in the best of hands with Kulani, and you probably didn't miss me sticking my nose in weekly for progress reports on your wounds."

"Morgan told me you were undercover. So what brings you here? Just catching up?" Dev knew differently. He could see the edgy look in Shep's eyes. His brother was hard to read by anyone's standards. He was closed up tighter than the hard granite that made up the Rocky Mountains where they'd been born. Ty and Reid were easy to read, like open books, in comparison to his oldest brother. He watched as Shep leaned forward, his thighs open, his hands clasped tightly between them.

"I'm here on business," he growled. "And I won't be able to attend your wedding because of it. Sorry."

Kulani came back carrying a tray with coffee in mugs, and cream and sugar. She placed the tray on the bamboo coffee table and invited them to help themselves. She'd also brought a plate of macadamia-and-white-chocolate cookies. She sat down on the other end of the couch and curled her legs beneath her, coffee cup in hand.

"You look pretty tense, Shep," she murmured between sips of the fragrant liquid. "Is that why you're here?"

Shep gave her a sideways look as he took his cup of coffee and several cookies from the plate. "You don't miss much, do you?"

Kulani grinned a little. "Call it women's intuition, Shep."

Snorting, he dipped a cookie into his black, steaming coffee and then popped it into his mouth.

Dev chuckled indulgently. "She's not going to let me get away with a thing with that all-terrain radar of hers."

Kulani laughed. "When are you men going to realize we women can read you like open books? You can't hide a thing from us."

Shep finished off his cookies and then got serious. He looked at them and said, "Morgan's sending me on an assignment back in Georgia. I know it's a top event, and I think it involves Black Dawn."

"Oh, no," Kulani whispered. "But...you captured the professor two days after he escaped us, Shep. I thought—well, that this bioterrorism stuff would stop with him being caught."

Shaking his head, Shep muttered, "Black Dawn is like the multiheaded Hydra, Kulani. Getting Valdemar was like cutting off one head. There're plenty of other heads on this bioterrorist group's body."

"So," Dev speculated, "Morgan's calling you in because he probably suspects Black Dawn is going to attack an East Coast target?"

Shrugging his big shoulders, Shep sipped his coffee and reached for more of the freshly baked cookies. Spreading them out across his thigh, he took one at a time, dipped it and ate it with obvious relish. "More than likely." His thick, black brows knitted. "I happened to be flying back from Singapore and I thought I'd lay over here a couple of hours before I catch the red-eye back to the mainland. Morgan's going to meet me in San Francisco to brief me. I guess this came up suddenly and I was the only merc around available for this assignment. That's all I know."

"You don't have a haz-mat—hazardous materials— background, do you?" Kulani asked worriedly.

"Nada."

"That doesn't make sense," Kulani said to them. "Morgan wouldn't assign someone to a top event like this without the proper background. Are you sure it's Black Dawn?"

Shrugging, Shep popped the last cookie into his

mouth and followed it with a swig of coffee. Wiping his mouth with the back of his hand, he offered, "Morgan was evasive when we spoke on the satcom link. But I heard the tension in his voice. He doesn't get uptight like that too often, and I've been around him enough to know that when he does, it's serious business."

Rubbing her arm absently, Kulani gave Dev a worried look. "This makes me glad you can't work as a merc anymore."

Dev understood. He had promised her he wouldn't become a merc and he had yet to finish telling her his plans. Weeks ago Morgan had offered him a managerial position in Perseus, to help coordinate the missions around the world. He was going to set up a satellite office on Kauai. The plans for the building were already with a local architect. Dev would be the manager. It seemed like the perfect nine-to-five job, so he could be home every night to share his life with Kulani.

Shep growled, "Well, from the sounds of it, this top event is gonna be a corker."

"Is it just you on this assignment?" Dev demanded, knowing his brother's penchant to always work alone.

"I have no doubt," Shep muttered, finishing off his coffee. Rising to his full height, he set the cup down on the coffee table. "I've got an hour to get back to the airport. I'll take my leave of you two. I'm sorry I can't be here for your wedding. I really am."

Kulani rose. Outside, the twilight was turning the sky to crimson and a ripe peach color. "We understand. Please be careful, Shep," she said as she went over to him. He wasn't the kind of man who invited familiarity or closeness, but Kulani disregarded the huge, icy wall that surrounded Shep. She walked up to him, wrapped her arms around his torso and gave him a warm hug. He seemed surprised, hesitated, and then awkwardly hugged her back. When Shep quickly broke contact with her, Kulani smiled to herself. Shep was like a grizzled old mustang stallion—too long out in the wilds without a band of mares to care for. Without anyone. Dev had said that an incident in Shep's past had changed the way he lived his life. He'd once been a fighter pilot in the U.S. Air Force, but something had happened to close him up and shut him down. Kulani knew he was a loner and sensed the vulnerable human being behind that icy cold gaze of his. At thirty-eight years of age, Shep appeared, at least outwardly, to be unreachable, shunning the more mundane, emotional aspects of being a human being. Still, he'd shown up here to see them, and when he'd congratulated them on their coming marriage she could see that he was truly happy for Dev and for her. Shep was salvageable—but only by the right woman, Kulani sensed. She hoped he would someday know the kind of happiness she and Dev shared.

Dev reached out and shook his brother's proffered hand. "Let me accompany you to the airport? I'll grab a taxi home."

"Sure." Shep smiled a little at Kulani. "Thanks for all you've done for him. I'm glad you're going to become a part of our family. The cookies were great. Thanks."

She nodded and walked them to the door. For a moment, Kulani saw a glimmer of the little boy trapped deep inside him. There was a human weakness in him, after all. She smiled knowingly to herself. Now, if he could just find a woman who baked homemade cookies, that would be the combination to the safe known as

Shep—a way of opening him up. "Just be careful, Shep. Will you call us when you've completed the mission? We'll both worry about you until we hear from you."

Shep opened the door and scowled heavily. "That's the problem, you know?"

"What's a problem?" Kulani asked as she followed Dev out to the porch. Around them, the sky was a palette of rose and peach hues now.

"Relationships." He gave Dev a wry look. "It's hell having the responsibility of a relationship. Our parents worry about the four of us all the time. That's why I never keep a woman around for long. I don't want those kinds of suffocating ties. I don't want her worrying her head off about me. Family's bad enough," he growled. "It's like a slave collar around my neck."

Dev gave Kulani a significant look that said he'd see her shortly. Kulani wisely said nothing. She lifted her hand in goodbye and watched the two brothers walk to Shep's rental car, a dark blue Mercedes Benz. Turning, she went back inside. Worry for Shep was already eating at her. She was relieved that Dev would never again have to place himself in danger and jeopardy. As she went to pick up the tray from the coffee table, Kulani fully admitted that she was glad that Dev would soon have a desk job. Setting the tray on the counter, she pressed her hand gently against her abdomen. She knew instinctively that she was now carrying Dev's baby. She felt relief that the baby would have a father who would always be there. A mercenary's life wasn't a long one, with dying at the top of the list of things to do. Sighing, she turned, rinsed the dishes and placed them in the dishwasher. Already, she missed Dev's presence.

* * *

"I'm home!" Dev called as he entered the bungalow later. He saw that Kulani had changed into a pair of cream-colored slacks and a rainbow-colored blouse for the evening. She was lounging on the couch with a bowl of popcorn in her hands, watching television.

"Hi!" Kulani held out her hand in his direction. "Is Shep off?"

"Yeah," Dev said. He took her hand and squeezed it gently. Limping around the couch with the aid of his cane, he sat down, placed the bowl of popcorn on the lamp table, put the cane aside and took Kulani into his arms. She came willingly. Sliding his hand along the slope of her cheek, he looked deeply into her soft, welcoming eyes.

"And you know what? I'm glad as hell I'm marrying you. I don't want to be like Shep—always alone. He never married. He's rarely in a relationship. And when he does have one, he breaks it off before it can get serious."

Kulani kissed Dev's hand and leaned her brow against his jaw. "He's a real loner," she agreed softly. "And I'm very glad you're not like him in that way. I'm glad you need me, and I need you."

Kissing her hair, her ear and then her warm cheek, he whispered roughly, "All I'll ever need is in my arms right now."

The words fell hotly across her. Kulani sighed and smiled gently as Dev held her tightly in his arms. "Well, if nature has anything to do with it, you're liable to be taking care of two of us real soon."

Chortling, Dev eased Kulani away from him and met and held her starry gaze. "I don't know how much more happy I can feel than right now."

"Oh," Kulani whispered impishly, "when I find out for sure, you'll be higher than a kite, Dev Hunter."

Regarding her tenderly, Dev slid his hand against her cheek. She pressed her face against his palm. "Even if you aren't, you will be someday soon. I'm not marrying you to have children. I married you because I love you and I want to grow old as hell with you. The children will come with time, if it's meant to be."

Agreeing, Kulani closed her eyes and was rocked gently back and forth within Dev's arms. "Our kids will be love children. An extension of what we have with one another."

"Want to call Morgan and Laura and give them the details on their trip here? The hotel where we'll have them stay with their kids?" he suggested.

Kulani nodded. "Yes, I want to touch base with Laura. She's a stickler for details, and it will be fun to talk to her about the flowers for our wedding."

As Dev rose off the couch to make the call, his mind warred between worry for Shep and the coming mission and his joy over his coming marriage to Kulani. The only solace Dev had in this situation with Shep was knowing that his brother was so good at what he did. He was the consummate mercenary—hard, icy and well trained. Nothing would get in Shep's way of completing a mission—or he'd die trying.

Tucking his worry away, Dev took the phone and brought it back to the couch where Kulani was sitting. "Here, give Morgan and Laura a call."

Smiling, Kulani took the phone. In this moment, she knew that the dark years of her life, like chapters in a book, were over now. Never had she dreamed of someone like Dev walking into her life. Kulani needed him. And he needed her just as much. As she dialed the phone, euphoria moved like a quiet stream through her heart. Dev was her solace, her sunshine. Her joy. Forever.

* * * * *

ATTENTION
LINDSAY McKENNA FANS!

MORGAN'S MERCENARIES:
THE HUNTERS

continues in November 2000
in Silhouette Desire®
with Shep Hunter's story!

THE UNTAMED HUNTER

Shep Hunter is as rock-hard as the mountains of h
Colorado home town. And he's a fierce fighter whe
comes to his missions for Morgan Trayhern. But n
that he's been paired up with Dr Maggie Harper—
one woman who can get through his stony façade—
heart is in for the biggest battle of his bachelor lif

Turn the page for a sneak preview...

The Untamed Hunter
by
Lindsay McKenna

——

Why, oh why, had she agreed to take this mission? In her angst, Maggie paced the length of her office, jamming her hands in the pockets of her lab coat. All she could do now was wait. Just wait. According to her boss, Dr. Casey Morrow, Shep Hunter would arrive at 0900 and then Casey would brief them both on the final details of the mission.

Maggie told herself that she had agreed to the mission because she knew Dr. Casey Morrow and Morgan Trayhern needed her help to stop terrorists from striking some unsuspecting city with a biological weapon. Maggie couldn't stand to think she would refuse a mission because the man working with her was an old boyfriend.

Actually, Shep had been much, much more than that, Maggie admitted to herself. She had fallen hopelessly in love with him all those years ago. He was keenly intelligent, competitive and he'd loved her with a passion she had never known since.

Sighing, she ran her chilled fingers through her loose, shoulder-length hair. "What have you done, Maggie?" she whispered through tightened lips as she ruthlessly perused her desk, which looked like it had been hit by a tornado. Restlessly, she picked up some papers and tried to concentrate on them.

The phone buzzed on her desk. She jumped. The papers flitted out of her fingers and wafted to the floor.

"Oh," Maggie said, scooping up the letters. Her heart was throbbing. She knew it was Casey buzzing her. It was time. Reluctantly reaching for the phone, Maggie wished she were anywhere but here right now.

"Maggie?" Casey asked.

"Yes?"

"It's time. Come on down so I can give you two the final briefing on this mission."

Shutting her eyes, Maggie whispered, "Okay…I'll be right there.…"

Placing the phone gently back into the cradle, Maggie tried to steady her breathing. It had been so long since she'd seen Shep. Had he changed? Had life softened him at all? Or was he still arrogant and self-righteous? A chill swept through her. She felt fear. Raw, unbridled fear. Chastising herself mentally, Maggie automatically touched her hair. Taking a look in the mirror that hung at one end of her office, she saw that her eyes looked huge. Like a rabbit ready to face a starving wolf.

Her fingers were so cold they almost felt numb. She was acting just like the college freshman she was when she first met Shep. Even then, Shep seemed to have the world by the tail. Hunter was always calm, cool and collected. Right now, as she swung open her door and stepped into the hall that led to Casey's office, Maggie felt disheveled, unprepared and scared.

Shep was a virus, Maggie decided with sudden mirth. She was infected by him and hadn't built up an immunity yet. That was why she felt vulnerable right now, she thought as she reached for the brass doorknob of Cascy's office. Her heart beat hard in her breast. Inside that office was Hunter. She felt hunted all right. Taking a deep breath, Maggie jerked open the door and forced herself to move quickly inside.

Shep contained his surprise. The woman who walked resolutely into Casey's office was even more beautiful, more poised, more confident than he could recall. Despite her small stature, she carried herself proudly, that small chin of hers leading, those incredibly beautiful hazel eyes of hers containing sunlit gold, earthy brown and emerald green within them. The years had been kind to her, Shep realized with undue pleasure as he rose from his chair.

Their eyes met for the first time. Shep felt his heart thud hard, like someone had struck him full force in his barrel chest with a sixteen-pound sledgehammer. He struggled for breath as he studied Maggie's oval face, her high, smooth cheekbones. The freckles across her nose and cheeks—those delicious small copper spots— were still there. Her eyes widened incredibly. He saw every nuance of every emotion she was feeling in her gaze. The fear was there, the uncertainty, the desire...yes, desire. He knew he hadn't read that emotion wrong. That made him feel good. Damn good.

"How are you?" he said, his voice deep and unruffled. Stepping forward, he offered his large hand to her.

Forcing herself to lift her hand, Maggie croaked, "Fine...just fine, Shep...." As her fingertips slid into his proffered hand, she was reminded how big Shep was.

And the touch of his fingers reminded her of all that they'd once shared.

Shaking away the thought, Maggie saw Casey stand, a smile affixed to her face, but trepidation in her eyes. One look at her boss's expression and Maggie knew that no matter what she once felt for Shep, she had to make this work. She had to get through this mission with Shep....

* * *

Don't forget The Untamed Hunter
is a November Desire™
—the Man of the Month no less!

Silhouette Stars

Born this Month

Don McLean, Buster Keaton, Clive James, Paul Hogan, Sean Lennon, Cliff Richard, Margaret Thatcher, Max Bygraves, Bill Gates, Bob Hoskins

Star of the Month

Libra

The next few months should prove challenging, you will need your wits about you and the support of those close to you. However, you will begin to feel that real progress is possible in your life and long held dreams can become reality. Finance looks good and there may be a chance for long distance travel later in the year.

SILH/HR/0010a

Scorpio

A great month for relationships, you will feel stronger and more committed, by being honest with your partner you will achieve new heights.

Sagittarius

Life remains complicated and you need to sort out your priorities. Loved ones will be able to support you but only if you show real appreciation.

 ## Capricorn

You're in demand both socially and at work, you may find you need to simplify your life in order to keep everybody happy and you sane!

Aquarius

Time to sort out your priorities, by trying to please everyone you are not really achieving much. Travel plans may have to be changed at the last minute.

 ## Pisces

You should be feeling optimistic about the way your life is going, especially in relationships where you realise just how much you mean to that special person.

Aries

Your natural charm enables you to win over friends and colleagues to your way of thinking making this month one of progress in many areas of your life. A shopping trip could find you bargain hunting with style.

SILH/HR/0010c

  Taurus

You may feel unmotivated and not so sure where your life is heading; don't despair, changes are just around the corner. Financial matters improve and you may receive something material from an unusual source.

Gemini

There are many positive aspects around you and by being confident you can succeed in all you desire, making this an excellent month. A friend has news that sets you thinking about how loyal someone close is.

 Cancer

You could be fighting to find some personal space as the demands from work and socially get too much. Sift out the important and allow the rest to drop away, leaving you time to refresh.

Leo

You should be revelling in the attention you are receiving as a result of recent achievements but deep down you feel that someone close is not being as supportive as you would like. Whatever their motives, now could be truthtime.

  Virgo

Romance is highlighted and you will feel pleased with the way a special relationship is going. Finances are looking good and you may splash out later in the month.

Look out for more
Silhouette Stars next month

▼™ SILHOUETTE
SPECIAL EDITION®

AVAILABLE FROM 20TH OCTOBER 2000

BABY BOY BLESSED Arlene James

That's My Baby!

Little Georgie was Colin Garret's son, but in the year Colin had been searching for him, Lauren Cole had been caring for and loving his child. A marriage of convenience was the only solution!

HIS CINDERELLA Cathy Gillen Thacker

McCabe Men

Wade McCabe was a self-made millionaire with matchmaking parents. But Josie Lynn Corbett Wyatt wanted to prove herself and considered Wade a potential *business* partner!

A ROYAL BABY ON THE WAY Susan Mallery

Royally Wed

Looking for the brother she'd never known Princess Alexandra Wyndham ended up commandeering part of Mitch Colton's home and heart. Could their romance survive the revelation of a royal baby on the way?

YOURS FOR NINETY DAYS Barbara McMahon

Stuck together for ninety days, Nick Tanner and Ellie Winslow resolved to make the best of it, but it was awfully hard to keep their distance! These three months could be the start of a lifetime…

DADDY BY SURPRISE Pat Warren

Devin Gray had long ago resolved to stay single, although his loveable, sexy neighbour was tempting him to change his mind even *before* adorable six-year-old Emily turned up claiming he was her father!

PREGNANT & PRACTICALLY MARRIED
Andrea Edwards

The Bridal Circle

Jed McCarron had just agreed to pretend to be pregnant Karin Spencer's fiancé and her child's father. Pretending to be her beloved didn't commit him to anything…did it?

0010/23a

AVAILABLE FROM 20TH OCTOBER 2000

Intrigue
Danger, deception and suspense

WANTED: COWBOY Kelsey Roberts
UNDER THE MIDNIGHT SUN Marilyn Cunningham
LOVE AT FIRST SIGHT BJ Daniels
SAME PLACE, SAME TIME CJ Carmichael

Desire
Intense, sensual love stories

THE UNTAMED HUNTER Lindsay McKenna
SECRET AGENT DAD Metsy Hingle
THE BABY CAME C.O.D. Marie Ferrarella
OCCUPATION: CASANOVA Alexandra Sellers
THAT LOVING TOUCH Ashley Summers
HUSBAND FOR KEEPS Kate Little

Sensation
Passionate, dramatic, thrilling romances

MISTAKEN IDENTITY Merline Lovelace
GET LUCKY Suzanne Brockmann
MARRYING MIKE...AGAIN Alicia Scott
LONG-LOST MUM Jill Shalvis
CATCH ME IF YOU CAN Nina Bruhns
THE REFORMING OF MATTHEW DUNN
Virginia Kantra

2 FREE

books and a surprise gift!

We would like to take this opportunity to thank you for reading this Silhouette® book by offering you the chance to take TWO more specially selected titles from the Special Edition™ series absolutely FREE! We're also making this offer to introduce you to the benefits of the Reader Service™—

* ★ FREE home delivery
* ★ FREE gifts and competitions
* ★ FREE monthly Newsletter
* ★ Exclusive Reader Service discounts
* ★ Books available before they're in the shops

Accepting these FREE books and gift places you under no obligation to buy, you may cancel at any time, even after receiving your free shipment. Simply complete your details below and return the entire page to the address below. *You don't even need a stamp!*

YES! Please send me 2 free Special Edition books and a surprise gift. I understand that unless you hear from me, I will receive 4 superb new titles every month for just £2.70 each, postage and packing free. I am under no obligation to purchase any books and may cancel my subscription at any time. The free books and gift will be mine to keep in any case.

E0ZEA

Ms/Mrs/Miss/Mr ....Initials.....................................

BLOCK CAPITALS PLEASE

Surname ....

Address ....

....

....Postcode.................................

Send this whole page to:
UK: FREEPOST CN81, Croydon, CR9 3WZ
EIRE: PO Box 4546, Kilcock, County Kildare (stamp required)